THE
RIPPING
TREE

NIKKI GEMMELL

THE BOROUGH PRESS

The Borough Press
An imprint of HarperCollins*Publishers* Ltd
1 London Bridge Street
London SE1 9GF

www.harpercollins.co.uk

HarperCollins*Publishers*
1st Floor, Watermarque Building, Ringsend Road,
Dublin 4, Ireland

This paperback edition 2022
1

First published in Great Britain by HarperCollins*Publishers* 2021
First published in Australia in 2021 by HarperCollins*Publishers* Australia Pty Limited

Copyright © Nikki Gemmell 2021

Nikki Gemmell asserts the moral right to
be identified as the author of this work

A catalogue record for this book is available from the British Library

ISBN: 978-0-00-851111-1

This novel is entirely a work of fiction.
The names, characters and incidents portrayed in it are
the work of the author's imagination. Any resemblance to
actual persons, living or dead, events or localities is
entirely coincidental.

Printed and Bound in the UK using 100% Renewable Electricity
at CPI Group (UK) Ltd

MIX
Paper from
responsible sources
FSC™ C007454

This book is produced from independently certified FSC™ paper
to ensure responsible forest management.

For more information visit: www.harpercollins.co.uk/green

To my beloved father, Bob,
who taught me the power and compassion
of non-judgemental love.

1934–2020

FOREWORD

Our grandmother didn't have long to live when she showed us a bundle of loose pages written in a wild and beautiful hand. We had just been to Willowbrae, that fine estate some two hours north, to picnic in its glorious gardens, but the weather had closed in and forced a retreat. Our grandmother had drawn inward at the mere mention of the house, which was most uncharacteristic; she'd shown no interest in going and had stayed firmly at home. Upon our return, she briskly urged us to take off our coats, putting them aside as if they needed cleaning.

'I know, I know,' she said, smiling as if indulging us, 'everyone wants an invitation to Willowbrae, everyone wants to see inside it. The turrets, the crenellations, the magnificent library, the avenue of elms, the circular flower beds. How lovely and calm and serene it all appears.' Her voice dropped. 'From a distance.'

We looked at her, unsure, for it was as if our grandmother was making fun of us. Her beautiful eyes were shining, but it did not seem to be in jest.

'I think perhaps it's time I read you a little story about your magnificent Willowbrae, my darlings.' Note, *our* lovely Willowbrae, not hers. 'A different kind of story. That you'll never have heard before.' Our grandmother shut her eyes and drew in a long breath, as if steadying herself. Our mother went to remonstrate but thought better of it and flurried off; they had obviously touched on this subject before.

Our grandmother turned to a small desk in a corner that had never been explored by any of us. She selected a tiny key hanging from her chatelaine and opened a locked drawer, revealing a secret chamber, then lifted out a bundle of rough, mismatched pages. She shuffled through them. They were crammed with a rush of fragments, as if written in snatches of secret moments. Our grandmother stroked some of the words with her fingers, flattening the aged, warped papers as if smoothing down their restlessness. Some paragraphs were written in ink, some in smudged and spidery pencil and it was all greatly faded, but our grandmother told us she could still make out the text, just, and her mottled and papery fingers flitted over the words as if conjuring them into life.

We expressed surprise that we'd never heard of these mysterious pages, yet they felt connected, somehow, to our picnic. We asked our grandmother again why she hadn't come with us but she just gave us an enigmatic smile and shook her head, all the while smoothing down the words, yet a little more firmly this time, as if her thoughts were suddenly snagged by something quite disturbing indeed. She looked up at us and said that everything was for a time and a reason, and now was the right time for this secret book; we were quite grown up enough for it at last.

'Oh, but it's a terrible tale, full of pain and anguish and trauma. It's a ghost story, a haunting, or perhaps a horror story – you be the judge.'

Someone – who shall remain nameless – immediately decamped, declaring they weren't in the mood for horribleness of any kind after such a lovely day; perhaps it was the thought of their beloved Willowbrae presented as quite something else that pushed them from the room. Our grandmother smiled in challenge to the rest of us.

'Are you ready?'

We expressed our immediate enthusiasm.

'Excellent. And it's quite the night for it, I think,' for the rain was setting in. 'Draw the curtains on all that thundery bluster. Gather in, make the circle tight. I'll feed up the greedy fire.'

By this stage our mother had quietly returned. Our grandmother held out her hand to her; it was squeezed in return.

'Who wrote this?' someone piped up.

'Ssssh, be patient.' Our grandmother shivered a little flinch, which only made us want to start immediately, for we loved our puzzles and games. 'As the guardian of these words I've kept them obedient and quiet for a very long time.' She looked at our mother, who nodded her assent. 'Too long perhaps. But I think you're ready now.'

Her voice cooled as she told us that our beautiful, immaculate Willowbrae was a house of denial, a house of amnesia, and that this was a cautionary tale. She told us that Willowbrae had closed its eyelids upon the truth and shuttered its past.

'This is a story that will freeze your blood and make you never want to return to the house again.'

We all gasped; our mother, meanwhile, was unreadable, busying herself in her needlework and not looking at any of us. The nameless one who had decamped had quietly returned, unable to resist the lure of all this.

'So make yourselves comfortable, my lovelies,' our grandmother continued. 'Blankets for knees, shawls for shoulders. Come, come, sit close. We need to be able to touch, to hold each other if we want.'

We settled in, quite thrilled at whatever was ahead.

'This is a tale of the past but also the future that will never be completely scrubbed out, and it will take us more than one evening to get through it. But let's make a start tonight, in this wonderful wildness, which is not so dissimilar to the beginning of this account. Are we ready?'

Yes, we clamoured, yes, yes!

Our grandmother's hands smoothed the pages repeatedly, as if spelling the sleeping words back into life.

'So. How to begin? This is an account of seven days in the life of a young woman called Poss' – we exclaimed at the singularity of the name – 'who arrived at Willowbrae wanting to be someone else. It's a story of the man she loved, who was not the man she thought. This is also an account of how the family that built your mighty Willowbrae learnt to live unpeacefully within it, as the walls of their beautiful creation grew taller and taller around them. Until one day they couldn't see out. Couldn't get out, or didn't want to. No one has told this story before, but this account is the truth and it's a difficult one and it was staring everyone in the face, but no one was interested in that, all those poor souls who populated Willowbrae long ago, that cursed place.'

With a trembling breath our grandmother turned to the first page. It had just three words written upon it, in what seemed a scrawled rush. *The First Day.*

THE FIRST DAY

IN WHICH I WAKE INTO A NEW LIFE

With a gulp of breath, like I'm trying to inhale the last dregs of life into water-logged lungs, I gasp, wide-eyed, at everything I've been through, the baptism like no other into a new life. Yet now. What place is this? Where am I? On this strange island, which could be a crucible or a prison or a nest or a haven of glorious newness and release, but I've no idea. Nor who the people are I've landed among.

A boy is right next to me, doctor-close. Eye-deep in stillness and stare. He has an angelic face – oh, such beauty – but unblinking eyes. I toss my head back like a pony spooked. The boy doesn't move, as if he's been told he mustn't, he must guard me and watch. A Bible a foot long rests on a table with my knife beside it. Thank God, my knife. The boy's eyes flick to the door. I try to smile but he doesn't give me anything, he's too intent on his task.

My eyes flit, trying to read my new world. Heavy mahogany furniture. A canopy on my bed that feels too weighty and too close, its curtains tied back with silken ropes. An enormous, black marble fireplace that would have cost a fortune to ship across the earth, with veins of white running through it like ice in a wintry sea. A doll's chair, or perhaps a small child's, on top of a cupboard, next to a matching table, utterly unused and as if on display. A faded teddy bear half sits in the chair like it would rather not. A mahogany cot in a corner with a similar air of abandonment. A doll inside it stares at me, with something akin to frozen shock, as if her little heart has quite stopped with fright. Dense floral wallpaper crams me in, its greedy chrysanthemums shrink the walls and it all feels so airless and stopped. Like a room an old person is left to die in. Wrong-footed. My arms are pinned down and the sheets are too insistent in their tuck – a restraint that's not accidental, it seems, but deliberate. A clock somewhere in the room slowly ticks and the boy is unnaturally quiet. Not a regular child.

I look to the windows with their heavy drapes matching the bed canopy. They cover lace curtains that are open a fraction. Hurting light beats down on a beautifully ordered, English-style garden that seems trapped in a heat-struck stillness. Yet a dramatic wildness towers beyond the neat lawns and circular beds, as if there is a continual tension between the two domains and the wild one is winning, just. I want to slip away into the newness outside, want to marinate myself in its lovely hot blare, but why are these sheets so binding, as if they need me held? A dog barks in the distance. Abruptly stops. My body feels colonised by ache and my head yowls with hurt. Can't wriggle free.

'Help me,' I say, but nothing comes out. I gasp like a fish on a wharf. A talk-thief has stolen my voice. And then I am floating, I am under again, I cannot get a sure grip on this new life.

I jerk awake. The boy is still here, staring. His eyes flit to my knife. My fists clutch the sheets in two whirlpools of dread that bloom underneath the cloth's surface.

'Where am I?' I mouth.

The boy brings his head closer as if he's examining some strange and wondrous creature from the depths, a broken mermaid perhaps, beached.

He's well-dressed. Indoor clothes, rigorously pressed.

'Help me,' I mouth again; the sounds still will not come out.

A hand cups his ear and he listens intently as if waiting for a sound from the dolphins or sea depths.

I rock from side to side and the bed shifts in a mocking ocean-tilt and I wriggle my arms free and hold out my hands like a sleepwalker stuck. Green and yellow bruises crowd my arms in voluminous clouds, a storm sky in surge. I grab the boy as if to test he's on the living side of warmth and connection, but he flinches back and looks at the door as if I'm some secret and dangerous thing and my touch might lure him across. To what?

Ah, maybe he's not meant to be here. I smile in collusion. A tentative flick of his mouth in return. Progress. I turn my head on a monogrammed pillow and blow out my cheeks. 'Faith' is beautifully scrolled on the linen from a careful hand. I squint downward and see that my nightgown has the same. Who clothed me? My legs press together as I try to think back, and back. To a ship, yes, and a man's spine. A door that was England yet not. Meanwhile, chrysanthemums press in and a clock labours its tick and the boy offers nothing and where are my clothes?

I need my father, corrosively. His Labrador-calm to still me, because the disquiet is too loud in this place. It's so opposite to everything that was our cluttery cottage back home in Knockleby, in Dorset, our squat, warm teapot of a house with its teetering piles of books and dancing dust and shafts of sunlight through the windows like great ropes of God's ship calling me outside. Which I obeyed often. But I never wanted to leave that tight little fist of a world; home held my heart. I'm in thrall to it still – but now this, the new now. That I can't read one bit.

I smile again at the boy. A smile that again is not returned, as if he doesn't quite know how. My father told me I have an open, trusting heart and that it would be the downfall of me one day – that I hurt too much – but I need connection here more than anything. 'Help me.' Nothing. 'Please.' Who is he? What made him this? Who are his adults?

Heavy curtains hold the day at bay, yet the French doors to a flagstone verandah are ajar, just, as if it's acknowledged I am a patient who needs air. Outside is the curious upside-down frontier my half-brother had spoken of so much when at home, a land of heat-baked soil and sallow colours and impossibly shaped animals and natives as black as midnight. But inside is triumphantly England, my land of florid wallpaper and crisp linens, mahogany and monograms, and its order is keeping this wild land in check. Outside taunts me with its aromas of alien air with strange plant perfumes upon it, and I just want to hold my face to its insistence, to lick it and lie upon its new soil, but these wilful sheets won't let me. Nor this child.

He's pale, as if he's been sick or unnaturally contained and has rarely been released into the light. His blond hair is too long for a boy and falls neatly – too neatly for my brother's stories of this rowdy frontier place. His tresses are so different from my own untameable crop, which is like an unruly child that can't help itself. I cut it myself, wrongly and bluntly, because my father couldn't be bothered with Knockleby's tut and tetch at his singular creation, the recluse's odd clod of a daughter. They never knew what to call me, and I couldn't care less.

But here, right now, a competition of stare. The boy's eyes are unwavering chocolate-brown pools, mine narrow with challenge. I suddenly waggle anemone fingers and cross my eyes and – what do you know? – it unlocks him. He laughs despite himself and tries to do it himself. Fails. Aha! The child inside is finally cracked out. I crook a playful finger; the boy licks his lips. I grab his wrist. He looks again at my knife as if it was a mistake to leave it there, then shrugs it off and dives deep, into a smile, a laugh.

I examine, close. His face is pale, yet his hands are honeyed up by the sun and his fingers are filthy like he's recently dug his way out of dirt. Hmm, mouldable perhaps to my independent ways, if I am to stay for a little while and who knows about that. Around seven I suspect. Ready for adventures and open, possibly, to a lovely grubbying up. He smells of soap. And all the while, light slips through a curtain gap as strong as a cat, enticing us both out.

'You're one of them mermaids, aren't you?'

Well, hello there. A voice at last, Scottish with the corners knocked off. And a mermaid. Oh, I wish that all the *Finbar*'s souls had been mermaids and mermen with the gift of dipping and diving unbroken from their ship. My hand suddenly shakes as I hold the boy tight, thinking back to what has happened, all of it. I have to let go, don't want to frighten him.

'Bet everything was smashed up real bad.' His voice teeters on the edge of eagerness. 'People. Cargo. The lot.' He crashes his fist in the air like a sky god crushing a leaf ship and all I can do is nod – yes, yes – and squeeze my eyes shut on yesterday's sun that was a pinpoint of brightness as I lay on the *Finbar*'s deck in my old, gone life, where my future was amber-set. When I had a voice. And a name – Thomasina Trelora – that won't be coming out any time soon.

No. Old Tom is gone. Vanished.

WRACKED

Thomasina Trelora's last day on this earth was yesterday. In another life when the sky congregated, grape-dark, as the ship's deck beneath her shifted and sighed like a saddle under weight. Jittery horses sensed strange earth, then were still, as crisp as an orchestra stopped. She sat up, alert. Because a plume of cloud had quietly assembled as if spumed from Hell's depths; it was hanging, waiting, over all the ship's souls. One hundred and thirty-two wildly hammering hearts, one hundred and thirty-two souls gazing up to that sky tinged its apocalyptic orange-pink.

How many are left? I spasm in a curl, not well yet and might never be. My nails draw blood in raw palms and I ball away from the stiff sheets and my teeth clamp down into bruised lips with the force of a rabbit trap. My ship, my ship. If I start crying now I won't stop and I need to keep my wits about me for it feels like my trial isn't over yet: it's the too-insistent sheets, and I'm all alone in this new world without a family or friends or support – and is this rescue? I'm not quite sure yet, so confused, my head, oh my head.

I shut my eyes again on the hundred-odd souls gazing up to a gathering storm they'd never seen the likes of before. Everyone was so eager to set foot upon the mythical Southland we could all smell so close – the wild, strange green – all so eager to feel solid earth under their feet. Except me, Thomasina Trelora, who wanted to be anywhere but here.

'How did you get to us? Was everything smashed?' The little sky god's grimy fist slashes and swipes at the air. The clock ticks, the chrysanthemums crowd. I stretch out my fingers to the boy, needing connection, warmth, life, and he lets me hold him, but he's cold so I rub heat into his flesh like a mother with a child. He smiles an intrigued thank you with his head on one side. I keep rubbing, it's all I can do right now; my body's too broken from the batterings of the previous night. My bed is rocking with the pounding of the sea and I'm clinging once again to my rescuing raft. I gasp, too much in my head, too much. Because I've always been able to read the sky yet couldn't yesterday; it was tinged an apocalyptic pink that seemed spewed from the Netherworld itself. The horses kicked out at the confining wood and I thought of Jack in that moment, my dear, sun-brimmed, stable-boy confidante; I imagined his speaking hands busy on twitching equine necks, gentling their rubbing and stilling his horses' fret, imagined him staring into rolling, fear-filled eyes. An anguished gulp of a cry.

'Jack!'

'Who?'

Can't speak.

'Land ahoy!' came the shout from the crow's nest and ahead in dropping light were grand horizontal striations as tall as a cathedral yet mightier still, battalions of rock, a world seamed mysterious and rich. The air was heavy with the brew of a storm and a heat with a back that needed cracking and the ship was suddenly frantic with preparation. It lurched. A horse's great scream and then suddenly close were the great castle walls of the cliffs and the ocean was upended, as if a giant sea monster had woken from a slumber of a thousand years and roared at its rude interrupting. I threw back my head to the shunting sky, to its biblical ferocity, but it was shifting too fast.

'Every man for himself!' came the cry from above, but it was lost to the wind as the sheer rock face towered and in the sudden spewy light what looked like a mighty gap in the land was not, but instead heaped rocks and sheer, unbreakable cliff. There was a gut-wrenching heave of the *Finbar* trying to turn, of copper-lined oak protesting against the mountainous force of a watered wall, and again a watered wall, and ropes snapped as the world spun in vertical mountains of spitty white. The rain came and its force felt like it wanted to smite into the ocean depths this universe of puny, praying souls, and flickers of lightning spat to break free from their cloud trap and this strange kingdom at the bottom of the earth seemed to be convulsing with rage at the frail mortals daring to trespass upon it.

All around me ropes snaked and horses were set loose and the ship's cow was unhammocked and chaos took over and won – I clutch the boy's hand and squeeze tight and he does not withdraw his fingers, he holds his post.

'I'm here,' he whispers. 'You're alright.'

No, I don't think so. I whimper.

Lifeboats spun and dipped and reared. The *Finbar* was trapped under a splitting sky and there was a babel of voices and monstered waves and the whites of horses' eyes and ribbons of flame across a vast explosive wet. The gap Captain Grent thought was a gap was not and more lifeboats were frantically heaved under the sky-assault, yet one by one they were slender leaves swamped. But the frail coracle of the lifeboat in front of me had to be different, had to, as my half-brother, Ambrose, pushed past towards it, propelling his fright-stopped wife, Mariana.

'Come on, you lump. Are you thick?' Was he aiming this at me or her? 'Get a move on, idiot. No shoes, of course. That'd be right.'

Ah yes, me, of course.

Forever the embarrassment to him, the encumbrance too loud and cloddish and clumsy and unladylike. Yet the anger was coiled like a spring that afternoon. At my half-brother who didn't care enough about me, didn't see me, what I really wanted for my life. At the future he'd planned for me. At all my dreams and desires locked up. Because this was to be my last day of being unwifed and soon there'd be someone else to take my brother's place in the Palace of Fury I am trapped in now. Ambrose had neatly arranged my new life, faraway in his distant colony. He had been living there for years but had returned to England to wed his Mariana and was bringing her back, triumphantly, to his fine colonial estate, alongside his encumbrance of a half-sister. But married, well, I'd be someone else's problem. Someone whom I'd never met.

Jack the gentle stablehand was suddenly next to me on the slippy sliding deck. I held his shoulders.

'We'll do this, Horse Boy.'

'Aye, we will, Wolf Girl.'

Jack gave me his smile that was like a door flying open to the sun; he made my soul bloom.

'Go on,' I urged, 'jump,' because Jack's whole life was ahead of him and mine was not and a lifeboat was waiting and he couldn't swim. I'd leap out after him, into a boat or not, because I swim every summer at home and could do this. I'd taught myself to swim as well as arc an arrow into a bullseye and ride bareback, wilded up. I was my father's grand hidden experiment while Ambrose was away at school then university then the colonies, growing his certainty and his confidence. And he couldn't bear how his odd little sister was turning out. The sheer embarrassing blight of me; such a humiliating, unquiet disgrace.

'Jump, Jacky boy! Go.' But he protested. I urged yes and yelled, 'Anything to not be in the same boat as my brother,' and Jack laughed at that and raised a thumb, for he'd seen it the length of this voyage; the man always at me, the harrower of my peace. I trembled a touch down his cheek, I could swim and Jack could not. As one world darkened, another way was lit on this my last day of choice. *Choice.* Such a gift of a word, and my mind was made up.

I said to Jack, 'I love you, Horse Boy,' and he took out his small folded knife and closed my hand over it and kissed my clench. I was petrified but tried not to show it, could no longer talk. The only thing left was to stare terror in the face and not think about it all too much, so I took a deep breath and prayed 'God help me' then plunged straight into the sea with a bulleting velocity. The wall of water rose to meet me, closing over me with its great weight and crushing me in its embrace and there were panicky bubbles of hoof churn and Hell breath then I cannoned from the stewy green into clutter and crying, into lift and brightness. Does dying give off its own light? If so, that ocean was lit with it. But I was released. Still, miraculously, holding Jack's knife.

Again I slipped under the great heave of water in my baptism like no other, and again, my arms flailing as if trying to find something solid to this furious liquid, to get a grip on life itself, but under I went again, and again, pulled down by the weight of my petticoats and skirt. Which way was up, where was the air? I could not fill my lungs enough before the gods of the ocean snatched me under yet again and tossed and turned me in their greed. I could swim, just, yes, but this vast ocean heave was like nothing I'd ever experienced; it did not want me here, alive. Finally I spluttered into the new light and floated with utter exhaustion on my back.

This distant island was welcoming me, just.

I gasp. Look around. Where am I? In my snug *Finbar* cabin with its tiny bed-shelf? No, course not. Blousy chrysanthemums, a hidden clock's tick, a boy with too-long, too-neat locks. Who is now frowning with his hands on my shoulders as if trying to still down my fret.

'I don't think you're right yet, Mermaid.'

No, boy, I'm not and may never be.

A dog barks again in the distance and my past feels already antique. A fly as big as an acorn whines and veers close and the child shoots up a hand and stills the insect like a steel trap upon a fox. The dog abruptly stops mid-bark.

UNGIRL ME HERE

'Can you walk, Mermaid?'

A voiceless gurgle as I rock again from side to side in the bullying sheets.

'Can you fix things? Are you magic? Because you're alive and it's only you.' The boy looks at the door. 'So far.'

I squeeze my temples, shut my eyes; can't hear this.

'They're still looking. They'll find them, I promise.'

He's trying his best. But, but. Surely not everyone? Jack, my darling, sun-brimmed horse boy with his long slender neck and the smile that brings his whole being to light. Ambrose and Mariana. I may not have loved them, but they were my only family left. The good-hearted, forever-mild Captain Grent. The children. Janey and Clara and Louisa, the scampy trio who'd stare at strange me, intrigued, at what they could possibly dare to be if brave enough. The babies of the ship so bonny I'd steal them from their mother's arms, craving the soft, vulnerable dips in the backs of their necks where my mouth would rest.

No. Not everyone. Another voiceless spasm and again the sheets are clutched. The boy says nothing. Alone flexes its claws. Surely some must have made it, clinging to their bits of wood then palmed by the coastal rocks? As I did. Surely?

'What's your name? I can't call you Mermaid forever.'

A name, oh no. I shake my head and curve my arms over my hair because a name will plunge me back to that life mapped out. Will bring me marriage to that man I don't want. No, no name yet.

On the wall in front of me is a painting, in a heavy gilt frame, of a tiny girl trussed up like a bride. She shares the boy's disquieting, challenging gaze. Silk flounces swamp her, just like the prickly doll staring straight at me from the cot with its eyes cold and dead and shocked. I squirm away from the unsettling gaze, too ungirled for dolls. The boy understands, he grabs it and tosses it across to me in a taunt and I toss it back to him, quick, like a ball – anything to distract him from the name interrogation. He catches the doll neat in a snatch and a grin cracks his face: he's revolted by it too. He snuggles the toy up too close to me, tries to get it to kiss me.

'Ow!' I wince.

'Sorry, Mermaid. Forgot. Bruises 'n' all. All over.'

I smile softly, it's alright, then open out my arms in a forgiving hug, but the boy hesitates about stepping into them, as if this is entirely new and unknown. My arms drop, I laugh, shrug. It's all too soon.

'How did you get here?' he asks. 'You arrived as if by magic. I saw you, from the bannisters. It was a right big kerfuffle. Right outside our front door.'

Flits of memory. A kerfuffle, yes. And before it a sliver of the *Finbar*'s broken skin hefting and heaving. Hauling myself onto a bit of deck with Jack's knife somehow sprung open as if it was stuck to my hand and I was never letting it up. Resting my cheek as the walls of wet pushed me backwards and forwards, too spent to propel myself closer to anyone. But the cries, long after the storm had snuffed itself out.

'Mama, Mama.'

'Papa.'

'Oh God, where are you?'

The wailing across the relentless water, the weakening, then the awful, slow stopping. The lonely silence. Ocean wide.

Islanded by the alone, I hold the eye of this reluctant boy and squeeze my hand and draw fresh blood in my fist. Surely not everyone?

Salt-caked eye slits, flaking lips that wouldn't close. And out of one eye, skewed, land looming then dropping, the ocean a giant hand clawing at rock battlements. A littered sea. An eerie silence, unsouled. Vast aloneness roaring at me. Then a low ledge like a cupped palm and a desperate swim that became a scramble over boulders clotted with oyster shells, nature's cruel barricade, and I was climbing almost vertical rocks and falling onto a mattress of stone.

What was meant to kill you could also bring you to life. On this my last day of choice, God had spared me and I had an obligation now to make the most of a new life in gratitude and grace for that greatest of gifts. Choice.

In the ebbing day, a crease in the sunset. Gold through a rip in the curtain. I watched the sun slipping off the earth, too quick. Sleep was sparse then not. The sea was flattened, apologetic, and I woke in a deepening black to a naked moon and a clutter of ship, ghostly stripped bodies, a stunned cow, a piano carcass.

Ambrose's hat.

In Which I Am Rescued

But then. A looming hulk of shape. Person, animal, sea monster? My scratchy eyes were losing sight, my torn skin was invaded by sting and there was no fight in me left. A reeky human smell. Familiar yet not, sweat and earth. That smell, too close. My body shutting down. But a human hand – oh! – gentle at my chest and back, sat me up and rubbed between my shoulders and pushed the curtain of hair from my face and insisted I stay awake. But my eyes, glued shut. But my mouth, stuck. My head flopped back and a hand caught it and tilted it forward. Spit, on fingertips. Rubbed my eyes into cleanness, into sight, and I blinked wide with relief and the world swam before me and it was like looking through a tavern's thick uneven windows and then in a palm before me was something – what? – to hold, look at, eat – yes, eat. Pale, unappetising, globulous. I didn't recognise it, was afraid.

I shook my head in a strop of refusal but the hand on my back kept rubbing and rubbing and the food came at me again and it wouldn't scrape past the thick dryness in my throat and I jerked my head back like a colt new to its bridle and gagged; I retched the food out.

'Jack?'

I leant on the strength in the arm and floated into a river of sleep. Jerked awake. The hand left and my torso tottered, my spine wilted, then fingers were firm on the back of my neck and near my mouth was the flattened palm with chewed up bits of food and I closed my eyes; the pieces were too large and I fell back into sleep's embrace.

Then lips. At mine. Oh. Goodness. What? This ... softness. This ... tenderness. I arced in some kind of instinct to meet the flesh that was saving me in a great transference of warmth and connection and trust; but, no, it was practicality, merely that. Masticated food was being passed to me, lip to lip, and I flinched and swallowed without tasting, then slowly like a horse ate greedily from a palm laid flat and as I did so I realised that the hand before me that had been rubbing my back and propping me up and cleaning my eyes with spit wasn't white – but black.

Black. I took the hand in mine and turned it over, held the rescuing fingers close. The hand was darker at the knuckles and ghostly pale underneath, as if the sun had never reached into it, or use had rubbed it light, and there was a paleness under the nails and near them and, no, actually, the skin wasn't uniformly black at all: the fingernails were yellowed and ridged and strongly thick as if from something else. The ocean perhaps, shells or sea creatures, a different other-life. I held the fingers in wonder but they had brisker work to do. I tried to read the new eyes, pools of darkness rimmed by yellow and deeply curious and not letting up. I was demanding more food and smiling and laughing at the sheer relief of being alive; he was laughing too. Then deep in the darkness the wet came again, the storm not quite done yet, in a last stutter of a taunt; the thunder murmured in the wings of the clouds as a feeble remnant of rain spat down. Yet this time I didn't huddle into the crease of the rock: I left Jack's knife behind me and moved out under the sky and lay flat on my back and stretched out my battered body and opened my mouth to the lovely rain, thirsty now. Him too.

That rescue shone. And in the thick of an alien midnight I was lifted into a coracle of softness whose powdery sides arced protectively over me. It was a canoe that was made of some kind of soft tree bark held together with a pale substance like clay, and by my feet a small, intense fire was blown into life. I held Jack's knife tight, like my hand was paralysed around it, and my rescuer paddled us strongly from the ledge and on his torso were beads of raised flesh, knobbles of skin that I wanted to touch but did not, did not.

Surrendering to the rhythm of the water. Closing my eyes. Reading the ocean meekening as we headed around cliffs into a lesser sea and the canoe sped to bluntness on sand and then stopped. I was slung over a shoulder with the indignity of a pig carcass. My consciousness was coming and going and the bone of my hip was sharp onto the man's collarbone and my saliva was a snail's trail down his back, which was all sinew and muscle and tiny salt-flecked hairs, and at one point – oddly, daringly, inexplicably – I licked it. I've no idea why; my body was taking over my mind. A sudden bird screeched its outrage, yet there was no fear in me at all, just a deep restful loosening that made me want to lie back and float in the river of this man's walking as his feet read the land strong. But a raging thirst. And a licking again of the sweat off his back. I felt in the long striding as if my flesh was melting into my silent rescuer's, then my consciousness seeped away and I was set down on the ground and went under deeply, momentarily, again.

Waking, with a start. To a high exposed moon and silvered, racing clouds. Waking to the abrupt contours of civilisation beneath me, a cold, hard floor. A door pretending to be England at my face. I'd been placed on flagstones under the mushroom of a verandah, with my fingers clutched tight around Jack's knife. A cliff of civility was before me, its threshold rigorously swept. No leaves, no dirt. My flesh ribbons from sharp rocks were bleeding afresh, but I was too weak to cry out.

My rescuer looked at me then walked away without glancing back. Too soon! I couldn't get up – tried, couldn't speak. He stopped – thank God – at an enormous witch of a tree wrapped in great slabs of bark like sheaves of vellum warped by water. It was as if they'd been slopped on haphazardly by some elderly and half-blind labourer. The rescuer ripped off four enormous tongues then placed the soft strips over me like a tender, loose glove and hovered his palm over my forehead and swollen lips and left with a low whistle, without looking back.

Oh.

KERFUFFLE

A light in a window but I didn't want to call out; wanted longer, for a moment, this island of wonder with its air more sea-filled than land-filled, its leaves bristly and blunt, its bark of astonishing softness and its assault of a strange smell that was human yet not, familiar yet not. And only when my rescuer was gone did the dogs bark. Then out they came, the babelous voices, the swirl of boots, the everywhere hands and eyes. Into me. Onto me.

A man's blackened fingertips were at me first with a murmured 'Christ o-mighty,' followed by a clutter of shouting and shushing – 'Cover her!', 'Poor mite', 'Blankets!' – and it was only then I realised my clothing had been shredded and I felt wrong for the first time, and shameful, on this great heaving wallop of a night. My fingers were prised from the knife and I was too weak to cry out and I curved my body like a fist away from them, from this great looming door into civilised life.

A woman's panicked scold cut above everything else – 'Get her warm. Quick!' – as my glove of protective bark slipped completely off and all the eyes were at me under their circle of light as lanterns and candles searched for a story, a name, a life.

'Who are you, lass?'

'Where did you come from?'

'Out here of all places!'

I searched for a voice to tell them who I was and how I got to their house. Instinctively I knew to protect my rescuer and my fingertips hovered at my lips in wonder, in memory hoarding.

Yes, it really happened, all of it.

ZOUNDS AND ZOOTERKINS

'I spoke to you first. You're mine now.'

I fold my arms at the boy's declaration. Don't understand it, never have – ownership, by another human – which is exactly what I'm fleeing from by not declaring my name.

'I got in first, Mermaid.'

He's half my size or less. My laugh shoots to the ceiling in a sudden raucous hoot; I am alive! Outside is the warmth of the sun and I'm ready to dive into it! With a possible new companion! I feel a volcanic surge of delight bubbling up within me; life is wondrous.

The boy twists the doll's wooden arm off as if he's done it before and flaps the disembodied limb then tosses it across to me. I wave it back. He claps his hands. I wink. We're partnered. The boy's grin is too big for his face, it floods his paleness with lovely ludic life; he's warming up.

'You have to stay with me, Mermaid.'

I frown in the thinking. Discomfort versus security, instinct versus want.

The boy fetches a plate of biscuits from a bureau. They're misshapen and lumpy, child-cooked. I devour them, a wild thing with hair flopping over my face, laughing through a spray of crumbs as my body wakes up.

'I always put in lots of sugar. Good? Yes?' A crumb-crammed grin. The boy flings back the curtains and releases the light. Raucous shrills and shrieks rise from a wall of trees at the edge of the lawn that's furiously neat, with clipped grass and flower beds and roses trained into arches. Yet the land beyond it feels muscular and dense, a wild band of green leering over the house.

'Who are you?' My voice finally works, just.

'You speak! But it's really low. Like a boy. But you're a girl. Did the sea do that?'

'My head hurts, which is making my voice go funny. But I don't feel like I'm quite of this earth right now.'

The boy gasps, half believing it.

'Can you take me outside?'

'What? When?'

'Now.'

The boy shuts down. Glances at the door – 'But there's lunch, and Mammy wants to dress you; she'll be here soon' – and I remember through an earlier jagged sleep a woman's hands swiftly shutting the curtains and a boy's voice: 'I was only trying to help!' Silence in response. The hands were luminously pale and cuffed by crisp lace and they abruptly smoothed my sheets with no maternal warmth and then the curtains were fussed over to close a sliver of a gap. It felt almost as if the obscene brightness of Outside might scald my delicate foreign eyes and I really must stay put in this darkened room that is trying so hard to be England, I must not move from it under any circumstances. Yet somehow, after the hands left, the gap in the curtains crept back.

Urgh, don't *lady* me, I'd thought at the time, whoever you are with your too-white cuffs. Because mud spatters and smudges are always on my clothes and twigs in my hair and caterpillars on my wrists; I love holding my face to the sky and being kissed by the wind and the dirt. Only my father understands this, and Jack, and possibly this boy with his intriguing hands of dirt.

'Get me out of here.'

He puts his finger to his lips and opens the French doors and I shut my eyes and breathe deep. It smells beautiful out there, laden with salt and life and a mysterious enticing green. Outside is winning, it will have me soon; I'm in thrall to new wonder and ready for this. I kick out my legs in their tight binding. These scratchy schoolmarm sheets will not win. But an ache all over is congealing and the boy says his mammy is coming soon and he's meant to alert her as soon as the guest wakes up; he's on watch.

'Not just yet. Please. Come on.'

'Alright,' he agrees, catching on. 'And we'll do so much when you're all fixed up. Cooking and fishing. Trapping opossums. Roo spotting. Snake catching.'

'Your mother lets you do all that?'

'I do what I want!' The boy speaks as if I'm to fill a great yawning gulf in his life and he has it all planned; I'm the water to his desert in this place.

'Where am I?'

'The big house. Willowbrae.'

Like I should know, like everyone does. A name of idyllic Scottishness that feels seamed into the weft of this land. 'Willows. Where?'

'They never grew proper. But the name stayed.'

'Oh. And can I please stand by the doors and look out at this Willowbrae?'

'Of course! But you need to get back into bed as soon as Mammy comes.'

I wriggle in the sheets and collapse and try again and the boy joins in and together we loosen the linen and I lunge out in an almighty kick and break finally from the cloth's determined grip. Sheets and pillows tumble to the ground. I stand. Just. My feet are unstable on the boards, as if beneath me still is the pitching deck, the sea not quite gone from me yet.

'Woah.' I sway. Drop. The boy catches me, just.

I sit on a stool and examine myself in a looking glass. Not good. A bruise smears my cheek and another is on my forehead. Seaweed and twigs are still stuck in my hair. 'Would you look at the mess of me.' I drag a leaf from a hair knot. 'Bloody hell.'

The boy gasps. Swear words, and in a girl-creature of all things. Salty sailory cussing that's now tipping him into thrillingly illicit territory. I laugh at his shock. He raises his thumb in appreciation; his creature from the depths has a rare kind of value now. I get up, sway, clutch the bed post, my world still pitched. 'Tarnation be damned!' Because the boy must have his show. He slaps his hand across his mouth and gobbles silently like a fish, as if he needs to cram in all these new words before they go. 'Zooterkins and zounds and, um, damnation by zounds!' I poke his tummy and tell him I'll be his very best new friend if he'll have me.

'Yes! Yes!'

'Well then, first things first. A name. Not mine. Yours.'

'Arran.' The boy spits it out as if expelling poison. 'It's all Papa's fault. It runs in the family and he wanted it. But there's too many Arrans and Callums, all the grand-whatevers grumpy and gloomy down the hallway. And I'm not them.'

'Excellent.' I laugh, rubbing my hands. 'A maverick. Just what we need to hear.'

The boy sweeps up his hair to cool his neck as a girl would. How brave he is and uncaring, growing his locks so long; unless someone's compelled him to do this. If he's chosen this look himself, well, there's an odd kind of courage to his difference, but perhaps out here no one's shown him how to be like everyone else. Arran grins. Seems so … alone.

'What's *your* name, Mermaid?'

'Oh, you don't want to know.' I smile serenely. 'Because I do not care for it.'

'Only bad people don't tell their names. Like escaped convicts. And no-good thieves. And dirty old gin distillers and axe murderers in the dead of midnight. Which one are you, Mermaid?'

'All of those. Scared?'

'Nah.'

I laugh. He's good. 'You know, I'd like to try something else for a while, young Master Arran. As a kind of … experiment. In fact, why don't *you* decide my name? It'll only be for a little while.'

He pauses, thinking. I'm thinking too. A new name decided by this boy might just work for the moment. Before I'm bridled with a surname I never asked for. Before me lies a possible extension of my freedom, for however long I can sustain it.

My breath shallows. I need this for now. Come on, Arran boy. Could I possibly, temporarily, be about to escape my fate? He's weighing it up. Finally nods.

'Poss.'

Just like that.

'Oh. Poss. Goodness. Singular. Mysterious. Quite unique. Ah, may I ask why?'

'Because you're like an opossum that comes in the night and scrambles things up and is really cheeky with lovely big eyes and I love them, they're my friends. Please. Possy. You've got to be it.'

I contemplate this lonely sprite of a child so eager before me. 'Poss it is,' I declare. 'I might just love it, actually, Arran. Naughty, night-time Poss.'

The boy tells me that no one ever calls him Arran except when he's in trouble, which never happens of course.

'Oh really?' I tickle him. And he's only ever known as Mouse, he says, his nickname, but no one remembers why. 'Little, possibly? Too much hair?'

He giggles. I run my fingers up his tummy. 'Mice make me laugh. But I can never quite catch them. They're very disobedient.'

We pump hands on a splendid new partnership then I bend and tickle Mouse's palm with my middle finger, eye to eye, and whisper that this very special, very private tickle will be our secret signal from now on. 'Our sign of adventurous adventuring and undying devotion. Forever.'

Mouse hugs me with a wrench that almost dislocates my neck, like he's never hugged in his life and is guessing it. 'And you can be my governess and talk all that boring lady stuff with Mammy. You'll be her gift, Poss! Her girl at last. She'll love it. A friend, for both of us. It's perfect.'

I step back. Contemplate this new arrangement. Possibility suddenly unfurls. Because there might be a future here, perhaps. As a lady of learning, a companion to the matriarch of this house. This could be a gift of certainty. Of employment and security and safety. What was I thinking earlier on? This is my big chance. The viciousness of the alone suddenly contracts; it's no longer brimming me up with its glittery weight.

'Excuse me, I'll only stay if there are four contracted hours of free time outside, per day, for the most terrifying of adventures. With one Master Mouse. Actually, make it five hours. Maybe even six.'

He rubs his hands in glee. 'Mammy always says this is no land for a lady.'

'I'm exceedingly tough, boy. I can handle anything.'

'Really?'

I lift him in a whoosh but I've been too ambitious and yelp in pain.

'You alright, Poss?'

'Yes, yes, shipshape. Just.'

He hooks his legs around my waist and I cradle his back in clasped hands then pretend to let him fall and, wincing, catch him.

'Again!' he commands.

'Sssshhhhh,' I say, giggling, 'or your mammy will put a stop to this.'

THE CORRALLED LIFE

Yet just try and stop me, I'm thinking, because I've never been able to contain my energy. Can't sit silently or be meek and contained, can't fold myself into daintiness. My limbs won't work that way, to the horror of everyone except Pa. And for my entire life until last year he was the retired school master on our rundown little farm, raising me without the guidance of a mother. He'd let me wear Ambrose's cut down trousers and I'd fill my pockets with rocks and shells and learn the land in boots he'd grown out of and I felt invincible and strong and earthed.

'I always wanted a brother like you, Mouse.'

His eager little face. 'And I always wanted a friend, Poss. Is this what it feels like? In your chest? Deep inside it?'

'Yes.' My fist balls into my blooming heart. 'Me too. We'll have so much fun.'

'Mammy never follows me. She has no idea.' Mouse looks at me, the cat with the richest cream. 'She's always in bed with her headaches. Every month, in the gloom, with her hand on her forehead and moaning. That's when, bang, I'm off.'

'Your poor mama. Stuck with a child like you.'

'I try to help! I'm a good boy!' Mouse smiles at me with his butter-wouldn't-melt face. I've got the measure of him now:

a little schemer and fairly crackling with loneliness. He just wants someone to show things to and fix things up. 'I've got sixty-three adventures ready to go, Poss. You and me, just like friends. Mammy's always wanted someone who'll stay,'

'Who'll … stay.'

'We're so far away. From everything.'

I glance across to the loom of trees beyond the lawn. What's out there? I've always owned the outside world, felt talled up in it, strong; and already Willowbrae with its heavy furniture and dense wallpaper seems like a fortress of claustrophobia in comparison. This morning, in my room, what were the woman's hands afraid of? The hands with their lace cuffs brisking the curtains shut, as if in terror of what's beyond the house, of what might be inadvertently glimpsed. They must have belonged to Arran's mother. But how will a woman like that cope with a someone like me? I've never fitted neatly into any lock and it's rare to find someone who'll just let me be me. As Pa did, and Jack. *Jack.*

I look across at his knife, my only possession in the world now. My darling friend must come back – an intake of breath, I shut my eyes. 'But I can't stay here forever, Mouse. And, actually, maybe your mammy won't let me.'

'You can't leave, Poss! You're not allowed! All the governesses always give up. Go away. Run away. But I'm *not* letting you go.' Mouse burrows his anguish into me.

'We'll see.' I stroke his back. Run away? What pushes them from this place?

'We can go to the kitchen after lunch. I'll show you everything. We can cook!'

A kitchen. I step back; no, not yet. It's the room I dread most because someone else invited me into theirs recently and I'm not interested in that world.

I have a kitchen of adequacy. I trust you enjoy baking. You will not miss England. We do a fine kangaroo tail stew and a Mulligatawny soup flavoured by opossum. There is much to learn. You will enjoy the challenges of living in this place. It is not without its beauty.

The letter had crashed into my world too soon after Pa was buried. My betrothed's hand was nervy, spidery, blotched.

There will be God's work aplenty for you. You will be kept busy all hours.

Really? And what had my brother told this man? What revenge was Ambrose exacting here? Then the line to make me go very, very still.

My land, though extremely remote, is a fine place to raise a family in. You will agree.

A curdling of revulsion. A mighty kick at the wall. The letter was flung at Maddie the sow, who promptly and loyally ate it. For God's sake, let there be choice with love most of all. Because every night I have a secret, liquid surrendering. Late, right before sleep. A surrendering that thrums me into someone else when I dream of Edward Tate, the school master, or, more lately, Jack with his open, freckled face. I know exactly who I want and don't, and know in an instant, and nothing will change my mind on it. I want a big life, driven by love, with a friend by my side. Not this. The pinched, ungenerous handwriting, the assumption this will work. And a vicar of all people, a man with a corralled life.

On the *Finbar*'s journey out, my sister-in-law – the eternally displeased Mariana – kept placing next to me her copy of *Women's Journal of Instruction*. Always open at some crucial page she wanted me to know about. The final time Mariana did this she handed me the book and walked away with a raised eyebrow, in challenge, leaving me with a folded-down page and a sentence underlined: '*Nothing will increase your influence and secure your usefulness than being in subjection to your husband.*' Well, that deserved a fling into the ocean and it had Jack and me whooping across the waves in delight. When Mariana was told the manual had regretfully been washed overboard, her head bobbed like a chicken with the shock.

The book's tenor was like every manual given to me by my sister-in-law over the years: *Your husband owns you. From the moment of wedlock all property and money will go under his name and it cannot be accessed without his permission.* Yet my father had raged against ownership, of anyone. There is some kind of willing erasure in my sister-in-law and it bewilders me – that a woman would embrace a disappearance into someone else's life. To Mariana there is a magnificence in the prize of wifedom; she sees men as a rescue whereas I am perpetually on guard, intent on rescuing myself. And what I sense most sinfully is that women who are independent thinkers can't get married, that it seems incompatible with their strength. And that some men like my

brother want to put me neatly in my place yet can't; they want
me to feel weaker and stupider but I know enragingly that I'm
not. Please let this docking not happen, I'd prayed yesterday –
only yesterday! – sun-brimmed on the *Finbar*'s deck. Because of
a fiancé unknown. A wedding unwanted. A life unhomed.

> *You need only pack only what is necessary. No niceties, no*
> *books. I have everything that is needed. I have managed to carve*
> *out an adequate, Godly life.*

Ah, so no curiosity-crammed life of difference then? Mere …
adequacy? I've always felt in thrall to the world, to its wonder,
want to gulp it whole. And no books? My betrothed already has
everything needed. So that would be the Bible then.

> *My dwelling has sufficient of all. The house is humble but not*
> *unpleasant. The Lord will keep you busy enough. Your most*
> *obdt. hum. Servant, in anticipation and in charity —*

Charity. Like this man is doing me a favour, taking my family's
square peg out of its round hole and resting my father's agitated
soul. Because he'd wondered in the end what would actually
become of me; as if, after all his unconventional methods of
raising a child, he'd suddenly gleaned my future and feared that
no man would ever have me. Risk me.

Ambrose had come home from the Southland to be married,
and then, upon our father's sudden death, had settled our father's
affairs – and mine, choosing for me a fiancé of thirty-three,
twice my age.

My brother's new wife seemed to take an instant dislike to her scraggly wild cat of a sister-in-law. It felt, oddly, like she was somehow afraid of me, of my indifference to her pursed ways. As a young woman soon to be married, I had to strictly conform to her world, and she would not stand for anything else, as if that would expose her somehow, perhaps, and her way of dealing with all this was endless little snippets of nastiness.

Mariana had whispered the morsel about my betrothed's age at supper, just before we sailed, her head on one side with a glint of chuff.

'You'll be well provided for, Thomasina. I hear he's rather ... large, apparently. And that his countenance is not entirely, er, becoming. Apparently he has some awkwardness. No matter.' Then she'd slapped down her pretty little gauntlet. 'It's what's inside that counts, of course.'

I'd exhaled like a draft horse through loose lips. 'What's inside? Do you know, Mariana? Do you want me to spend the rest of my life with a ... a stranger?'

'Just wait and see, Thomasina. Thomasina? Are you listening? Get your head off the table. You have so much to learn about life. You're such a ... *child*.'

'I'll remove my head from the table when you start calling me by my name. Which is Tom. *Tom*. It's simple. Three letters. Quite possible, even for you.'

Mariana had stormed out of the room. I poked my tongue out after her. I despise my sister-in-law. Can almost smell the fear of difference on her, fear of a peculiar female difference which must be squashed in all circumstances.

In the weeks before sailing, Mariana snipped away constantly at me, trying to mould me into something tamed and knowable and quiet. There were tuts and taunts at the whoop of my too-loud laugh. At my leaping a stile or dangling upside down from a branch. At the shock of trousers, when Mariana arrived at our farm unannounced. At my feet astride two galloping donkeys. At the unseemly scrawl of my hooked left-handedness, which has never been corrected. And at the indecent boom of my singing voice joyed-up too much in its church.

And so, to Mariana's triumph courtesy of an arranged marriage at childhood's edge. Mariana's strange sister-in-law will be bridled at last because she's too uncontained, too much; she'll be married off to a vicar who has a name and age and not much else.

But now this. A new future can be attempted, for a while, that no one will have any say in but myself.

I drop Mouse lower then catch him neatly in a snatch. He shoots out a laugh.

Maybe, actually, everything will be alright in this place.

I hope.

In Which the Cuffs
Present Themselves

Footsteps along the corridor, brisk with purpose. The bedroom door is flung wide. Mouse has been cradled in my arms but jumps out of them the instant the door is opened.

'Mammy! I didn't do nothing.' Mouse swallows his words, panicked. 'She got up by herself. It wasn't me, it was her!'

Maternal fists accusing on hips. 'The room is a mess. You know I can't have that.' A nervous, guilty hoot of an apology from me, which is abruptly stopped as the mammy hurries over to the French doors and shuts them and locks them and the curtains are once again snapped tight on the light. 'Lord, this room.'

She's tiny and round, as pale as her son and meticulously turned out, a crisp, shiny apple of affront. Her unnaturally red cheeks look vigorously scrubbed and her pale hair is ruthlessly scraped from her face. Nothing about her looks ready for Outside.

'You didn't tell me our guest was awake. And not only awake but up. *Up*. You were meant to tell me, Mouse. Mouse?' The woman's voice is running away from her, slipping into shrillness. Mouse says nothing. 'You were meant to watch. Not do anything. I have to keep this girl alive.'

I go to say something but stop. Mouse's head bows in the knotted silence. I find his fingers, squeeze them. They don't squeeze back, as if he's now afraid of even that. A hand is appalled at the woman's mouth, like she can't bear the shock of this mess, the sheets pulled back and spilling onto the floor alongside strewn pillows as well as the doll in disarray and the eiderdown on the cot mussed up. And what does she know of my rescue last night? I shut my eyes for a moment on a slow lick of skin the length of an arm – how did that happen, what took over me? – then open them again to this new knot of a family, to Mouse's sudden shrinkage and this woman's tutting affront. A large black cross on a rope of jet hangs from her neck.

'And you, child. Girl child. Tall girl child.'

'I'm not a child.'

She looks at me as if she sees right through me. 'Really? As ragged as a child. And certainly standing like one. And torn to bits. Can you speak? What's your name? What's Mouse done to you? Dragged you off into the mysteries of his world, eh?'

Mouse holds my nightgown like a dog on a lead and pulls me back to him. 'I was Doctor Mouse, Mammy. Like with you. I call her Poss because she can't remember her real name and she arrived in the night and she's got a head that hurts.'

'Poss? So now I have a Mouse and a Possum under my feet. A right menagerie.'

'Yes!' I laugh then stop.

'What's your real name, child? We need to find out who you belong to. And get you fixed. Your head took a blow.' The woman's hand hovers at my cheek, then smooths back my hair, and smooths.

'I'm good at fixing things, Mammy, aren't I?' Mouse babbles, nervous.

I lurch back with my fist balled above my eye; it's suddenly thudding with pain. 'Please, ma'am. Your boy was helping. I need to gather myself. Rest. My head —' It's now pulsing in an iron grip but my voice comes out blunt, wrong, verging on rudeness; it's the freshly pounding forehead that's curdling it. The mammy is fairly bristling with her need for an adult interrogation and I know that a well-bred young lady's speciality is niceness and acquiescence, the big yes, but I just can't be any of that right now, in the skin of the new me. Oh, I need to be good at being alive! Yet all my instincts are telling me to retreat and rest, to fix this aching head.

The mammy tilts her face, observing. 'Lunch is served in half an hour. You'll need some clothes, young Miss.'

'But —'

'If you can hold a boy of seven, you can hold a lunch. I saw you, child.'

The mammy officiously pushes up one lace cuff then the other and removes my fist from my temple and places her flattened palm on the felling spot, and presses. It's good, cooling. She's helping me here and my shoulders soften. Perhaps I'm reading this all wrong.

'Thank you,' I murmur.

'My bark can be worse than my bite, you know. Never forget that.' A curt smile, then she lifts up my hair and fusses with it as if imagining what it would be like, styled.

I do enjoy someone running their fingers through my hair and I lean into the intimacy of the touch. Close my eyes for a moment, relax.

'Lunch is at one. It won't be a long affair, then you can spend the rest of the day in bed.'

A flicker of acknowledgement passes between us: that we're females together in this. A consoling arm of steel is slipped around my waist and Mouse sneaks his hand into mine but his mother brushes him away – *Scat! She's mine!* – because there's the uncontainable mess of a mysterious guest alongside strewn bedclothes and open curtains and this woman will now be taking over, thank you very much. It's all in the rigour of the lace pinned at her neck and the hair with not a strand out of place. This wild child before her, from the ocean depths, needs to be enveloped in civilisation. *Her* civilisation. Not Mouse's.

WILTING

The woman leads me to the bed and at the strength in the encircling arms I wilt; the ocean is back through me and I sway and fall to the sheet like a mole wanting to tunnel into its home. Home. So removed from all this. When I depart this world, I want my body slipped into the sweet wild earth of my unbound girlhood, my balming earth, but I fear I'll never get back to it now. This is my only certainty here: that I'll never again sleep in the home that holds my heart hostage, my little teapot of a cottage with its snug windows of warped glass and sooty candle nooks and narrow stairs to my attic lair; I'd always leap over the bottom five in my race to clatter into the day. I nestle on the bed now, want to weep. With my father I was exactly the person I wanted to be; I was found. And now I need some kind of ballast; I am lost.

'Name? Age?'

'Sixteen.'

A softening voice. 'I think there's still something of the child in you, yes? You do look very young. Poor poppet, what you've been through.'

My hair is smoothed behind an ear, and smoothed, and I nudge into the sudden tenderness like a dog wanting a pat. The woman's fingers hold my head firm on either side and find both

46

temples and rub in a circular motion and I shut my eyes and surrender to the authoritative, feminine touch that's melting away my headache. My mother died of a lung disorder when I was four and all she left me with was a craving for a fingertip's slowness down a cheek and a fierce female holding where everything is soothed right. My father left me with the memory of freedom in a life flavoured by the earth. He didn't want his girl in corsets that restricted her breathing, or skirts without the convenience of pockets; he wanted my hands ready for the world. *You must have pockets for your fossils and sticks, to collect the world, Tommy Tom.*

And now an unreadable woman fusses around me. Her hands straighten the bedclothes and rearrange items on the bureau and tuck Jack's knife under the Bible as if she's sullied by the sight of it, then she goes to the curtains and completely shuts out the light. 'What dreams, child.'

'Pardon?'

'This morning. You were crying and calling out. Clawing at the air to be saved.' The mammy mimes madness in restless sleep.

'Oh. I've no memory of it. Goodness.' I'll have to watch for any signs of slippage. After my father's death, my brother had one thing over me when it came to stubbornness and strop. He threatened to have me locked in the County Women's Asylum more than once – and as my legal guardian he could have done it. *That look, Thomasina. It's too much. Would you care for the asylum perhaps? Would you? It can be arranged. Just try me. Go on.*

I always knew that a charge of insubordination or wilfulness was enough to have me vanished; women around me had been swallowed by less. Beth Tine for being a grass widow – although why should she have been punished when her husband was the one who got bored and ran off, leaving her to look after two small children? Mary Harris for rebellion against domesticity. Em Snow for fret sickness after her baby came. Hetty Raddle for fret sickness when her baby didn't come. Ada Wilton, hysteria. Cara Larkin, hysteria. And what exactly did that word mean?

My brother's solution to the vexed matter of my existence lay in a parish in the colonies, regrettably far from his own estate but close enough to occasionally keep an eye on me. I could never be left in Knockleby completely alone, unwatched and penniless. Ambrose had burdened our father's house with debt to fund his new life in the new world and now there's no family money left. And I was not allowed to be left behind to become the village eccentric in perplexing boy-clothes. But what Ambrose doesn't know is that I'll only marry for love, and want, and that decision will remain sacrosanct.

The mammy absently examines my hands as if looking for the indent of a ring swept off. 'What happened out there, child? How did you come here?' She shakes her head. 'Perhaps some food will shake the tongue out of you.' She informs me that her name is Alexandra Craw and asks if there is anything I need? 'Water, Bible, a hymn?'

I express gratitude for her kindness; it's brushed off.

'I've always wanted a girl in this house. We'll do very well together. You have lovely eyes, but what a hoot of a voice you've got. If I shut my eyes it could be a gentleman's.'

'I've heard that before.'

'Have you now? And your laugh.'

'I'll try to contain it.'

'Hmm. That may be impossible. Now to business. Name? And don't you be saying Poss.'

I flop back on the pillow, my fingers over both eyes as if pressing them into my skull.

'She's had a knock, Mammy,' Mouse intervenes.

His mother sighs that she'll crack the mystery out of her guest yet, but in the meantime Willowbrae has a brand new girl to contend with and fancy that. Just fancy.

'A brand new ...?'

Mouse whispers to me that his mammy lost her dear little Faith when she was bitten by a snake that she thought was a stick. The woman adds that her girl had been three and would be about my age now and the pain has never faded, it's grown over her heart and fair stopped it. Her girl, her only girl. 'Then you arrived, Mouse. To flood my life with —'

'Another stinky boy! Three of us now, Mammy. *Three*.'

'I am *not* counting. And you are *not* the stinky one. That would be your two brothers. You drive me to distraction in many respects, Master Mouse, but not that one. Most days I'd drown you if I could, mind ...'

A glittery silence. Mouse goes very still, bites his lip. And in that moment I see the isolation of the neglected child, the baby not desired enough. I want to clasp my little friend fiercely and tell him how grateful I am to have him, a proper brother at last. I wink. He smiles bravely back, shaking his head as if he's used to this. I feel filled up suddenly with the thought of this rare, dear find, so plucky before me, more brother than a brother — because I've chosen this one.

I ask if Outside is as forbidding as the tales I'd been told on the ship and it prompts a symphony of horror from them both: stories of brown snakes that kill in six minutes and spiders that leap and falling death-branches and sharks with ravenous teeth. In fact Mrs Craw isn't sure why she ever settled here, why she was dragged from her lovely, benign northern world into this. She's barely still as she smooths the cot's quilt and runs fingers along surfaces that have no dust. She picks at some embroidery left on a chair and stabs the needle into the mesh, blooding her finger and sucking it with pursed lips. 'Everything goes wrong in this God-forsaken place. Can't even get the sewing right.'

I suspect she's a woman who can't control the world outside, only inside, in this house. God help her with me. Her hands clap at a mosquito. She misses, claps again and triumphantly displays her palm's bloody blot.

'You're very good at that, ma'am. I need to learn.'

'Years of practice. Don't worry. I'll teach you everything you need to know.' Mrs Craw's voice drops into something else. 'And alongside the blood-sucking mosquitos and the spiders and snakes out here … there are the Blacks. Savages as dark as the devil, Poss. You never know where they are or what they're doing, and that's why you'll be staying close. In this house. With me.' Mrs Craw brusques to the French doors and stares out through the curtains. She turns abruptly, propelling Mouse to the door – 'There's a water jug to fill' – then she raises an eyebrow at me. 'So, Miss …? Anything you've got to tell me?'

She wants me alone. All to herself.

THE MOTHER I NEVER GOT

Mrs Craw jostles flowers as big as fists in a vase. They're pulsing with colour and a rude waxy vibrancy; they're too fecund, too much. I shrink back in the bed and shake my head. I have nothing to tell her. The curtains are again rearranged, keeping whatever is out there at bay for the moment, because she must.

'I love the light, ma'am. Love being outside. Actually.'

'It's just the bush, poppet. It's too easy to get lost in. Now, down to business. You arrived on our doorstep barely conscious. Who helped you here? Someone did.'

'Here? Where exactly *is* Willowbrae?' I reach out my hand, test the waters; can I swerve this talk? I want this house to be a haven, a harbour, to rest from the toss of my future. I'm penniless and have possibly lost all my remaining family – a fact that I don't fully understand – and I need a home now, the solace of certainty. 'How far are we from everyone else, ma'am?'

Mrs Craw laughs and says that we're a long way from anywhere else and I'd better get used to it. That her little Poss is on Craw land now, which has far too many men on it, and it's about time she had some female company at Willowbrae because it's been quite a while, so I'd better take a good long time to get fixed. 'Understand?'

'If you say so.'

Mrs Craw looks at me. 'Yes. I do.'

'But what about all the others. On the ship?'

'We're seeing to it, child. Rest assured.'

I nod, not quite sure of the nub of this woman. Who is she, exactly? Mrs Craw tells me that all the pesky townsfolk will want to get their claws into me but I must recover here under her watch and, besides, her littlest could do with some company. He has no one to play with and is always under her feet and needs exhausting by someone else; he wakes up far too early for everyone here, day in and day out. 'It's so hard ... this land. Mothering is hard. Of impish little boys in particular. So many little boys in my life.' Mrs Craw's fingers knead her head as if clouds of panic are congregating at the mere thought. She says she has my recovery planned and by all means take my time. I rise unsteadily and head to the French doors and push the curtains back, suddenly needing some fresh air.

'There's nothing out there, Poss. This is a vast endless island of ... nothing.' The woman parts my hair over my shoulders and smooths her fists over both bunches, and looks, and looks, and smiles, as if lost in something very private. Then she runs her finger down my bruised cheek, stopping over my swollen lips. 'Does your mammy need to be informed?' It's a voice that almost can't bear to say it.

'Of what?'

'Of your ... aliveness?' A weighted silence, followed by Mrs Craw's smile. 'No. I didn't think so. It's the hair that told me. You don't care for it much, I can tell. The brush I left for you is quite untouched.' She indicates a hairbrush left beside a hand mirror on the bedside table; I hadn't noticed them until this moment. 'I suspect you've never been taught how to properly do things like hair, have you? A lady of refinement would have seen to it immediately, before anyone caught sight of her. And a mother would have told her that. Am I correct in assuming that you're in need of some mothering, perhaps? I'd love to have a girl about the house.'

I smile. Mrs Craw's fingers shake my tresses into further wildness and I accidentally knock over a glass as I move away – 'Sorry!' – and she holds in a tut.

'Not very good with life sometimes, ma'am. I need to get better at it.'

The older woman folds her arms. 'Maybe I can help you with that.' I shrug helplessly; Mrs Craw nods as if a deal has been done. Asks about my father but my face tells her to go no further, that it hurts too much. 'And do we read, by any chance?'

'I have French and Latin. And sing. And play the piano. You'll be begging me to stop.'

'I knew it. I told my dearly beloved, always absent and eternally distracted husband you'd be educated.'

'How did you know?'

'You've got a bump on the side of your writing finger. See.' Mrs Craw whips up my left hand. 'The devil's hand. And it looks like no one has ever prevented you from using it.' She tuts a mock.

'Oh goodness, ma'am, no. Never.'

'You happily wrote with it?'

I shrug, smile.

'I miss nothing in this house, young Miss. My husband must see this.' She rubs her finger gently over the writing bump before reluctantly letting my hand go. 'You'll meet the good man soon enough, at lunch. He's never around except for a feed. Always out there, somewhere, always off.' Her hands flap at Outside as if pushing it away. 'And it's not just the finger that told me you read. It's that sharply intelligent face.'

'Oh, I like that "sharply intelligent" bit. Please keep repeating it. Often. I think I'll enjoy staying here.'

Mrs Craw laughs. I pick up the doll from the floor and hold it out and she takes it from me and pushes its wooden arm back on.

'It's always coming off,' she murmurs. 'It was my Faith's.' She suddenly holds me, a touch too long, as if she's going to crack in this moment. With the kindness. 'Goodness.' The woman's eye-prick of tears, she holds them back. 'You've certainly come at the right time, girl. And who needs a proper name anyway? You'll be gone if we learn of it, I suspect. Someone will claim you and we can't have that, can we? You're our little miracle for now. A sign from God that we must, actually, be doing something right. And yes, Poss will do very nicely for now. As a name. It's all we need. For now.'

I step back. Smile, hesitantly. This woman understands erasure; she'll go along with it. I glance outside. Am sure I catch movement, by a tree, a flit of a shadow swiftly enveloped by the bush. I push back the lace netting to get a better look and accidentally tear some from its hooks. 'Oh! Sorry! So clumsy. Pa's always saying that.' A laugh shoots out and Mrs Craw visibly swallows and tells me tightly it's fine, easily mended.

'I'm always making a mess. I'm so sorry.'

'I'll manage.' A pause. 'I think.'

'Thank you, thank you.' A glance back at the tree.

'Now, lunch. You need to meet your rescuers.'

I turn sharply. 'My who?'

'The family. My posse of little boys. Who are very impatient to find out exactly what the storm washed up. Which is you.'

'Oh.'

CLAD

The pounding in my head is subsiding. I can feel an old self unfolding; something is spining me up. I can do this lunch. Want to thank my native rescuer, wherever he is now, and want to meet the rest of this family. I just need my clothes.

'I've had your old ones disposed of.'

'Oh. Why?'

Mrs Craw picks up the brush and starts fussing about my hair. 'They were no good anymore, Miss Poss. Shredded. They've gone.'

'Oh.' So. That's it. The last possessions from my old world, vanished. Except for Jack's knife under the Bible, my precious gift and comfort.

The woman plucks twigs and bits of seaweed from my hair then breaks apart knots and firmly brushes; I tilt into the confident stroke. No one has ever tidied my hair before like this; this is attention, consideration, this is a mother's touch. I shut my eyes in gratitude.

'Thank you so much.' I smile. 'I can't wait to go exploring here, ma'am. Outside. In some new clothes …'

A sigh. Outside is a problem for Mrs Craw. 'You'll be needing stout boots for the snakes. And a net over your hat for the flies.

Stockings for the greedy prickles, gloves or your hands will be covered in spots, and a parasol against the horrible light. But why go out anyway, Poss? I manage not to – well, much – and it's done me no harm. And your trunk hasn't arrived off the boat, has it, and I'm shorter and fatter than you. So we're stuck. No clothes. What to do, child, what to do?'

I agree that the trunk situation is most inconvenient and I must have words with that storm. Mrs Craw chuckles. 'You'll do, lass.' I tell her any old thing will be fine, even men's clothes just for now. 'I'm used to it outside, from home, when my Pa let me borrow my brother's old clothes.'

A firming behind Mrs Craw's smile. 'Your father, eh? But it's my house now. My rules. And you'll be staying put for the time being, my scampy little Poss. Quietly, and alively. Inside. As young ladies must.'

I beg Mrs Craw for any old clothes, just for now, until we get something made up. She ignores the plea and natters away about eighteen years of hard labour in this place and how she prays for salvation but do you think it ever comes. And as Mrs Craw chitter-chats about pianofortes slipping into tunelessness and curls dropping in the heat and mould on boots, there are mysterious shrieks from a new world outside, at raucous play, calling me into it. My head cranes as heat presses at me like a wall and a spider of sweat slips down my chest. This room feels so stopped in the midst of vivid life, as if it's all somewhere else.

Mrs Craw checks her watch. 'Goodness, lunchtime. Where did the day go? What are we going to dress you in? I'm going mad in this heat. Think, woman, think. Mouse! Where is he when I need him? *Mouse.*'

The boy comes running and before his mother can get in with her words I blurt loudly that I have nothing to wear for a dining room, I'm not Mrs Craw's size and from what I can gather there are no other females in the house.

'Just wear trousers!' Mouse says, as I knew he would. Mrs Craw retorts that they have standards at Willowbrae; she'll get some cloth sent from town and in the meantime one of the boys' belts can go around my waist and it might just do to bunch in a skirt, which will be far too short actually, which is no good.

'So then what, ma'am? With a skirt that's too short and too wide.'

'I was skinny once, you know. A long time ago … too long ago.' The muttering, the pacing, the sizing up of the curtains.

I tell her I can wear boys' clothes if it's just for now, and just the family. Easily. 'Please. I'd love to.'

A pause at this madness. Mrs Craw cocks her head, in a sudden realisation. 'The ocean has addled you, child.'

'I can't go to lunch in a nightgown.'

'It was Faith's!'

'But she was … a babe. When she, she —'

'I had her trousseau made up. All her things. Early. In joy. Do not speak ill of her.'

'I'm not. I'm sorry. Ma'am. I'm really not.'

The air is taut with misunderstanding.

'I can get some of Tobyn's old things, Mammy. They're in his drawers. Poss is a friend, a boy one. For me, just for now. It'll be one little lunch then she'll get normal again. Let me get her some of Tobyn's things. Please.'

'I know where the clothes are in this house,' the mother retorts while not taking her eyes from the audacious wonder of her house guest. I drop to my knees and mock-pray, hands clasped at Mrs Craw's cross, tickle her fists annoyed at her hips. Which somehow draws out a grin. Just. She sighs and bites her lip, fighting this, then says, 'Alright then, just this once – but this is *your* horrid idea, Poss, not mine. And as soon as the cloth arrives, this insanity will stop. Which could be tomorrow, God willing, or the next day at the most. Because I can't take much more of this.'

I stand and nod my thanks, beaming. Possibility suddenly flexes its claws. At what I could become, at what I'll be allowed here, and at my little partner in crime who'll so eagerly do my bidding. Mother and son depart and ten minutes later the door is kicked open by my messenger, young Master Mouse, who's balancing a tower of men's clothes.

'Delivery! Your new uniform. For all the adventures that are coming!'

'Wait, aren't I meant to be indoors? Quietly and, what was it, alively?'

'It's easy to sneak out,' Mouse responds. 'And I've always got my hat on, so she never sees the sun on my face. She thinks I'm heading off to the veggie patch. If only she knew.'

'Oh. And you're not?'

'What do you think?'

I smile. We're partners. And now I have clothes to roam this land strong in: sturdy, Mouse-chosen garments. If I'm dressed too much like other women I always feel itchy and fidgety, bound and slowed, but I won't be with this lot. I shoo Mouse off and hurry on the trousers, roll up their bottoms and tighten the belt then drop the shirt over my head and lace up the worn boots. Stamp my feet. Laugh. Feel suddenly ready and capable and strong, someone else entirely. I do a gleeful handstand with my feet resting lightly on the wall. This is who I always was on the farm and who I am again and this new world will just have to deal with it. I right myself and punch the air like a boxer, the joy roguish through me.

Mouse runs back, stops short. 'Zounds and, what is it, zounderkins. And zooterkites!'

I grab him in an exhilarated twirl.

'Again, Poss! Again!'

IN WHICH LUNCH IS ATTEMPTED

Mouse and I walk to the dining room. The boy gauges the mood before me and holds me back, holds me tightly in his child world and not the adult.

'I dressed her,' he explains. 'She's called Poss. I chose the clothes. And the name. Because she can't remember who she is but she's mine now and no one else's, alright?'

I say to blame everything on Mouse as my hands flutter to my hair and try to smooth it down because I know this is what Mrs Craw would want, yet my action feels like it's all too little, too late, and I stop in confusion and awkwardness.

But a hedge of men rising, three of them, all tall. But their faces. At my clothes. Mouse drops his hands; Mrs Craw gestures to the men that this wasn't her doing and takes her seat. A stand-off of silence. The others sit too.

'No one told us we were getting this,' says a young man finally. He's dressed in a sloppy uniform and has a freckle-crammed face and looks as if he's truly a child of this wild frontier land where the rules aren't quite followed, as if it's claimed him, it's won, despite his decorous family. A twitch of a smile. 'Mammy?' Then a giggle-snort.

His father – it must be – glances sharply across at him. The older man has a scar down his face as if the flesh has parted with the cleaving and no surgeon has ever seen to it and it has been left to heal by itself in a brutal unright state.

I look back at the younger man. He has a flop of unruly dirty-blond hair with a cow-lick that gives him a boyish look. He hasn't quite grown up. His eyelashes are long; a mother would have melted at them in the boy. His ill-fitting uniform is threadbare and faded as if he too has landed from another place, not this genteel house at all.

But the looking, like a tongue on my eye. I blush. It's noted. I've been here before, with Jack, and Edward the teacher; this personal felling feels familiar. I'll not be drawn into it, will not. Need to keep my wits. A vibration of knowing passes between us. The young man turns to his mother. 'What were you thinking, Mammy? My trousers, my shirt. On a girl of all things. And Pa already has problems with the hair on your youngest. Everything's upside down in this place.'

I hoot an awkward laugh that rings out to the ceiling; everyone stares. I stop, not good at this, decorum, among these people. Mrs Craw raises her hands and says she's never heard a laugh like it, and I'm not sure if this is a good thing or bad from the tone of her voice. I announce that I'm happy with the clothing, for the time being, that it's my request – and I feel like a new person talking here: taller, spined up, earthed.

'You sound like a boy.' The challenge is thrown across from the pretend soldier, who fingers a tarnished gold button hanging by a thread as his mother fiddles with her cross while praying silently to her God with moving lips. The son is all looseness;

he gets away with a lot, I can tell, he's been very loved. It's in his easy energy and the flip of his hair and his playful hands as they tent their pockets. As he looks at me, and looks. Curiosity, challenge, attraction race around the room to the unknowing of everyone else.

'I don't have any of my own clothes right now. I'm sorry.' I flex a booted foot.

'Right. So you just march into the nursery and steal everything. And it'd have to be my favourite things, wouldn't it? Mammy. Explain.'

Mrs Craw runs her fingers along her cutlery as if stroking two tiny pets. She doesn't look at her son; she straightens her cutlery, and straightens it. 'Tobyn, this has little to do with me.'

Mouse suddenly pushes himself in front as if shielding me and declares it's all his fault.

'I suspected as much, Master Mouse.' The soldier waggles his finger. 'A thrashing before sunset for you, and from your favourite brother no less.'

My groin is liquid as he veers back to me; I'm all appetite. Just as I'd been with Jack on the *Finbar*'s deck, just as I'd been whenever Mr Tate tipped his hat. I try to batten it down as I stand before them but the two of us are speech marks aimed at each other across the jumble of everyone else. This boy-man has rules to abide by, I can tell: to never be completely serious, and to never quite grow up. And he's spelled by my clothes, I can see it.

'Boys, boys.' Mrs Craw claps her family to attention then presses her palms to her temples. 'Our young visitor wants it this way. For now. She's had a knock to the head and mightn't be quite … fixed. Yet. But this will only be for a day or two, until some cloth arrives. She has forgotten her name, so we have agreed to call her Poss. A name which Mouse has kindly suggested. Thank you, Mouse. But no one needs to know about the clothes. Our guest has no luggage. So. We can make this work. Poss will be staying with me in the house, out of harm's way. Resting and the like, while we make her some proper clothes. It's only temporary.'

I tell the family I'll be no trouble and thank them repeatedly for taking me in.

'How did you find us, Mermaid?' the boy-man asks.

I tell them it's lucky I can swim – 'Swim! Goodness!' – and explain there was a bit of deck I used as a raft but beyond all that it's a muddle. 'My head has holes in it. Right now.'

'Perhaps your memory will come back with some food,' Mrs Craw prods, and I concur and say that as soon as the situation is sorted – the others found, from the wreck – I'll be on my way.

'Thank you. So much.'

'Well, thank *you* for enlivening this remotest of outposts.' The soldier's smile is arrowed right into me. He runs his fingers through his hair; oh yes, he's been cherished. His disobedient limbs seem too gangly for a coat too short in the sleeves, as if he's had a sudden growing episode and his clothes haven't quite caught up. He winks and I mock-frown; it feels as if all my nerves have been released to the surface, they have no helmet. I'm raw, exposed and must not be here, must make sure nothing about the past slips out. 'You've got your claws into this one well and good, haven't you, Mammy?' the son says.

Mrs Craw sighs and rolls up her cuffs then thinks better of it and unfolds them. I stand before them all with my boy-booted feet planted strong and my hands behind my back, feeling like someone else entirely from that trapped girl on the ship, far removed from the young woman Mariana's manuals requested me to be: '*What is especially to be avoided in ladies is an unquiet, bold and imperious air, for it is unnatural and not allowable.*' So. I'm trying a new self. This boy-man before me represents only one thing – distraction – which I can't afford in this place. I must be alert.

'I'm Tobyn, since you ask. The eldest son. The favourite son.'

A clotted young man hunched next to him raises his eyebrows. This one doesn't care for me; he'll endure my presence but not welcome it. He's the potato to the fresh celery of his brother, pale and round and bespectacled. I'd lose him in a crowd and not remember his face. It's surprising how one brother can be perfectly cooked, yet the other a little off, like a boiled egg too viscous. And he's a little grimy-looking too. As if he doesn't care a jot for any of the niceties of the life his mammy tries so hard to maintain; he looks like he goes about his own business here, apart.

I curtsey in confusion, stop. Hold out my hand. Drop it. Feel suddenly woozy; it comes over me in waves at unexpected moments, as if the storm and the sea have not quite let go of me yet. I press my fist into my forehead to steady myself; no one asks me to sit.

The disengaged brother looks sideways with assessing eyes; he unnerves me, leaves me hanging. Book-bowed or music-bowed, he seems resolutely of the indoor world and I can imagine him a piano teacher or training for the church. I smile in greeting. He gives me nothing back. Like my being here is irritation and nothing else.

'How did you find us?' the father asks, finally. He saws the underside of his little finger on the table's edge as if the digit is addled with some strange infection and he can't contain the impulse. 'Young lady?' He gathers himself with his hands triangled at his chest like an accountant in a collecting pause waiting for his day to commence. He's a stick of dry, stringy beef among them, tough to chew. He looks around at his family, clocking each member with a proprietorial air. I imagine they're everything to him in this far-flung place. 'How did you get to us?' the man says slowly as Mrs Craw methodically picks a crumb from the table.

I stammer that I'm struggling to remember anything.

A pause. 'So when do you think you'll be sufficiently recovered?'

'As soon as I can, sir.'

He nods. Swipes at a fly, misses, tries again. Mrs Craw leans across and claps it crisp between her palms. Tobyn swallows a laugh. As if nothing has just happened, the older man tells me that his name is Callum Craw and I thank him for his largesse, babbling my gratitude.

'You can stop now,' the eldest son teases. 'Father gets twitchy when unknown people crash into his world. He's not good with strangers.' Tobyn's eyes laugh, but the older man's do not and I see exactly now what I am to him. An intrusion.

Yet I feel an impishness restless in me as I stand among these people, talled up in my boots in my lovely new anonymity cloak. Because all the stops on my life are vanished for a brief time; I'm Pa's Galatea made flesh and out in the world, finally.

The doughy son bites at a sliver of loose skin on a finger. It's oddly blackened. Mrs Craw asks him to stop.

'And who is this?' I enquire.

'Virgil,' Mr Craw responds in lieu of the man who does not speak. 'He likes to listen as opposed to talk.' This son still does not speak and is strikingly different because of it, a reaper of quiet.

Mr Craw turns his focus to me as if to draw attention from his taciturn son. He invites me to sit. He says he trusts I'll be comfortable at Willowbrae; I respond that his wife and Mouse have been excellent nurses.

'The best!' the little boy chimes in. 'She's not allowed to leave, this one.'

The matriarch says that Mouse needs a friend because she's heartily sick of his imaginary ones and her Poss has come at exactly the right time. Her hand flutters to her neck. 'Yes? Callum?'

A spider of a prickle again, picking its way up my back. They're so removed from anywhere else. Could this work? Could I possibly live here in this remote place?

Tobyn teases that I'm not allowed to borrow anything more of his unless he's asked first. He says he knows girls – 'unlike my brother here' – and they're such boisterous, rough creatures, always getting muddy and moaning and messing things up. 'So unlike us gentlemen. Impossible to manage. Isn't that right, what's your name again – Poss?' We laugh together.

Mouse looks at us in confusion. A dawning on his face. Competition, and a closing over at the thought.

An older man enters, quietly tending to the dishes on the sideboard. He's bald and compact with a reddened face roughened by what looks like years of drink, yet his hand movements are graceful, speaking of other, finer lives. He nods a smile to me and details the courses in a soft Irish accent, his voice barely heard. Mulligatawny soup from India, kangaroo-tail stew direct from the bush (Mrs Craw pulls a disgusted face at this one), hominy, cider-baked pork with crackling, pickled cabbage, and plum pudding and jellies for dessert.

'What's hominy?'

'That's a maize pottage, Miss.'

'Thank you. Are you the only servant, sir?'

The man looks at me. 'Yes … Miss.' He goes to say something else and stops. Appears to be shrinking into the wallpaper, to make himself as invisible as he can among these people, as if he doesn't want a bar of any of them.

Mr Craw signals a quietening into grace. It's recited with a fervour that's like an incantation of protection. 'We pray no evil shall befall us nor any plague come near our dwelling. We pray we shall walk in God's protection all the days of our lives.' Mr Craw lowers his hands in a sweep of the table as if trying to spell calm into the furniture and the very marrow of the walls, and himself. I glance outside. What a lonely place this is, islanded by the loom of its forest. Mrs Craw kisses her cross. Mouse's eyes are closed in obedient prayer, his lips moving over silent words at odds with his father's, as if he isn't listening at all, preferring his own secret God.

'Are no other women here, ma'am?'

'I can never keep a female. It's too wild and difficult, too remote. Flea's the only one who's stayed. Our faithful Labrador. And he's only got two months left before he gets his ticket of leave. We're family, aren't we, Flea?'

I take a plate from this Flea. He feels like a tinderbox of restraint; his silence is a presence. He's missing the middle digit of his right hand; it's gone right down to the knuckle.

Mouse catches my looking. 'Flea tells me a shark bit it off. Or a tiger. Or a crocodile, was it?'

The man says nothing as if he hadn't heard.

'You will be staying on with us, won't you, Flea?' Mrs Craw's fingers drift to her hair, smoothing the smoothness. Flea smiles slowly, as if anything he might say will be too much. Mrs Craw turns with reddening cheeks and says too brightly to the table that Mouse is in need of a governess. His letters are slipping. His French is non-existent.

'In other words,' Tobyn says, and laughs, 'in need of some taming.'

Mrs Craw says with brittleness that some female company would be a lovely thing indeed and that the dogs, despite what her husband thinks, do not count. Mr Craw doesn't respond. The lines are deep between his eyes, as if he's permanently clenched with worry; a lifetime of frustrated living is in his face. He doesn't seem free at all as he rubs his finger on the table's edge with a tiny tightening of his cheeks, not free like my father was.

Mouse asks me once again to stay, as if he doesn't want to be left alone here. What have I stranded myself in the middle of? I feel oddly vulnerable right now, lost in a strange land and totally alone in it, with not a rag to my back. Yet before me possibly is an income. A position. A purpose in life. A warm bed in a fine home and good clothes: an escape. This is about survival. Mouse looks at me. He lifts his palm and silently tickles a finger from the other hand upon it.

A smile, a deep breath. 'I'd love to stay, ma'am. Try my hand at being a governess — if you'll have me. Because after all a boy must have his French. And Latin. Both of which I have. I was taught by my father.'

Mouse pulls a vomit face that only I see; I stifle a laugh.

Mr Craw looks at his wife then at me then at Tobyn and back at me. 'Alright, alright. For you, madam. We shall try this temporary arrangement.'

I laugh in delight and Mrs Craw claps her hands in triumph and relief. 'Excellent. Welcome to the big house, Poss. After lunch you must get back to your room and continue your recovery. While we prepare. So you're strong for the days ahead.'

'Yes, ma'am!'

'Straight to bed. Alright? Then tomorrow you can look about. Your new home.'

I lean back in my chair and shut my eyes as a glow of relief seeps through me. An anchor, yes, an anchor to my life, right here and right now and I smile at the gift of it. I've always had an irrepressible joy seamed through me and now it's bursting out and despite myself I laugh. A loud whoop to the ceiling, I can't contain it. Tobyn raises an appreciative eyebrow as Mouse flits his eyes between us both.

The Second Day

IN WHICH A VISITOR DISTURBS

A scrubbed quiet. I breathe in a skinful of new air. How long have I been sleeping? It feels like days, weeks. I claw at the untied curtains of the bed canopy encasing me like a shroud and sweep them aside and climb out, to the French doors, pushing back Mrs Craw's light-trapping curtains. Beautiful tall light is outside and the day already feels stale; Willowbrae is lazy with stillness. Heat sheens my skin. I flop back to my stewy bed of sweaty sheets. A tap on the French doors could be a pebble thrown. Hello? Am I imagining it?

No. There it is again.

I rise. Fling the French doors wide and breathe in deep the lovely new air crammed with its alien fragrances. Look down. Gasp. A rat in the last throes of life lies on its side on the flagstones, its fur slicked wet. Yet the day is dry. What? I step outside. Is this allowed? Don't care, I'm out at last in the blaring light and slap at a mosquito on my arm; it smears in a bloody streak. I clutch the verandah post. I'm suddenly woozy all over again with the sun's hurting glare and the earth rising up to whoosh at my sea legs.

I bend to the animal. It's barely breathing, drowning in water or its own death-sweat and soon the ants will be at it. What happened? The rat's belly heaves as it draws its last painful

73

breaths; it's beautiful, perhaps some native vole I don't recognise, not a rat at all. I need a book. In my room I've found the Bible and three manuals: *Female Beauty As Improved by Regimen*, *Etiquette and Ceremonials* and *The Woman Beautiful*. The last will do. I lever the rat onto it with the other instruction book and walk across the lawn and set down the animal under a bush.

Why was it by my door? Nature, or careful placement?

Pa taught me to study the world restlessly, to question, to not meekly accept. I crashed late into his life 'for a purpose', he'd say, and laugh, 'to teach me about little girls and their strength'. Girls and their strength. Which none of these manuals of womanhood, written by their men, ever talk about. As if they can't bear to acknowledge it; as if they want to make little girls quite something else.

Studying, restlessly, oh yes. I look about; no one's in sight. Yet the animal's placement disturbs me. My back prickles up.

It feels like someone is watching, close.

IN WHICH THE WORLD IS SET TO RIGHTS

'She's fixed!' Mouse declares, popping his head around the bedroom door. Footsteps stride along the corridor and he slides into the room, closes the door. 'Watch out. Mammy will take you all for herself,' the boy whispers in warning, 'to keep the terrors of Outside at bay.'

'Not if I can help it, Stink Mouse.'

He laughs. Oh, I've got the measure of him now. He's my good fairy putting everything in order and all he needs is the gift of attention. 'We've got to get out today, Poss. I've got so much to show you.'

'Door!'

Mouse opens it as Mrs Craw pushes inside with a breakfast tray of cold cuts. Under her arm is a skirt with a crude band of cloth attached. 'It's mine, an old one, with a bit of rag sewn on it to make it decent. I fixed it up at three in the morning during a sleepless night. You've been addling me so much. I want you to stay, my wild little Poss. I like you, you funny thing. But you're so … I don't know, uncontained. Or something. Which feels dangerous. Like you're heading for trouble. And I want you to stay with me but I just, we just, have standards —'

'Ma'am, please. You really don't have to.'

'I insist. And you, Mouse, scat.' Mrs Craw snatches up a hairbrush and drags it through my hair – 'Ow!' – explaining that tangles must be tamed in this house. 'You're at Willowbrae now and you must reflect it.'

I bite my tongue; I'm a guest, must make this work. Mrs Craw tries and tries to smooth my hair but it refuses to conform. Strands keep escaping and ridges of stubbornness keep appearing; it won't lie flat. I laugh helplessly. 'It's just how I am, ma'am.'

She groans. 'Get dressed,' she says, crisp, abandoning the hair and tossing the skirt across. 'Make yourself presentable. For me. For us.'

I run after her, to the bedroom door, but go no further. Mrs Craw's not in the mood for further talk. I shut the door to a sliver and watch. She bumps into Mr Craw, who's on his way down the corridor for a day of work. 'All under control?' he booms.

'Yes,' his wife responds, tight. 'I think.'

A pause.

'Is this going to work, Lex?'

'She's the little girl I finally got. I have been praying. For years.'

'I know.'

I have a vision of silk ribbons and suffocating lace; my hand taps in agitation at my throat.

'I've got a headache coming on, Cal. Everything's been so … agitating.'

'Go to bed, Lex. You were up all hours last night.'

I quietly shut the door on them both, my fingers still at my throat.

TOBYN'S GRIP

A musical knock on the door. I know who it must be and my stomach rolls at the thought. Of course it is Tobyn. I command him to enter, if he really must, and he flings wide my door and playfully salutes. He wants to steal me for a stroll around the garden – 'Really, now?' – and he'll be back in fifteen minutes on the dot, but what he doesn't know is that I'll be ready early, of course, on the verandah outside my room, my insides liquid at the wait. Or maybe he does know, from his lopsided grin and his impish wink as he departs.

He's not back in fifteen minutes. Twenty. Twenty-five. I'm a hostage to his forgetting and can think of nothing else, ridiculously nothing else. Where *is* the man? I slump on the sweet-smelling grass, the waiting inside me like a dog with its head on its paws. This is some game and I'm his pawn and there's no shyness to the light pounding into my skull and my head now hurts and where is he?

And then, and then. The nonchalant saunter across the lawn as he juggles two apples, as if it's only been a matter of minutes. All is wiped, of course. I spring up, hands on hips. 'I've been waiting a long time, you know.'

'I do.' He tosses across an apple, which is caught in a crisp snatch, and Tobyn bows in respect. 'I had to do something for my father.' A pause. 'Apologies.' I smile in forgiveness; there is nothing else I can do. This man has been absorbed by me like smoke; in the pores of my skin I am caught.

The garden is a skirt of neatness around the house, all circular flower beds and stone benches and urns. It's not what I need; it bores me. The wildness beyond it calls me out into it with its bird shrieks and shrills, its thrilling loom, its dangerous sense of coolness, and I straighten as we near it. Odd, untidy trees of a strange almost-green crowd the lawn's edge, as if the sun has bleached them of fecund life.

'I want to show you something, Poss.'

I look back to the big house as we head further and further away from it. Someone is madly thumping a piano as if they're broken with fury or trying to crash into the tension that exists between Tobyn and myself, and I wonder how Mrs Craw gets any sleep through it. 'Is that Virgil?'

'Yes. He's angry. Mama will yell at him to stop any moment now.' Sure enough, she does.

We walk to a far corner of the garden, a dog compound with 'Barkingham Palace' painted on it. Tobyn explains that he's responsible for the name and that the dogs – Sage, Chili and Parsley – love him the most; he's their favourite because he raised them. The animals leap and mock-bite as he lets them loose, then he whistles for them to follow and they fall into easy obeyance.

Tobyn leads me to a wilting rose garden. Walled off and long neglected, by the matriarch I suspect, though there must have been a time before Mrs Craw gave up on Outside and turned inward and nervy and stopped. Perhaps this garden was a gift long ago from her husband, to beguile her with home comforts. But it hasn't worked. A golden spider's web stretches between dead rose bushes with an enormous, tiger-striped arachnid at its centre. A fly struggles in the silken threads, but the more it wriggles the tighter it's enmeshed. I stare, fascinated, but do not help; it's too far gone, tangled in its silken trap. The spider waits. Poised. 'It's called a golden orb spider,' Tobyn explains, 'because its belly looks like it's about to explode.'

Heat presses in. A snail's trail of sweat drops down my chest. Flies worry at my face and I swat them away. Tobyn lets the dogs loose to their rummaging – 'Off you go, ladies' – but the one called Chili stays close. I fondle the flap of her silky ear and tell Tobyn she's my favourite here now, tell him that his crown has been lost.

'She'll have to go then. Immediately. That's it. She'll be shot at first light.'

'What? You beast! No!'

'Well, there could be a reprieve. If my crown is restored as the favourite, immediately. Hmmmm?'

'Do I have to?' I mock groan.

'Oh yes.'

'Alright then, alright.'

Tobyn punches the air in triumph and grabs my hand and leads me through unruly thorns to a sun-blasted wall; with docility I follow. He turns to me and bows in delight; I bat him off. 'Away, away with you! You're worse than the flies.'

'But you're going to like this.'

If he asked me my real name right now I might well tell him; I'm that gone, ridiculously gone. We stop. At … what?

Graves.

'Oh!'

A line of tiny stone tablets, a foot or so high. *Nelly. Amelia. Eleanor.* Engraved. No surnames, just dates. Every few years. I drop down to their tiny, doll-like simplicity. Chili licks my cheek and I hold her tight.

'And now Mammy has you,' Tobyn teases. 'You'll be a great comfort, I think.'

I squeeze Chili's softness. Am suddenly claustrophobic. Are these his mother's children?

'She's lost so many over the years. From the womb. Who knows if they were girl babies, but she names them all. And then of course there's little Faith.' He indicates a more substantial grave in a corner. The earth around it is clean and swept; barely a leaf falls upon it, as if the air here is hushed.

'There are dogs too,' Tobyn indicates. 'All girls. My mother only allows that.'

'Oh.'

'You're her lovely new little pet.'

It shivers me up and I'm suddenly annoyed at his game, whatever it is, and yell after him as he strolls nonchalantly away, 'Why have you brought me here?'

'I don't know.' He turns back to me. 'Something to do.' His smile is breezily unburdened, there's not a scrap of weight in it. 'Come, sit with me,' he says, with his pleading eyes and beautiful lopsided grin that makes me forget everything else. I soften and follow him to the lawn and we lie languid out of sight of the house behind a native tree as straight and pale as a shin bone. We're like two shawls tossed aside in the heat. I shut my eyes on the tall blue, and the shapes of the leaves dance in flames over my eyelids.

Occasionally Tobyn dares a touch, a caress, just. It is very polite. It is the first time I've been touched in this way – this hesitant, enquiring way – by a man. The jolt of it, my breathing dips; what is this vividness now mining its way through my body, turning me into someone else? I'm on the cusp here, dipping into being lost. One eyelid is suddenly kissed, soft, then the other. Oh! The audacity, the loveliness, the theft of my calm. I can scarcely breathe; something is turning my body alive in a way that is new and strange and I don't know what to do next, how to respond.

Tobyn falls back. Grins, just that, as if it is enough of a lesson for today. I gasp – 'What?' – then do nothing else and he says nothing back but I hold that secret gesture of his eyelid kiss in the fist of my heart, for in that moment I am lit by the rescue of it. My whole body feels blazed by newness. This could work, being here, all of it.

We gaze at each other. Shy, both, at some secret line of tenderness that has been crossed. Smile, just. I imagine trailing a fingertip down his cheek in a slow memory hoarding. Do nothing, hold back. How is it possible to fall in love with the curve of a neck? So quick. A freckle tucked into an eye's corner? His laugh at my looking undresses me and I blush. I want to be unpeeled by him, layer by layer, and my stomach is rolling at the thought. I feel a dangerous slippage. Fight it. His attention is swerving me off my course of focus and containment and grit in this new land, of keeping my identity at bay for as long as I can. Yet my resolve is melting at the sight of this man like hot water thrown over snow, and it feels extraordinary and wrong and too soon that he could have this power. It is pure, surrendering … want. I push him away. 'Tobyn, stop.' Again. 'Tobyn. I don't like it.'

He gets up abruptly, tells me he has to head out bush now, to help his father. He'll be gone all day.

I return to my room, my heart singing. This rescue will work.

But as I go back through the French doors, I notice the table with the Bible on it. For the first time since yesterday.

The knife's absence.

Jack! Why didn't I hide it? Who would take it? The young girl in the painting looks at me as if only she knows. I pound my head with a furious fist, how stupid I was to leave it. My lovely, quiet, good Jack. The last thing left of him, left of us; and Tobyn's kiss now feels like a transgression God Himself has witnessed. Oh my Jack. Grief closes over me and my knuckles ram my cheeks, trying to stop a cry breaking out.

In Which Mouse Lures Me
Into a Big Adventure

I slam into Mouse in the corridor as I run to find the knife. 'Poss. Quick.' Mouse jitters. 'Mama will be in bed until lunch. She's having a sleep. Come on! Our big adventure!'

'But my knife —'

'What?'

'It's gone.'

'Someone would've tidied it up. Don't worry, it'll be around.'

'Oh. Alright. If you say. Later, good, later.' All afluster. 'And what's this thing you want to show me?'

'My secret island!'

'Well, I can't miss that. I guess.'

'We'll find the knife. And you're not the only amazing thing around here, you know.' The competitive blurt.

I laugh, wasn't expecting a something else. 'Really? As exciting as me?'

'Better.'

Well, well, he's got me well and good. 'Let's see it then.'

The young master wants me launched immediately. 'But get your old clothes on. From yesterday. The exploring ones.'

'What? No!' I glance at the door.

'Mammy won't notice. She's having a sleep. Come on, quick. We've got to do this before lunch.' The boy plonks on a wide-brimmed hat that's seen better days. 'Damnation be damned! Quick!'

I laugh at the childish attempts to match a master in the swearing stakes and shoo him out while I dress. Fling on the trousers like I'm stepping strong into an old self; I move differently in these clothes, without encumbrance. Summon Mouse back.

On his way in, he glances at his mother's shut bedroom door then leads me onto the verandah's flagstones and puts a finger to his mouth. I nod. A treaty of silence, of course. A wink. As we slip away to see the best thing in the world that isn't me by a long shot.

We dash across the lawn. A heavy smell hangs in the air, of oil baking in the heat, and another mosquito veers and I pause and a fly toys with my mouth and it feels like all the elements are conspiring to keep me from this land; to have me bound in my room, neat and safe.

My guide has leapt ahead into his gleeful forest and vanished. A hand pokes from the foliage. 'Come on, before Mammy wakes up!' Every joint is haranguing me as I clamber over roots as thick as legs and break through cobwebs several feet wide and climb rocks as tall as horses. My beckoning boy seems haloed by his loneliness and is acting now as if I'm the best thing that's ever happened to him and he's seizing it. 'Hurry up! Quick!'

But no. A stopping. For I'm standing on the soil of the upside-down land in a way I'd never dreamt of only a few days ago. I'm unbetrothed and unfettered here, with no name and no past. With a new future in this land. A secure position. A roof over my head and I smile at the thought. If a match were struck to me in this very instant I might well combust. But then I remember all the souls from the *Finbar*, still unfound, and my smile is snuffed. Mouse's hand reaches out. It's gratefully caught. I hold his palm gently to my cheek, over my bruise. Hold on to life, generosity, companionship. The simple blessings of all that, as necessary as sunlight, a blanket in the cold, a mother's arms.

'You alright, Possy?'

'Yes.'

'Mammy says everything'll kill us out here.' Mouse grins like he knows better.

'I'm tough.' I flex my arm muscles; the boy feels them, impressed. And on we go, flitting through the thick ferny undergrowth among its shadows deeply cut with light, in patches, like a pond's sudden warmth. Some trees have bright orange bark but others are starkly white as if naked. High stone ridges tower to the right of us, giving the impression that Willowbrae is always being watched by something above it. There are great looming rocks the colour of brooding skies, dappled like ponies and hovering on the cliffs as if ready to topple and crush any intruders upon this land; some are as tall as houses. Branches snag, mosquitos whine, heat assaults. Is there anything benign in this place? I stop in a pool of light and hold out my palms in benediction to this lovely new sun, so different to my own land. Mouse stands beside me and copies. I softly sing to him:

When that I was and a little tiny boy,
With hey, ho, the wind and the rain,
A foolish thing was but a toy,
For the rain it raineth every day.

Mouse asks what song it is and I tell him it's from a play by William Shakespeare, who he says he's never heard of, and I tell him someday I'll teach him about plays just like my father taught me, and I sing again:

> But when I came to man's estate,
> With hey ho, the wind and the rain,
> 'Gainst knaves and thieves men shut their gate,
> For the rain it raineth every day.

Mouse claps his hands and exclaims that it never rains here, mostly, that it's blue skies all the time and I snatch him up – 'Really, truly?' – and lift him with a whoop then drop him squealing in a crisp catch.

'Again! Again!'

I oblige in air so fresh it's like it's been scrubbed, and hold out my fingers in awe at this magical world, to its beautiful bright air that is fixing me up.

'Were you a convict?' Mouse lashes an imaginary thrashing.

I laugh – 'No!' – and pretend-thrash him back as birds around us shriek. There's so much raucous bird-talk here. Flits of colour: green and blue, yellow and red. There's laughter – *wooo a wooo aa aaaa* – with iron in its raucous mock, a vast echoing symphony around us, the two innocents on our quest. Mouse points out and names for me rosellas, kookaburras, magpies and cockatoos and says there are also snakes with bellies blood-red and stingrays with sword faces and sharks with rows of gigantic teeth – so much to marvel at – and asks is my land as good as this, ever, can it beat it?

'Well, my friend, England does feel very tame in comparison. And dark. And cold. The clouds brush the rooftops all the time. Which means you never get light like this, which means you never get shadows like this.' I point to the abrupt delineation between dark and light then push up my sleeves and hold out my arms to the sun in a great and unseemly freckle-harvest. 'But I'm always on the side of the light. It's where you'll find me.' Mouse follows suit then hurries me along. 'But what about all those snakes you go on about, Mister?'

He strokes his chin like a surgeon confronted by an impossible ailment. 'Hmmm. Death extremely likely. In ten minutes perhaps. Actually, no, five!' I mock-choke him and he rolls his eyes heavenward then springs awake, grinning his angelic smile. 'But no snakes around our house! Papa got the lawn from Ireland. From the peat bogs. It's our magic grass. He had it shipped especially. For Mammy. Snakes won't go near us.'

'But hang on. This is the woods.'

'The *bush*. You have so much to learn, Mermaid. Rule number one: just *stomp*.' Mouse demonstrates and I copy, more vigorously. He whoops and takes off. Wolf Girl flits, Mouse flits faster. We bash shoulders companionably and he wins, just, then the two of us stand on a crest and gaze out over the endless ocean to a far horizon then swivel to great fingers of a river plucking at the soft land then a blue line of hills folding off behind more hills, and more, and more to the west. I hug my arms. I muse that it's an awful lot of woodland – 'Bush, Poss! It's called the bush!' – before us, and around us, spinning in wonder at the sheer, breathtaking enormity of it; you could disappear into this land and never be found. The bush suddenly feels impenetrable.

If something happened here, within this family, no one would know. I glance across at my lonely boy. 'Where's the town? How far away are we, Mousey? From anything?'

But the white-blond curls are disappearing fast at the bulleting questions. 'Far, far away.' Mouse shrugs the questions off.

We continue on, closer to the rim of the harbour's bay. I catch silvery glimpses through the trees. A spider with tiger-striped legs sits in a web in a tree fork beside me; the creature is as big as a handspan. I reel back.

'They're everywhere,' Mouse laughs, 'they won't hurt you.' He plucks a hollow shell off a tree's trunk and latches it onto my sleeve with tiny claw hooks; I pick it off and marvel at such an ugly, brittle thing. 'It's a cicada shell. The insect's old skin. They crawl out of it when they grow up.'

The wonders this land contains. 'Mouse, I just love this place.'

'I knew you would!'

Leaf canopies toss their heads in the breeze like ponies wanting home, pointy leaves scratch our arms, springing branches thwack our faces and everything feels like a test. Yet I'm slipping through this alien sharpness almost as surely as this home-footed child, my soul unbound in it. Because I'm free. Because I have a new name and a tall sun and a secret kiss on my eyelids, as well as a little brother-boy in whom I've found something like reciprocated love, and it's all, all brimming me up.

Just a few days ago I was lying flat on my back on the *Finbar's* deck with my palms open to the sky like a rude Jesus on His cross, harvesting freckles in the glittering aloneness and dreading everything about my future life. Ambrose hated me sprawled on the deck like that, more boy than girl and wilded up. He was a dog lead to my future, like he was constantly tugging on the lead and bringing me up abrupt with all his snips and snaps: *Ladies should not appear in public like this. You're so ugly with that hair. No one will want you. Your voice is defective. You'll be a failure in life.*

A hedge of men's will surrounded me on that journey out. And their genius solution to my infuriating existence – a wintering into marriage, with a man I didn't want. Yet now, now, a brand new life!

Mouse and I stand on a flat rock, on the edge of a small cliff, peering down. We're too close to the ledge's dizzying drop and the wooziness comes over me again and I step back, pulling Mouse with me.

It's the water. Too soon. I clutch my hair, contemplate. Below us is a thumbnail crescent of golden sand with a cluster of creamy, oyster-clotted rocks at either end. There are steep cliffs to one side of the beach that plunge down to perilously sharp rocks, but on the other side, where we are, there's a slightly gentler approach.

'Come on,' Mouse urges.

'Do we have to?'

He nods. I follow reluctantly. We pick our way down a grassy goat track over boulders and dead, fallen branches. Mouse wants me to wade a short distance into the harbour to an outcrop of a rocky island, as big as a ship, whose presence so close to the shoreline seems to meeken the beach's water into calm. A band of trees clings to the island's centre.

But the water. There's too much memory in this and I shy away from the lapping edge as the horrors of the *Finbar* come back at me, and back, and back.

Mouse isn't interested: today's a fresh day with something wondrous in it. 'It's only knee deep. It's low tide. Come on.' He yanks me abruptly, yet I have a flash again of the voices crying for their mothers and their God. The voices quietening, the too many voices. The voices stopping.

'You aren't allowed here, are you, Mouse?' Because this may stop him perhaps. My boy doesn't look at me.

'Come *on*, Scaredy Cat. This is my secret place. Better-er than anything.'

I suck in my breath, brace myself. Right. He's not budging. I pull off my boots and step hesitantly into the water crammed with its memories. It's warm, inviting. The sand is soft through my toes, clouds have fled the tall blue above us and the world feels contrite, as if sorry for the great unhinging of the other night. A deep breath, and soon we're scrambling onto the island's rocks.

'Watch the oysters, Poss.'

Too late. A foot is sliced to add to the slices of the other night. Mouse is mortified. He goes to rip up his shirt but I brush off the ribboning red. 'It's nothing. Lead on, Captain Mouse.' Which the boy does, thrilled at his fresh crowning.

'Captain Mouse at your service!' He grabs a stick as his sceptre and marches onward to a place of mysterious pause. A glade in the outcrop's centre.

It's a fern-filled dip like the hollow in a neck. Its energy is arresting, removed. A deep silence pools in it. I suddenly want the alone here, not this noisy chattery boy, want to cloak myself in the thick, repairing quiet of this space, unencumbered by my scampy companion with his thrashing stick. Mouse tugs me forward, his voice suddenly sucked from him as if he senses it too, finally, that he's intruding here.

But then, but then.

I flinch back as if unexpectedly brushed by fire.

Oh no. Oh God, no. Mouse mustn't have seen it; oh God, he mustn't.

I pull him back. Stopped.

What a Swan's Wing Cradles

A woman.

Her baby.

Lying on the ground, asleep. No. Yes, surely yes. I hover a touch. Flinch back. They're natives, I've seen black people before. The other night, in the rescue. As well, my father had a rare friend, Olediah, from West Africa, a servant of a sea captain. He'd been kidnapped as a child and for years he had uttered only dog's howls, but gradually he was tamed into service – and when the captain retired, Olediah went with him. They settled near us and Pa befriended him out walking and he was enfolded into our lives. My father taught Olediah his letters. When he visited I always wanted to sit nearby, to gulp him, everything so curious and different and lovely and strange about him. Hair that wouldn't be tamed, skin the colour of midnight, his pale and worn fingertips. It was all so wondrously something else to me, yet not.

But these two people are different. The woman is darker and almost completely naked except for a band of cloth around her forehead that clears her face of hair, which is close-cropped and clustered about her head in tight whirls. She wears a necklace crammed with little white cones of shells, jumbled with black ones, four strands. The baby is naked and at her mother's breast as if she's just dropped off it into a milky stupor. She has one thin strand of the black and white shells about her neck, and long black lashes in sleep.

But no. Not sleep.

I step back. It feels like a stone is at my chest now, compressing my breathing. Who else was here? Mouse has gone very still, very quiet, turned in on himself, in shock perhaps. I reach for his hand; he holds mine tight as if I am holding him up. The little girl is coiled like a closed fist with her tiny fingers bunched under her neck and the woman is curved like a comma around her. They lie on what looks like a swan's wing. But black. A swan. It's an oily, green-sheened spread of feathers, so different to the carefully tended graves from this morning, and the woman and child are lying down like they've found the softest of mattresses available in relief. The enormous wing has been ripped from some great bird's body but there's no carcass and the two people lie upon it as if in gratitude, as if this is correct and ceremonial and right. Is it some kind of ritual? I step closer. No, no, it's not a swan's wing at all but damp, blackened leaves which I thought were arranged in a pattern but no, they're not, oh my head, what is happening to me? This confounding, contrary land, and I feel wrong in it. And this is not sleep. My fist gouges into my temple in confusion, in shock.

Mouse whispers furiously as if the land itself is listening in. 'Oh! They're here. Oh, oh.' Great gulps of breath. 'This is my hiding place, Poss. My secret place. I wanted to show you. But, but they're here. They should be taken away. But they're not. They're stuck. In my place.'

'Taken by who?'

'Why are they here? I don't want them.'

'Mouse, I do not know why they're here.' My calm has gone astray.

'Are you a magic mermaid? Can you fix this? Wake them up?' Mouse's voice peters out at my face, at my hand over my mouth as if I'm quelling vomit, at my fingers pushing away his talk. Is someone else close? A prickling picks its way up my spine and I turn. Want to shake this boy and his unseeing innocence, want to shake an understanding into him. Because these two people before us are definitely not asleep, they cannot be woken up.

A keen of a wail. I have no idea what to do. And I'm alone here, with a boy who doesn't understand, and with whatever else is coiled on this island. I can feel it, something else is here, close. And the baby's plumpness is pressed into the woman's belly in some furious shielding; why? The woman's back is arched around her child as if in some final, frozen spasm. I want to drop down to them both. I've never known that kind of fierce maternal ownership and it feels like a protecting. From what? I look around, my heart tripping over its beats. We need to get away from here fast, need to find help.

But I can't leave these two on their lonely wing of leaves. They seem so isolated out here, and by the look of them they were formerly in robust health. What's felled them? I hover a hand. No, can't touch. Have to, in case of some leaking of warmth, so I can bellow it back into them. Come on, girl, do it. But their flesh is cold and firm and vanished of spirit; it's taken on some new and weighted solidity, and of course it's too late.

Mouse gazes at me, eye-deep in confused stare once again like that boy I first knew from my sickbed. They're dead. *Dead*. What happened here? Their placement is so odd, as if the mother's body wants to swallow the child's flesh in an embrace of furious protectiveness. From what? It's a fierce mother's clench, of the kind I've never known and have craved my whole life. It's so intensely human and familiar, despite the nakedness and the oddly lengthened breasts on the woman; she's had many children no doubt. This is an embrace of fierce denial, hooked around her precious child. A baby with a curl of yellowed hair that's tucked behind a tiny ear that I want to touch, caress, yet do not, and both have blackened lips that I want to brush into life but cannot, in any way, cannot.

Mouse bashes his stick furiously at some ferns.

'Stop it,' I snap.

The boy looks up at my new coldness. I've become someone else, because there's something bigger than him now. My fingertips dart at my cheeks, tap tap tap. We're intruding here and these bodies need a burial, a slipping into sweet earth like the graves from this morning, yes. Do these people have a family close: a husband, a father, a tribe; someone who loves them as ferociously as this mother loves her child? They seem so hidden in this secret glade, so deliberately alone.

Mouse bashes and bashes with his stick. I bite a nail, tear a skin flap clean off. No, Mouse and me, we shouldn't be here. I reach for the boy's hand to still him. 'Do you know what happened here?' The boy shrugs, afraid; he's the student suddenly ignoring the schoolmarm. 'Mouse. Answer me.' The boy scowls at his mermaid's swift cooling into adulthood.

'Things always happen out here,' he shrugs. 'It's the bush.'

I ask what he means.

'It's just the bush.' A stand-off. 'Can you make it go away, Poss? This is my secret place. They're spoiling it.'

I stare at him, disbelieving.

'Please, Poss, make it all go.'

He's talking like a stupid child now, restless to move on. The pirate eager for new treasure, the sea captain wanting his eyrie back. He runs his fingers along a fern and strips it of its fronds so it's just a bare stick then does it to another and another, regressing into that impenetrable boy from yesterday morning, lost in his shock. I grab his wretched stick and toss it away.

Mouse repeats, slowly, 'It's the bush, it's what happens,' staring at me like he's seeing a new person entirely and has made a mistake. I hold his hand firmly. He *will* observe some kind of decorum here; the solemnity of these dead people in their chapel of enveloping green enforces a pause. Surely? But Mouse is uninterested, champing at the bit. It infuriates me. This situation needs respect. But this hasn't gone according to plan for him. I'm no longer the mermaid stranger in awe of the boy's treasures and all his secret places, no longer the magical person to impress. I'm vastly someone else, more adult than child, and he doesn't care for it.

CANDLE-SKINNED PEOPLE

'We have to find out what happened here, Mouse.' My hand scrunches my hair, hurting and hard, as I try to think.

'I've got other bits to show you. New places. Come on. Before Mammy gets up.'

What? Just leave the bodies here? Is Mouse mad? I'll honour the tenderness in this mother's embrace; I must. I've been granted a second stab at life and have to put that gift to use. Pa told me once that the great reckonings of a life, at the end of it, are how well a person has loved, how they've demonstrated it, what kindness they've practised. So my pledge is to do good in this new land and love well, and my fresh and miraculous existence here will be distilled to this.

I stare at the baby, at the fierce maternal holding of her. It's always arrested me – at a church picnic or a spring fair or waiting in a shop – I've felt a clench in my chest, a little flare of envy. What it must feel like to surrender to that enfolding and what it must feel like to give it. I've been thirsty for it ever since my mother died.

'Come on, Possy. Let's get out of here.'

No. Not yet. Because a watching dog is inside me now, waiting, searching – for clues, signs, anything that will distract me from the grief washing over me when the thinking crowds in too much. All the flashes of Jack and Ambrose and Captain Grent, of Turnip the twinkly kitchen hand, of Janey and Clara and Louisa and all the babies brought to this island for their bold new lives. The screams. The whimpers. The silence. The silence. The silence. And now this, a mother and her child – and I can do something for them at least, perhaps; I can work this out and have them laid to rest. And it might fill up my brain; yes, it might crowd everything else out, keep my thoughts from rushing back to the storm and its too-silent aftermath. Perhaps. 'Things like this don't just happen, Mouse. We need to help these poor souls.'

'Souls? It's the bush, Poss. Like I said. It's what happens out here. They're not us.'

Right. 'So what are they then, Mouse? Animals?' He doesn't answer. I step back as if grubbied and bump into something solid. Gasp.

A tree. With enormous shaggy branches that loom like a many-armed ogre. It's similar to the one in the garden at Willowbrae, the one that clothed me on my first night, but this one is enormous, ancient, magnificent, like it's grown here since life began on this earth. Bark hangs off it in great powdery tongues as if its skin can't quite contain the great force pushing out from its heart, as if there's a core pulsing with secrets and power and vivid, hidden life. I remember my rescuer's hands placing bark just like this over my brokenness, in a blanket of benediction. And now I will pass that gift on. A long strip of the tree's skin is peeled off and held to my cheek in a memory hoarding.

'That's my Ripping Tree. It's what I call them, Poss. They're magic because you can use their bark for a million things. Shelters and sleeping mats. Canoes. To cook things in, under the coals. And for torches for fishing at night, to lure in the catch. Just about anything.'

And to keep babies warm, I think. And to wrap dead people.

'The Ripping Tree,' I whisper, wrapping my arms around its muscular softness and pressing in my cheek. What eccentricities this upside-down land brews: witch-trees that deskin themselves like reptiles, swans' wings that are leaves of a devilish black, spiders as big as handspans. I peel off another slice of bark, like a leaf from a medieval chapter book.

Jump.

At a young girl. Beyond Mouse's Ripping Tree.

She's midnight-black, just like the woman, and naked as the day she was born. Goodness. I nudge my friend. He gasps. The girl is staring at us both, in Mouse's secret place. A dawning. *Her* secret place. *Theirs*. The girl is staring at the intruders, moon-pale and jittery and wrong, candle-skinned. Watching what we'll do next. She's holding something in her hands, a small bowl of some sort. I stutter a something, a rasp of a hello and stumble towards her and stop, feel suddenly awkward. The girl is statue-still and slightly taller than Mouse, who's staring, stopped, in shock. Like she shouldn't be here, like she's a ghost.

'Why are you here?' His voice is suspicious, unwelcoming. The girl says nothing. Does she understand? She stands immobile yet poised, ready for flight. Her body is all muscle and sinew, lean and tough; her legs are slightly apart and her bare warrior feet are strong on the earth. *Her* earth? I feel suddenly ashamed of our intrusion, because that's what it feels like. I look into her eyes, girl to girl; I'm the most grown up one here and want this child to understand that somehow I'll honour the protectiveness in the dead mother's embrace. *Her* mother? I catch my breath. Oh Lord. Is this a *family*? I hold Mouse back with both hands stretched sternly behind me, want the girl to know I care. Smile, hesitant. Don't want her fleeing. What would Pa do?

I close my eyes and surrender to instinct. Go back to the Ripping Tree and peel off some silky tongues of bark and place the sheaves over the bodies like a tender, loose glove and hover my hands over the mother and baby in something like a prayer, and breathe deep. Is this right? The girl and I lock eyes and I place my hand on my heart and close my fist in a clench of sorrow and she nods, a touch, she's noted it. She bites her lip; I do too. I turn back to the bodies, checking the arrangement one last time, then look again to the girl.

She's gone.

Without a sound, not even a twig crack. Oh! Too soon. Come back! I run to where she was; she's vanished. But on the ground is the tiny bowl she held in her hands – but it isn't a bowl at all, it's a nest. Made with twigs and clay and the fluff of feathers threaded through it like tiny pillows of tenderness. I leave it. It doesn't feel like it's mine to remove; a mother, somewhere, might need it.

Mouse shrugs and shakes his head like he has no idea what's just happened or who this late arrival is or how she's attached to these people, if at all.

'We have to tell someone, Mouse.'

'Why?'

'These people are dead.'

'Lots of things are dead in the bush, Poss. It's how it works. Can we just get rid of them? This is my place.'

Of course. I nod, grim. He's been showing me his rare find of a secret glade and now something else, most annoyingly, is in it. As the two of us stand side by side by the Ripping Tree it feels like we're almost two different species, from different worlds, with no common code. But I can't stand it, the obscenity of his casualness. What world is this? 'We have to tell someone. A grownup. We have to help these poor people, and that little girl. Maybe she's related to them.'

Mouse's shock. He backs away. It's all in his face: I'm now the encumbrance and the opposition, and after all my promises. Telling will spill his secret place. Alert his mother to how far he actually goes. Spoil everything.

'Your father can help us, Mouse. Your father needs to know.'

But Mouse is suddenly shaking his head and garbling, 'No, please, not the Chair.' He's stumbling that his father can't have them, they're not his father's to take, they're not supply and Papa can't know any of this, can't find out. Mouse is tripping over his words in panic. 'How do we make them go, Poss?'

'Chair?' I ask. 'Go back, what's this chair? And supply? What's going on?' Mouse stutters that the chair, it's his father's, in his study, and he suddenly barrels into me weeping like a child overwhelmed, as if everything in the blink of an eye has become too much. 'Don't go, don't leave,' he sobs. 'You're my friend, the only friend I've got.' Someone else entirely.

I hug my poor confused little Mouse, the calming big sister to the baby brother I never had, and he clutches me like I'm the only thing left in his world. I hold tight my little friend who believes in mermaids and magic, my angel dipped in goldenness with his long girly curls and his trembling mouth. All the childish contradictions, and I soften at them; Mouse is so young, a baby, with so much growing up ahead of him. What does he know, really?

Only what the adult world has taught him and he can't be blamed for that. If he thinks these natives are mere animals, native fauna to be discarded, then it must be coming from someone else because these attitudes aren't instinct but learnt. Pa taught me that. Who is civilised here and who isn't? I hug my Mouse's yielding flesh. There's still time to open him up to a gentler way of thought, surely; it's still possible to veer an unknowing child.

And on a bed of black leaves two bodies lie before us in a defensive curl, and wait. For what? I look around. A twig snaps.

'Hello?'

But nothing declares itself.

GROWNUPS VERSUS CHILDREN

I clamp Mouse's hand. He can't pull free, he's locked. The dynamic between us has shifted and I'm the adult now to the child because someone has to be told about these bodies and I need to know what's happened. Something feels like it's curdling here; it's in the spidery prickle up my back as I look wildly about.

'Come on,' Mouse whines but I'll not change course, it's too soon to leave. I feel oddly protective towards this woman in the glade and can't abandon her yet. A different kind of death is coming for me: the death of my freedom, when I slip into the sleeve of my real name once again, as someday I must. And who knows if this woman was once treated as not fully human, just like myself; a woman with roaring wants, just like myself. She seems so alone, with her daughter, in death.

I linger a hand above the bodies in a sorrowful farewell then sweep up Mouse's stick and bash furiously at the undergrowth, hurrying past more ripping trees, monstrous beasts with their skin peeling off. Mouse skips ahead of me. I stumble over oyster-helmeted rocks, ignoring fresh ribbons of red, and splash across the shallows with salt-stung flesh. Tree branches flick back at me in sharp taunts as if to say, 'Go home, girl, you'll never get used to this.' Yet I won't be slowed. I clench the hurt in my freshly aching head and run on, and on.

'Poss, what's wrong? Why are you holding your head? Stop.'

Finally I do. Mouse's eyes peer at me in concern.

'My head hurts again.'

'Can I rub your temples?' he soothes. 'I'm the best at it. Mammy calls me her medicine. I'll kiss your forehead too if you like.'

I relent, sit on a rock. Mouse's fingers stroke my temples like a trickle of soft water and I shut my eyes and surrender to his touch; he's done this before, he's been taught. Between two grave palms, Mouse kisses me on the forehead and I still down into calm at his caress.

'I've only ever had imaginary friends, Poss. You're my first real one. I get up really early and wake everyone up and they all hate it, but I won't for you, I promise, I'll let you sleep.' It's brotherly love and need and it's slipping under my skin and I yield to it, because I crave a connection too. I felt like the loneliest person in the world just a few days ago, on the ship, a young woman about to be married who would never be allowed a life with someone like Jack; I felt like the loneliest person in the world as one Thomasina Trelora, heading into her newly adulted life. To be wifed.

Mouse tugs at my hand and we flit afresh through the spiky green. He tells me through ragged breaths that we'll do so many things together: chess and charades, croquet and sea captains, fishing and pirates and baking and the like.

'Baking!'

'I love it, Poss. Flea the lifer teaches me, and Mammy says yes because it's the one thing that won't kill me in this place. Because it's not the bush.'

'Lifer?'

'Well, he gets free after fourteen years, with his ticket of leave, and he's only got a bit to go. He helps us.'

'What did he do?'

'Highway robbery. I think. Or something. No one tells me anything. Maybe it was his wife, maybe he chopped off her head and boiled it for breakfast. He's my friend. He lets me roam the bush and he's good at secrets. I love him. He knows everything.'

I raise my thumb to all of it, despite this lifer in our midst.

'Hooray!' Mouse skips ahead to Willowbrae. I remember that I'm wearing the boy clothes and have to walk across the lawn and into the house, in daylight, and my attire is shouting many things and none of them good, but mainly: Harridan. Unhinged. Madness and Insolence and Wilfulness.

I have to watch everything here, must think before I act, which Pa always said, laughing, was so hard for me. I mustn't put a foot wrong, mustn't let anything slip.

WEIGHING UP

No one is about, thank goodness, as we slip inside the French doors to my room. We need to tell someone, fast, I say. Mouse asks why.

'What do you mean, why?'

He looks at me, beseeching me silently not to blurt anything out, not to spoil his hiding place. I jab my finger at him; he won't be getting away with this. In an instant, another boy. Deflated, stopped. Sulky. 'Do we have to?'

'Yes.'

Mouse licks his lips. 'Even Pa?'

I bite my nail. 'Yes.' Tear off a skin flap.

'Sometimes, Poss, I don't like what grownups are.'

I ask him what he means but Mouse won't elaborate, he just asks why I care about the two people by the Ripping Tree so much.

'Because they're exactly that. People. And they're dead.'

And because there's so much tenderness in the mother's embrace. And because I can't vanish the whorl of the baby's curl from my head. And because of the little girl's stare before she vanished. And because they're a family, I'm sure, and that lonely girl is now out there somewhere and most likely keening for a maternal touch and she's reeling and unanchored just like I've been my whole life.

I shoo Mouse from my room and change back to the girl his mammy wants to play with.

Wanting the alone, the vast salve of it.

IN WHICH THE FAMILY IS TOLD

'We pray no evil shall befall us, nor any plague come near our dwelling. We pray we shall walk in God's protection all the days of our lives.'

At lunch Mr Craw is lost in thought, Virgil is not bothering with anyone, Tobyn is all winks and grins – the boy who's never quite grown up. I can't respond to his playfulness right now, my head is too swamped by the bodies in the glade. Mrs Craw enquires with her fist pressed into her temple if their guest has had a rest. I tell her swiftly that no I did not and actually there's something that needs attending to and I do not drop my stare from Mouse, I won't let him off.

'We saw some dead animals, Mammy,' Mouse jumps in, 'and Possy got a fright. She'd never seen anything like them. That's all. I took her to my magic kingdom. Crawdonia.'

'Oh, poppet, there's nothing out there my menfolk can't fix. And as for Mouse, he's always imagining things. What he's got in that brain of his! Imaginary friends, goblin lands, monsters, creatures of all sorts. He reads far too much.'

Mr Craw raises his head.

'As for the animals, leave it to us,' his wife continues. 'Don't you worry; my lads will bury anything that distresses you.'

'Will we now?' Tobyn teases.

I hold up my finger to him to stop; this is no time for play. 'Something needs sorting first.' I look at Mouse. His lips are rolled in, he's shaking his head, yet I will not be a shy volcano over this. 'We found two people.'

'What?' Mrs Craw exclaims.

'When we were out. Taking a walk.'

Mouse draws in his breath; I'm betraying his secret place.

'Where? Intruders?'

'Who? Escaped convicts?'

'Cal? Callum!'

The patriarch's knuckles are snow-capped mountains as he clutches his knife and fork like two spears guarding his face.

Mouse stares straight at his father. Challenging, pleading, disliking … surely not?

'I'm afraid,' I venture, 'they weren't —'

'What?'

'Alive. They were black. Natives.'

The stem of Mrs Craw's wine glass snaps yet she does not mop the red liquid that spills from the surface of the table like blood onto her lap.

'They looked like a mother and her child.'

'God help us.' Mrs Craw drops her head in her hands, keening a soft moan, needing this stopped.

Virgil stands with an abrupt scrape of his chair and flings his napkin to the table. His father reaches out and pulls him back. He does not release his grip and Virgil's whole being tightens as if he's holding in some explosive force. Tobyn sputters a shocked laugh, while Flea is still, watchful, silent, glancing at me then back at the family then to me again as if he can't quite believe I've done this, spoken out.

'Where are they?' Mr Craw asks.

'At the Ripping Tree.'

'The what?'

'Mouse's big tree, with the bark like paper, on the island by the beach.'

'Noooooooooooo!' Mouse's squeal is high-pitched and anguished above it all at the realisation I've crossed some divide into the adult world and he wants me firmly held in his childhood one and I'm now lost to him and he's broken by this. Some wall has been breached; his friend and ally has crossed over to another place. And I hadn't quite noticed the destruction in it. The boy runs from the room, banging hard into his father, yet he keeps on running to get away, flinching in revulsion from all of us, the adults and their mess, as if, in his eyes, we're all stained by this.

'What's this about?' Tobyn asks. 'I've been in town too long. What have I missed?'

I take a deep breath. Think back to the simplicity of our moment sprawled on the grass, when everything felt so uncomplicated and ready and fresh. I inform them all that there are two dead natives over on the rocky island in the harbour and I don't know why they're there but it looks like something terrible may have happened to them because they look young and in good health and something just feels wrong about it.

'Was there blood?' Mr Craw asks.

'No,' I say, watching the father's hand firm on Virgil's arm.

'A sign of a struggle?' Again, no. 'Then why are you saying this? That something terrible happened. How do you know that?'

I'm blindsided by his pique. 'I … I don't. It just feels … odd.'
I say that Mouse didn't want me to tell but I had to. 'Something
needs to be done, doesn't it?'

There is no turning back from this now. Mr Craw looks
at me like he knows this and that it has only just begun. Mrs
Craw jabs an accusing finger at her husband. 'They're back. You
promised. Do something. Be the man of this house. Sort it like
a man should, Callum. Get off your backside and do something.'

'They never left, Mammy.'

'*Stop it*, Tobyn.' Mrs Craw's vicious hiss, a new mother
entirely. 'You know nothing,' she spits. 'You never have. How
many, Callum?'

Her husband sighs as if the weight of the world is now on his
shoulders. 'None left, madam. I've told you.'

'Mammy. They've all gone,' Virgil says low. 'Haven't they, Pa?
You're protected. Your husband makes sure of that. Protected.
Always. Mammy.'

Everyone turns to the man's quiet words; the first he's spoken
in my presence. He's clotted with something and furious, as if
speaking is a great effort and every word must count.

'Why are they here, Callum?' Mrs Craw twists the lace at her
neck almost to a ripping.

Mr Craw's palms rest concise on the table as if trying to stop
it rising of its own accord. 'Madam, they're not back.'

I ask what is going on here. I add that my knife is missing,
the one thing I still had from the wreck. Mrs Craw snaps it'll
turn up and not to worry; Tobyn says cordially that things are
always going astray in this house. Mr Craw looks up at me
as if suddenly remembering I'm here, the pesky intruder in

his world, the serenity-thief he doesn't want. He turns to his wife and sighs. 'Madam. You must trust that the Good Lord will protect us. That *I* will protect you. Now, I'm going to go immediately to this island. I'm going to look at these so-called bodies. And I'm going to fix things up. Like I always do. My love? Listen. Don't I? Always. You know that.' The last sentence is flung like a whip.

A cry from outside the door. Mouse is listening, of course, and his father will now find the bodies and his secret sanctuary of a place and it's everything he dreaded yet I don't know why, and something feels very wrong here: no one's reacting like they should. What did the little boy say again, at the Ripping Tree? Something like, *He can't have them, they're not his to have.* The world feels askew. And my grand plan that I can make myself anew here, in this strange world so far from anywhere else, feels like it's suddenly running aground.

I look around. Flea is busying himself between the sideboard and the table, covertly watching us. One of them knows something, or several do. Or none, like it just happens this way, of course. Flea catches my looking and begins clearing up, his actions contained within a small, crisp space as if he doesn't want any part of this.

Mr Craw tells me that I must take him to this Ripping Tree after ruining lunch so effectively for everyone – 'and thank you for that, thank you very much'. I do not break my gaze as he looks at me like I'm more trouble than I'm worth and he can see something ahead that I cannot. I nod, at all of them, steeling myself; I started this and can't back down now. Can't flee from this and apologise that it was all a mistake. I'm snared.

'I'm coming to your Ripping Tree too,' Mrs Craw declares, her voice unnaturally deep like a cello's lowest thrum. She looks at her two eldest sons. Tobyn is shaking his head at the hopelessness of it all: his family and Willowbrae, the whole damn lot of it. Virgil is utterly quiet, with a fist pressed to his chest as if trying to soften a thudding heart. 'I'm coming too,' Mrs Craw repeats strong. 'Callum, I need to see this.'

IN WHICH A FAMILY EXPEDITION
IS UNDERTAKEN

'It can't be true, it can't be true.' Mrs Craw repeats her mantra over and over as if something in her head is unhinging itself and floating loose. I tell her it is indeed true and I'm not sure, actually, whether I can find my way back to the Ripping Tree, I'll have to think. She asks for Mouse to come immediately, in a voice with iron in it, and after a long pause the boy enters the room and slips his hand pointedly into mine and not his mother's nor his father's.

Mr Craw orders his elder sons to fetch the dogs. Mouse pulls me aside ahead of the rest and whispers that I'm spoiling everything, and I say tightly that I'm fixing everything, and he says they don't want anything fixed, there's nothing to fix, we should've left everything as it was. For everyone's sake.

'What does that mean?'

Silence.

The only inhabitant of Willowbrae not with us is Flea, who's slunk off to his kitchen. A hot wind pulls and tugs at our grim little posse like a nagging child up to no good and wanting in. The estate's three mongrelly bloodhounds strain at their leashes, all held by Virgil, who says nothing and is apart from everyone

114

else. I do not speak as I stride ahead with Mouse. Every so often the little boy jabs me with savage fingernails to convey a frustration that does not abate. 'Thanks for nothing, Poss.' Stabs of whispers. 'They never see it like I do.'

I stop. 'Who's they?'

'All of them.'

I have to tread carefully, to spool the boy out, to soften and amuse him. 'You say they never see it like you do. But how do you see it? You didn't seem to care much about those dead people when we first saw them.'

The boy wails at those two words – dead people – as if he can't bear it. 'How do you know I don't care?'

I wipe a slick of sweat-heavy hair from my face. 'Mouse, I know nothing about this place. That's why you're here. To inform me.'

Mrs Craw strides forward and pushes her hand into her son's, in ownership, and pulls him away as if she's had enough of this idle talk, all the secret collusions that are leading to no good. She drags Mouse beside her with a wrenching grip while battling her way through the bush as if she can't bear it, this entire treacherous world that will bash at her or sting her or crush her or worse given the chance. She hates it: it's in the spite of her hand as it furiously swipes and swats away. The hot wind is no help. It's whipped itself up into a squall of mischief and dust in a right blustery, nasty day, as if some great spirit is departing this earth and the world is fractious with it.

I make it to the water, just, with Mouse's sullen pointing every so often; he doesn't want this. Mr Craw looks at the shoreline then back at his wife in her skirts. She raises her hands to the heavens and groans, gathers up her clothing and walks straight in like a ship leading an armada into battle. Then yells at everyone to get a move on, she hasn't got all day, and meekly the posse follows suit.

By the Ripping Tree are the bodies. Just as Mouse and I left them. Lying on their feathery fingers of leaves with the smell of death almost sweet in the heat. I want to drop down and stroke the long black eyelashes on the child's cheeks and the tiny shell of her fingernails and the mother's foot cracked from a lifetime of strong walking in this place.

I glance at the Craws. They've all stopped, except for Mouse who's once again bashing his ferns with his stick, lost in stare at his bush. Virgil is very still, very contained, up the back, inscrutable and silent with a handkerchief over his mouth. The dogs, tight on their straining ropes, are eager to investigate this. Why doesn't anyone want to deal with it? Do they know who's responsible? I ask loudly if anyone knows what might have happened. No one answers.

Tobyn drops to the bodies, a knuckle at his mouth. Mrs Craw holds her fingers to her lips then whimpers, 'No, Cal, no.' She clutches her husband's hand and he winces at the grip but does not shake his wife off. Mr Craw's free hand rubs at the edge of his waistcoat as if the unbearable itch has begun tormenting him again and will not, will not, let up.

A rustle of something, standing the hairs on my arms to attention. Someone – something – is watching. Does Mouse sense it too? I whip around. 'Hello?' Not even a twig crack. The dogs breathe in great huffs and slobber their thirst.

'Poss? What is it now?' Mrs Craw's enquiry has steel in it.

I shake my head. If the girl is watching then I must protect her with my silence.

'Callum, can you do something for once?' Mrs Craw asks. 'I can't live like this. I'll have to go home, and I mean … Home. My nerves won't stand it. This … impotence.'

The man's almost imperceptible tightening of his cheeks as his fingers rub, and rub, in deep thought. He says nothing.

'We could try and find out what happened,' I declare. Tobyn nudges the woman's body with his hat as if to check she's really dead and not asleep; Virgil steps forward. The dogs tug, he holds them back; the tinderbox of restraint. I squat beside Tobyn in something like partnership. 'What do you think?'

He shrugs and says it's the bush way and it isn't always what you think. 'Be careful with this one, Poss. You had a blow to the head.'

'Eh?'

'It's just the bush.'

Just as Mouse insisted earlier, yet I can't shake the tug that there's more to this. I look for clues on the ground, anything.

'How do we even know *someone* did it?' Tobyn says. 'Maybe they did it to themselves.'

Mr Craw adds, 'It could be poison berries. A snake. A spider. You have to learn that, child.'

But none of this rings true. If the mother was bitten by a snake then how did the baby die? Was the poison leaked through the breast milk? Do such things happen? And she holds her child so tightly, so protectively. From what? Why are the Craw men so dismissive, and why does this feel like such a lonely, unwanted death? 'The natives would know the dangers of the bush, wouldn't they? Surely?' I saw it in my rescue. The balancing on surf-pounded rocks, the deep rhythmic drawing of the canoe's stick, the sure feet walking through the night bush.

Mr Craw steps between me and the bodies, as if to shield them from me. 'Not always, Poss. Just like us.' He tells me very slowly that things happen differently out here, that what I think means one thing could be something else entirely, something completely innocent. I cock my head. Something about his measured tones feels like a dismissal, and a threat.

'We need to find out what happened, sir. There might be someone here …'

'It's just their way,' he counters. 'Tobyn, could you accompany our young guest back to the house. She's had a rough baptism when it comes to this place and needs a lot more rest. Take the little fella too. Now.'

'I'm all growed up, Pa. Let me help.'

Mrs Craw stifles a gasp of dissent.

'We're fine, my son.'

'Please, Pa.'

'Stop it.'

'Pleeeeaaaaaaasssse.'

'No.'

A flinch of rage, held in check; a hand ready to slap that stops inches from a tiny face. The father stares us all down, willing us into silence. 'I'll take care of this. Poss. We've no more need of you now. Thank you.'

Something is not right. They're all so tense. I snap away from Mr Craw and stand on a rise and confront the vicious wind. Flinch I will not, break I will not; inhaling the spite in the stiff breeze and bending as it nudges a tear down my cheek. I'm sure the little girl is close, staring through the trees at the candle-skinned people standing around those she loves the most.

And wondering what comes next.

DECISIONS

I turn back, face him. 'Sir, I don't want to leave just yet.'

The man is very soft and very clear in his response. 'You do as you're told, child. Go back to the house. Now.'

Tobyn turns hurriedly to his baby brother. 'Have you seen these people before?'

Mouse cries that he doesn't know anything about anything, that he wishes none of them were here, in his place, his secret place and it's the bush way and so what and he wishes they'd all go and that it wasn't like this before, it's all ruined, everything. He's flinging a jumble of words and swiping his hands at his face as if he wants to brush this entire landscape off, and these people, and this world; it's all too much.

'Leave him be,' Virgil says quietly from a deep, removed stillness. He hasn't moved the entire time we've been here. His handkerchief is still at his mouth as if it's some kind of personal crutch between civility and chaos and he's holding on tight. 'Shall I bring them in?' he asks his father.

'Yes.'

'Bring them in?' I repeat. 'Wouldn't we be better off burying them here perhaps? I can run back and get a spade.' Virgil shakes his head at me like I'm stupid and really should be gone from this place. 'They need to be buried,' I reason. 'Someone – something – has killed them and we need to find out what, to stop it happening again.' I'm speaking to all the Craws now and anyone else in the bush and they stare at me perplexed as if they don't know what to do with this outburst, as if something weightier is pressing in on their world and I have no idea of it.

'Is any of this useful?' Tobyn looks at his father. My head lurches back: what? Virgil snarls at him to shut up. The dogs bark; Mr and Mrs Craw scold them in unison to stop, which they do. The father says to give him a moment, he needs to think, and everything between them suddenly feels stretched and breakable and taut.

'Poss, get back to the house. Now. You've done enough.' Mr Craw brushes me off. 'All of you in fact.' The man is close to breaking point; the rubbing of his hand grows more vigorous on his hip; does he even know he's doing it? 'Virgil, stay. And the dogs.' Something here feels like slippage. Mrs Craw's hands are at her head and she's keening softly in words I can't make out and she's ignored by all the men as if they're used to this.

I cannot fight this; I'll have to go. I slip my arm around Mrs Craw's waist as a crutch to her fragility and lead her past the Ripping Tree, want to lie her down on the moss and strip off some bark and wrap her in it. She leans on my shoulder in a great exhalation of weariness. I turn back briefly to the men, shrouded by the grimness of their task.

Virgil removes the tongues of enveloping bark I'd placed over the woman's nakedness then lifts her body into his arms with an arresting authority and tenderness. Another man entirely.

Woken up, into something else. And the dogs, their leashes dropped, look on in abeyance.

From the beach we turn back and watch Mr Craw splashing after us across the shallows, with the little bundle of a baby girl too heartbreakingly small in his arms; her tiny feet flop in the solemn air. Mrs Craw pulls away and notes her husband holding the child and at one point lets out a sharp cry, of something like defeat.

'Pa, stop, please,' Mouse wails from the bushes.

'Let me do what I have to do, son,' the father says.

I locate the boy from a startle of blond hair amid the trees; this feels like a wound. I walk to him, and take his little hand in the grip that began our friendship, the secret tickle in a palm's pit.

'Stay with me,' he whispers, 'please.'

I look back to the fist of the hidden place that a moment ago cusped two dead people in it. Who was the woman shielding her baby from? I just wish this family would show a little more curiosity and concern but, no, they're not explaining anything. And they're barely tolerating me at this moment. Why? My breath catches in a gasp.

'What?' Mouse asks. 'Poss?'

I tell him I'm not sure his father wants me at Willowbrae.

'Oh, that's just him. He's always grumpy, but I'm not.' Mouse's face is suddenly open like a sun slipped from the cloud; he's my little helper once again, wanting to set things right. With great effort I smile at my friend and tell him I'm not leaving him, that he's got himself a new governess here, but he'll be whipped to kingdom come if any dead mice are found in my desk. 'What's a desk, Miss? I've never heard of that.' His giggle blazes him into life.

I glance across at Mr Craw holding the baby as if he's never held a baby before, and at Virgil carrying the woman as if in ownership, and at Mrs Craw shredded by all of this and at my little Mouse clutching my hand for dear life and not letting up. Then at Tobyn, reaching up and pulling at the branches above his head as if he's really not part of whatever is going on, as if he really doesn't care enough. I bite my lip, trying to work him out. Work everyone out.

I'll be staying in this strange world, oh yes. I'll be striding along the fighter's path. Because Pa would expect nothing less. And because in the bushes, quite possibly, a little girl is watching and she may need my help at some point. A little girl who nodded at me once, just, in something like trust.

I retire for the rest of the day and ask for supper in my room. Need to be away from the lot of them right now, cleansed of the swirl of this place by enveloping solitude. I look out the French doors, wondering where my rescuer is. Has he moved on? Does he know the woman in the glade? The children?

Night presses in. A moonless, cloud-covered dark.

I miss my father so much it hurts in my chest. I tip my head back on tears. Want Pa's guidance here, want his gentle, teasing laugh. Everything aches.

A deep sleep will not net me, no matter how hard I try. Not even the thought of my rescuer's strong striding through the dark will send me off tonight. He feels utterly gone now, too; and I, all alone.

THE THIRD DAY

AN INCONSISTENT THUD

I stir from a sleep webbed by wakefulness, thinking too much of the bodies in the glade and thinking too much of my Bec. For it isn't the first time I've seen a mother and child this way. Deep in a January frost – could it already be two years ago? – Pa and I were out walking and came across my dear, dear friend, my Bec. On a day when the world was shrouded in stillness we found her lying with her newborn baby under a tree near our farm, on a bed of shy snowdrops. She must have given birth all by herself, before her time, and I can only think that she'd been trying to get to us but then couldn't get up. Her dear little son was frozen stiff in the tuck of her arm, baptised in hoary white by the brittle frost.

Heart aching for them all, I fall back into a churning slumber and am awoken by a thud against the French doors. A bird. It's a bang of extreme violence, as if the creature has been flung at the glass. My chest constricts. Not again. 'Who's there?' No one. Of course.

I reach for Jack's knife and remember it's gone and no one yesterday could give me a proper explanation apart from 'It'll turn up.' The girl in the painting now looks at me with what seems like the softest of smirks; like she knows something I don't. No. Stop. My palms push into the skin of my forehead as if trying to steady my brain.

My flitting heart. The flagstones outside are stained with splashes of blood. The bird is beautiful, its wings tipped with the blue of a summer sky. It also has a furious-looking beak and a sickening fragility to its drooping wing. I hold the creature's brokenness to the nest of my chest – 'Oh, you, you' – and press its faint, enormous heart bewildered by ebbing life into mine. Who did this? Or was it just the bird itself, confused, flying directly into the glass?

I hurry across the lawn to the bush. With scrabbling hands scoop out some loose soil to bury it. Yet the creature is still alive. What am I doing? Becoming? I press the heel of my hand into my pounding chest; stop. Think.

The bird is rested on a mattress of soft bark torn from a ripping tree. The creature's beady eye looks up at me as I back away and hold my palms over my head as if trying to shut out the sin of abandonment. Uncertainty is taking hold of me in this place; I feel infected by it. What's going on here? I look around; there's no one of course. I gulp a breath but can't fill my lungs. It's as if they're thickening up in this place, in panic; something is closing over them. My eyes shut and I see again the sinews of a moving back on a storm-meekened evening. Where is he, my rescuer?

IN WHICH VISITORS ARRIVE

I fall back into an exhausted, scrappy sleep then wake with a start: Mrs Craw is calling me from far away, the front of the house. I have guests. Who knows I'm at Willowbrae? Jack? My brother? Captain Grent? They've been found! Survivors, hidden in coastal pockets, I knew it. Mouse runs in, shaking me into a sitting. 'They're outside.'

'Who? Who?'

'Quick.'

I pull on the trousers and run to the front door, tucking in my shirt as I go. Stop abruptly at a melee of carriages and upturned faces as I freeze on the top step of the verandah. Oh, no one I know. The voices rise in a questioning cacophony, hemming me in. Who is she? Is she alright? What's her name? *What* is she wearing? I look down at the clothes thrown on without thinking. Oh no, oh no.

The crowd has gathered on the gravelled drive with carriages and horses in a messy group to the side of it. I'm stopped between the two Ionic pillars that frame Willowbrae's front door. Behind the restless crowd is the lone ripping tree I remember from my first night here, on its very English lawn. It is striking in its difference, as if someone once decided it was just too beautiful to destroy in the vast clearing of this land.

I stare in silence at all the new faces. Breathe very shallow, very still; trapped. This is Scandal. Mrs Craw is standing in the thick of the visitors, helpless to intervene while her husband says nothing up the back of the crowd; he just stares at my trousers with a face of stone as he rubs a tormented hand on his waistcoat. I hold my head high because there's no turning back from this, I'll have to brave it out. I gulp, step forward. This has to be carefully done.

The people-clot advances; I don't know a soul. Strangers' hands dare a touching at the mysterious mermaid from the depths – alive, miraculously, and in boys' clothes no less, and that hair, good gracious. Mrs Craw tries to keep them at bay but can't. Her husband watches from the back. Mouse is behind me. The older sons have vanished.

'The child needs rest. Her head is addled, which explains the clothes.' Mrs Craw looks furiously at me – this is Disobedience – and holds her hand high but is ignored by the crowd. A strand of her hair has fallen loose and her hands are shaking. Mr Craw stares at my trousers.

'What's your name?'

'Who's your family?'

'Who else is alive?'

'Where are you from?'

I glance from face to face, at this crush of curiosity, all these people flinging their questions. Perhaps everyone here has been hoping I'm theirs; at the news of a rescue they've rushed to Willowbrae in a wild wishing. Could I be their own private miracle?

'She's not Sarah.' A woman falls to the ground, sobbing; another tries to smooth my hair. 'Poor mite.'

A man in a sweat-stained hat takes this as his cue. 'How did you survive the hateful sea, lass? Who's your family?'

An elderly man points an accusing cane at me. 'Come on, what happened?'

Mouse cries out to leave me alone but no one hears him except me and I'm the crowd's now as much as his, the circus act, the mermaid beached. They tell me the *Finbar* missed the harbour heads and turned in at a lower point of land that dips and is impossible to see in a storm; there's no lighthouse in these parts and Captain Grent got it wrong and what he thought was a gap in the coastline was actually a sheer rock face. 'Visibility was down to nil. Poor captain, poor soul.'

'Souls.'

'Bodies are being washed up. Unclothed.'

'Sssssh. Not yet. She's too young.'

'She needs to be in town.'

'Horses are on the rocks, their legs stiff as posts. A cow with a barrel of a belly.'

'They're still trying to find survivors. All down the coast. You're the only one.'

'So far, pet, so far. There's more, I don't doubt.'

I shiver a flinch at the bash of the voices, at the greedy faces all wanting me to be someone else. Want to burrow back into my room and shut this world out. But, but. All souls lost. *All?* No. The crushing weight of proof is like an ocean of hurt hard on my chest. I crouch by the front door, hands clamped over my ears, trying to shut them all away and moaning softly; in an instant Mouse's palm is strong on my back and Mrs Craw gentles me into standing. 'Are they really all gone, ma'am? All?' The woman's forehead is creased and she shakes her head. Can't quite speak.

I have held on to the thought that all along the coast there might be pockets of people palmed by the rocks, just like myself, my brother among them and his thin-lipped Mariana; and that my strange, fresh existence with a new name and a new future was somehow temporary. Until everything was righted, and my old world came back. But no? My brain hurts. Am I freed? Bound? Grieving? Not? A deep low keening is expelled from my belly, an animal wail.

'She's not mad,' Mrs Craw explains, 'just broken.'

But all the ballast of my days is gone. I want to ask, 'What of my brother?' But do not, cannot. Through great gulps of anguish, there must be silence about my past. But all gone? Even Captain Grent? Can I live with audacity now, anonymous forever and totally unanchored? On nothing but wits? Ambrose. Not Ambrose. And Jack. Dear Jack. 'No, no,' I keen.

A lean whip of a man curdles into view, knotted with anger and suspicion. So, they haven't finished with me yet. He's all eyes, his lids dropping to my chest and it feels like intrusion and I want to shove him away in a strop. 'You must have had someone's help,' the man says. 'Where are they? Hiding? Are they convict stock?'

I'll not give him the dignity of a response.

'She's staying with me,' Mrs Craw warns him in ownership. 'There's no one else.'

What has this stranger heard of my rescue? I recall a scrap from Mariana's sea-flung instruction manual: '*You must not hold your head high, so as to avoid sexually exciting strangers. You must learn the shame of your body and its functions.'* What shame and what functions? Yet again the man's eyes drop.

'The sickroom, child, immediately.' Mrs Craw pulls me to my feet and I'm a grateful horse to her trough but the others will not let her win this just yet.

'Is anyone else saved?'

'Who are you? Come to town with us.'

'Yes, come to town, girl.'

'Did someone bring you here? Where are they hiding?'

Because of course a young girl like me couldn't possibly manage a rescue by herself. The alone roars at me. I look across to the impenetrable bush, to the city of birds protesting in their high heat. These people want me in town, but what does that offer? Officialdom, interrogation, a need to dig me out. Meanwhile there's a little boy with a steadying hand by my side, whispering, 'Come on, Possy, we need to get out.' Then he raises his voice indignantly. 'She's staying here, she's not better yet.' Bless him, but the people won't let up; I can smell the greed of their curiosity. And my new life with its new name will unravel among them, I can feel it already, and Ambrose's marriage plan will be enforced. Is that man among these people, waiting in the shadows for his own private miracle?

'What's your *name*, child?'

'Spit it out.'

'Why were you sailing here?'

Mouse's protective blurt. 'Her name's Poss and she's my friend and she can't remember nothing 'cause she's got a bump on her head and I'm fixing things up. So leave her alone.'

'Arran!' Mr Craw exclaims, to quieten him, but the boy continues bravely on.

'She wants to be better. Here. With me.'

Mrs Craw laughs to the crowd with her hands thrown up, as if in surrender to the whims of a child.

Yes, I nod, yes, this will do. My head whooshes, I reach out to steady myself.

'Lordy, she's going to faint.'

'Water.'

'Someone, water.'

Need to cave myself.

In Which There Is a Rescue of Sorts

'God's liquid.'

A man's tallness at the back pushes its way through and they're all parting in his wake. A man's tallness is holding out a silver flask like a fervent cross and it rattles awkwardly, too close, in a way that makes me think this man is not used to chivalry nor sharing; he's not done much of either. I shake my head. 'No. Thank you.' Am I presenting as so unhinged that I need a reviving of the whisky sort?

'The good Lord's liquid. Yes. It will do no harm. Girl. Child.' This awkward bear of a man is urging with insistence but no smile and makes it seem like a cursed rejection if I deny him this grace. I give him nothing. There's no connection with any of these people. All souls? Everyone on the ship? My head is still full of it.

'It's water. Yes. Just that.' The man is not liking the resistance, as if he's not used to talking to the likes of a girl in her trousers, or to anyone. His body is slightly twisted away as if he'd broken his mother by being birthed and is deformed from the experience. Perhaps he's sailed to this rogue place of rejection so he doesn't have to face the world; perhaps he's running from something. Could the same be said of everyone here? They're all wearied and creased; no one looks crisp. Except Mrs Craw, a little apart, with her hair now righted and her still-snowy cuffs.

The man smiles at me shy and sideways, perhaps regretting his forwardness already; he's looking out, just, from under a block of black hair. He cut it himself, I can tell, with hands mixed up in the mirror, just as I've done more than once myself. I soften at that. Allow him a grin. It lights up his face. 'I've not drunk one drop,' he says.

'He's one to trust, lass.'

The twisted man turns to the woman who has yelled her endorsement and he tips his hat then looks at the crowd and somehow silences the communal restlessness.

'This soul, this poor saved soul, needs some rest.' His tone settles them. 'She needs to gather her thoughts. To remember. Not now. It's too soon. But eventually.' The man glances at me sideways; it feels like a secret. Or perhaps not. His eyes look away, perhaps he's gone too far.

I gaze at him, closer. At his shyness. His strange power to silence. His authority that stopped the crowd short. He's a vicar, of course. His dog collar is barely visible under the layers of bush clothes and smeared with dirt, but it's there, just. No woman has kept him neat. Lately or ever. But a vicar. I step back. Just what I do not need right now.

'We need to ascertain something of this matter. Per-pertaining to your, er, circumstances.'

A vicar. Here for his private miracle? No, he'll not be digging out my 'circumstances'; there's nothing he needs to dig for. But does he know who I am? A hand covers my mouth. I certainly won't be asking his name. I'm a bird suddenly fluttering and panicky in a cage. Does he suspect? There's never been a portrait of me. Do I look like Ambrose too much? My hands tremble at my cheeks. I'm too wild and unkempt for the likes of my brother. Few would guess we were siblings without knowing us both; each of us has reddish hair but Ambrose's is darker and straighter and more tamed and a stranger wouldn't make the connection. Surely? Perhaps, oh God, in the smile which is our father's; but Ambrose rarely smiles and we don't share a mother.

I'm ready for flight. Look to the bush, want to be swallowed right now by its cool caress.

'Can I – I … Your name?' The vicar's question drops into gentleness. Right. Quite hopeless with talk and he'll get silence in response, thank you very much. He can barely bring out his next words, as if some creature is hauling them back in his throat. 'If – if you … remember it. No?'

Every fibre of my being is on high alert. I jerk my head like a wild horse suddenly bridled, can't trust my voice.

'I – I travelled to Willowbrae at first word of a survivor,' the vicar says. 'To see if I could help. In any way, any of the poor souls. Who – who might need it. God's help. Then we heard that you – so far – are the only one. Yet here we all are … crowding you …' His eyes are nervous; his hand rests above my shoulder but doesn't dare a touch. 'It's alright to weep,' he says to me quietly. 'You've been through so much.' The hand touches me then springs back as if shocked at its own confidence.

I look at him. Feel cracked by obscene kindness here, all of a sudden; my body without warning wants to soften into this man. I feel pricked, spent, as if a whole lifetime of tears is about to tip out. I will not let this happen in front of him.

'It's a terrible thing. What you've been through.'

The man's massive, bull-like shoulders are misshapen with a stoop, like he's been told for too long that he isn't good enough and wants to fold himself away from his dreadful, twisted bulk. I feel shadowed beside him yet want to lean in just as I used to with Pa, and rest. He offers me some water again, seemingly at a loss over what to do next. His face is deeply crevassed as if the effort of just surviving here is burden enough, as if he's seen too much already in this place.

I shake my head at his courtesy, thinking of all the words in the letters that have ordered me into a new life as wife to a husband I don't want. Could this awkward loom of a man possibly be him?

'Big crowds. Not – not good for anyone. Yes.'

I nod. Possibly, whatever, I don't know. I shake my head, anything to not talk.

He starts up again, perhaps feeling that the gap between us is unbearable and must be filled up. 'Talk can just slip away, yes, like a runaway cart. I'm not good at it. Not very helpful in a vicar, of course. Ha. Which is perhaps why I'm here. Not England. Yes.' A shy laugh.

My lips are rolled in, I won't cry, yet a pricking threatens a tip.

'Were you … travelling with someone, lass?'

I will not have the weeping released.

'Who was meeting you?'

I narrow my eyes as thinking as a cat.

'Of course. What you've been through. Too soon. And Mrs Craw —'

I look up sharply.

'Your rescuer, is the best for this. A venerable matriarch. Yes. Of this colony. A – a fine woman.'

I tilt my head in wonder at his stilted talk.

'We'll leave you. Hmm. In her more than capable hands. And then, perhaps, we'll speak. One day. Yes?' His clogged voice, like he's been alone for too long and the shutting off has wormed its way into him. He murmurs in conclusion that everything from the *Finbar* is possibly lost, everything, and I must prepare for this. With pained eyes, he whispers, 'I'm sorry.'

So. I'm left alone among them all, voiceless and nameless, stranded from that time when I was known as Thomasina Trelora of Knockleby, Dorset, the recluse's odd daughter. And I could remain nameless and anchorless among them all unless I declare myself now, tell them my real name. Or I can choose to remain silent in this moment and become, miraculously, someone else, with a new future and a new life, even if it's only temporary. Oh, the freedom to be seized in that!

Choice.

'Let us not give up hope.' The vicar nods gravely.

A flutter in my stomach. I can't bring myself to enquire of the man's name, can't bear to hear his response, because perhaps he is my future locked.

The contingent from town mills about and urges me to recover back in civilisation and their voices are too loud as they press me to be questioned by the harbour pilot and the coroner and the police and the newspaper folk. But no. Not now, not today. I need to hide a while longer from a future mapped out and they'll not be getting a name from me just yet.

Mrs Craw knows this by instinct; she holds up her hand in a determined stop. 'This girl could not be in a better place than Willowbrae. With me. Is there anyone who doubts it? If so, speak up.' She's looking straight at her husband, who's a pillar of flint as he stands there saying nothing, and no one argues with the steel in her voice.

'There's no finer woman, lass,' an older woman concedes. 'No finer family. You're in good hands. The best.'

Mr Craw's cheek twitches as his wife's palm is held imperiously high in dismissal, without a dressed-up goodbye. He remains silent, staring at his wife and his cheek twitches, and twitches. Then she propels me away with iron in her grip.

'How did you survive?' The words are flung like a whip at my departing back. 'What did you do that my precious Sarah did not?' The anguish in the cry.

I freeze. At the stirrings from the others. Then the tension is released like a grain sack split by a vicious knife. Did I see a man's son? Another man's wife? A baby nephew? Did I help?

From the back of the crowd the vicar implores them all to be quiet, to grant their new arrival peace and to be thankful I'm among them, but on they go, and on: the whip at my back.

'What did you do to survive when all those other souls did not?'

I shrink into myself, supported by Mrs Craw and my Mouse. Too emotionally battered for any of it, too stricken to tell them that I survived, perhaps, thanks to all the summer days back at home, as soft as a pocket, when I taught myself to swim in my farm's little brook, which was allowed by a father who didn't mind me toughening up. It was a life of climbing trees and making fires and skinning rabbits, and now my pa is in his green-coated resting place in Knockleby's churchyard, utterly gone, and so is everything else from my life.

And I'm alone. Without even Jack's knife, my last possession in the world. I have to light my own lantern in the dark and I'm not quite sure how and it all feels so hard at Willowbrae, suddenly, but I can't tell anyone this.

Mrs Craw firms her arm around my shoulder and propels me inside, shutting the visitors out.

'Thank you. Leave us be. My girl has had enough.'

My girl. I can't recall any woman ever calling me that and, oh, the softening into the thought. Yes, please, may I be someone's girl. Yes, please, may somewhere be my home. My anchor, my place of rest.

AN ONION IN REVERSE

Back in my room it is like a cloud has scudded across the sunshine, all warmth from Mrs Craw is vanished. 'Get dressed. Immediately. Properly this time. That was humiliating. Don't you even dare think about wearing those ... those ... abominations, ever again.'

The change is instant, as if all through the townfolk's visit she'd really just wanted to be this. Punishing and cold and withheld. Mrs Craw informs me it's time I became a proper lady and stalks off. 'Stay in your room,' she commands as she departs, 'I'll be back.'

I try dragging the brush through the knotted tangle of my hair at the back; it doesn't work, it gets stuck.

A few minutes later Mrs Craw returns with some garments crudely modulated. 'I haven't finished but they'll do. I was up all night. Once again. The things you drive me to.' The woman's cuffs are sternly tugged over her hands and her hair is smoothed.

'I'm so sorry. I just threw on those old clothes without thinking.'

'Well, you must learn to think, mustn't you? If you're to stay under this roof. If you're capable of it. And I'm not sure about that.'

And so to a layering into submission like an onion in reverse. First a too-loose chemise, then a corset with its seams folded over because it's too wide for me, yet Mrs Craw has sewn it into an unforgiving tightness and now I can't move loosely nor bend.

'How am I meant to tie my boot laces, ma'am?' I'm ignored. 'Ma'am?' The older woman is good at selective silence. It feels practised, a settling into a familiar deflection. 'Ma'am, it's hard to breathe. It hurts.'

'If you can talk, you can breathe.' The abrupt answer. 'You live under my rules at Willowbrae. Not yours. Not anyone else's.'

I think of the alternatives – town and its crush of curiosity, or telling the truth and being married off. What is better? Under Mrs Craw's firm hands I'm rendered helpless and bound and weak as the older woman nods to herself. 'Now we're getting somewhere.' Next comes the undershirt. A cage of a crinoline – 'too short but it will have to do' – then three petticoats because she wants to see what they look like together, then her fourth-best dress that smells of old sweat and has a band of mismatching cotton as a hem to cover my scandalous legs. 'Which this entire household, and district, has seen too much of already now. Thank you for that.' A sash to neaten everything, imprecisely, and not to Mrs Craw's standards of containment. 'It'll do. For now. And thank the Lord you're a girl, finally. I can see it at last.'

I try to take a deep breath but can't. The entire effect feels scratchy and pinched and wrong. Moving is an effort because an item of clothing rubs against every attempt; ease is something to be fought for.

But I'm learning. I don't need this battle right now. Can't afford to make an enemy of this matriarch whom I might need soon enough and who hasn't had a living doll to make up for over a decade. I sigh a flattened thank you; Mrs Craw declares tightly that I look splendid now. 'It's good to start afresh, isn't it? My girl. You'll be doing everything right from now on, won't you?' Despite my protests the woman removes every item of male clothing from the room and places it by the door.

'Not my shoes!'

'We need to have you sorted, Poss. Completely.'

'But I won't fit your feet! And I can't go barefoot. What about the snakes?'

Reluctantly Mrs Craw concedes this point yet tells me there's not much need to be going outside, a proper lady has no want of all that wildness.

'Really? But what about yesterday?' And I ask her in the blurt of a moment what happened to the two people from the glade; what happened to the other natives, were any left?

My questions are unanswered but they set off a new pique. Mrs Craw propels me in front of the looking glass and braids my hair then flurries it out and braids its recalcitrance once again. It feels like all the woman's frustrations at being unable to control this situation on several fronts are now directed entirely into the flattening and taming of my hair with a cruelly insistent comb, making my style as rigidly controlled as her own.

'Ow! That hurts!' It's ignored. 'Ooooooooooooooooow.'

Mrs Craw persists until I'm helmeted by a dull, smooth shield of unremitting ugliness. I'm amazed that no blood has been drawn. I stare at the stranger before me in the looking glass. It feels like the world of the big house is closing over me, that I'm being remade into what I never wanted to be, and I want to tear at this new girl, scrabble her off. I tug at the stiff silk; Mrs Craw smiles, wilfully unseeing it. 'A lady at last. For any future – unexpected – house guests.'

I excuse myself tightly through held-in tears that I don't want her to see. Say I need some fresh air and push my chair savagely from the dressing table and stalk out. Her voice follows me down the corridor.

'We won't have a repeat of this morning, will we, Poss?'

IN WHICH THE MEDICINE IS DRUNK

I stride along the hall then take a hunch that the room off the parlour will be the library Tobyn has told me about: a place to escape to because it's rarely used. I'm rewarded with a corner room that captures the sun from the north, a haven of books and maps and globes and an enveloping winged armchair that arrests time by dragging me into its deep rich depths and holding me captive.

It reminds me of my father's library, which Ambrose disbanded soon after his death, selling off whatever he could to pay his debts. This one is a monument to Mrs Craw's insistence on perfection, with its air of rigid calm. Everything is in its place. Whereas Pa's bookish lair had toppling stacks of tomes and papers held down with horseshoes and iron nails as big as thumbs and a swirl of ammonite fossils and giant shells alongside a filthy dog quilt that Bess, our old wolfhound with the speaking eyes, slept on like a queen in her treasure chamber. Ambrose wouldn't let me take her with me on the *Finbar*; he said she was too old. Whatever love I may have had for my brother was extinguished at that moment. I miss my Bess so much, miss burying my forehead between her ears when I needed comforting, miss lying the length of her in front of the fire's warmth.

Pa's library contained diversions of wonder on its many bowed shelves, pages stretching into chapters and sometimes entire volumes in long, golden days of instruction and warmth. I need that nest right now. Need a room of books that's a sanctuary, a harbour, to rest from the toss of uncertainty. I took from Pa's room his cherished volume of Shakespeare and a nautiloid fossil that was the first he ever found; both were lost in my luggage when the *Finbar* went down.

In Willowbrae's library, on a round table next to my chair, is a collection of exotic insects impaled on steel pins, each one trapped under a cylinder of glass. They're colonising the small surface in a flare of colour and wonder and sheen, each beautiful, frozen creature with a pin driven through either abdomen or heart. I shiver. Turn from them.

To a lithograph titled *Warratta*, with folds of blood-red stamens bowing like pilgrims in worship to their central god. Jack said he dreamt of one day 'drawing strangeness, like that Mr Banks. I'm going to do it, Tommy,' and I laughed and told him nothing must stop him, that he must get on with his plan. My dear, vivid-hearted friend, with his lovely long neck and Adam's apple I always wanted to touch but never did, for it felt too intimate and revealing to do that. I wish I'd told him of my affection, the gladness at the mere sight of him. Did he know of it?

I squeeze the flesh on my upper arms until it hurts. What purpose was my saving? The thinking in my head is too glary, too much, and I knuckle my fists into it. One hundred and thirty-one of them. Gone. One hundred and thirty-one. I shrink into the armchair, trying to shut everything out.

Mrs Craw enters the room and tells me curtly that I have an unexpected guest but she will not say who. And they would like to see me. Alone.

I unfold myself and rush to the parlour. Could it be Jack, miraculously rescued from the sea, come to find me?

WHAT WE DO

The vicar. Oh. Mrs Craw is right behind me, hovering to be sure and planning to stay for the entire exchange. I say, 'Thank you, Mrs Craw,' and she smiles determinedly with a curt nod; she will not leave me alone with this. I see.

I turn back to my guest. So. Not Jack, or anyone else wondrously rescued, and I can't hide my deflation. The huge bear-man is stranded in all his clotted awkwardness, as if trying to diminish himself in this too-small, too-floral room; he's the wrong size for it.

'I – I turned back. From the others. I had to see you. One more time. Today.' He puts his cup and saucer of tea on a slender colt of a table and spills the liquid onto the tablecloth and uses the edge of the material to wipe it up then thinks better of it. His broad hands are too large for the fragile porcelain. He rummages in his pocket and holds out a piece of folded paper then retracts it then holds it out again and to relieve him of his agony I reach for it.

'For me?'

The vicar snatches it back, an embarrassment of confusion. No wonder he could never snare a wife, he'd be too scared to ask – but I do understand that the pen that unlocks courage is sometimes not found face to face. 'Your clothes. This morning. Goodness. I've never seen a girl ... woman. Like that.'

'Well, I've been put to right now. By the mistress of the house.'

'Yes.' Is there a flicker of disappointment in his reply?

'It was scandal, I know. But it allowed a wonderful freedom of movement all the same. You men are so lucky. I could stomp and run and climb. It was extraordinary, the difference!' I tip forward, irrepressibly, as if to sweep the vicar into a dance and Mrs Craw tuts at me like a teacher as our guest leans back as if he couldn't possibly be touched. He laughs unsmoothly and tells me that I seem like some wild creature, some kind of animal let loose – and that it's alright, mind, it's not an insult.

'None taken. So, why exactly did you need to see me, Vicar?'

He says in a stutter of a rush that he's checking on me, that's all, because the crowd was overwhelming, and ... and ... he just wanted to check. Again. He's hoping I'm having a good rest amid everything. Yes? 'I hope so. For your head's sake.'

I smile. His hesitancy and earnestness make me want to be big in front of him, loud and cheeky. I check myself and report that I'm slowly recovering, thank you.

He says arrangements are being made. In town. By the authorities keen to set the horror of the shipwreck to rights. Somehow.

'Oh!'

I'm to have a nice room with a lady, a widow, a good woman. If I want.

'Do, do you?' He says it'd be advisable, as soon as Mrs Craw decrees, which should be soon. 'Yes?' We stop. Stare.

Mrs Craw butts in, cutting across our looking. She reassures the vicar that there's no need for a nice room, far away from the big house. I'll be taken good care of, she says. I'm to be a governess here, to her young son. I'm needed very much. 'It all works out ... perfectly.'

But, but. Stewing with the knowing yet not knowing. Do I want to leave here so soon and immerse myself into fresh trauma, could I bear it? To break the impasse of saying nothing or too much, I ask what it's like to be a vicar here.

He answers, hesitant: it's a challenge, there are many factors to contend with which are not present at home. 'Do you want to give thanks to God for saving you?'

I smile gratefully. 'Yes, very much. I need the privacy of ... of a helping hand. To, to God. In thanks.' Fervent and hoping and glancing across at Mrs Craw. She nods, in respect for prayer, and quietly withdraws.

Alone at last.

'Thank you for coming,' I say to him in a rush.

'I thought you might welcome a – a ... change of scenery. I mean, face. Yes? Someone new. To talk to. Perhaps.'

I laugh. 'Yes. Thank you, yes.'

The vicar says in a rush that I'm not, possibly, the only one feeling lost and I agree but can't quite look at him and then we meander with talk of God and rescue and gratitude and guilt and it's easy with him, so easy.

'I do feel religious, Vicar. I do. Just not with the church. Sometimes. Oh, I feel blasphemous to even say such things!'

'Don't. Please. I understand something of what you talk of, yes.'

'Really? Sometimes I feel things so strongly but don't dare to say my thoughts, ever, for fear of the walls listening in. Of … God listening in.'

'You can talk freely with me, Poss. I will always promise you that.'

I look at him. He blinks a smile. Something uncurls in me; I trust him. 'I feel contrary, Vicar. Sometimes. Dangerously so. God is deep in me, right here.' I thump my chest. 'Just not' – my voice lowers, I cannot look at him – 'in the church. There. I've said it.'

There is silence in response, silence for me to fill, for the vicar is nodding without looking as if he wants me to go on.

'I'm just not sure about the church, Vicar. Sometimes. Who runs it, who decides. Because … it doesn't feel like my God, sometimes. In there. What they talk about. What they tell us to think. My God is better than that, I feel, better than … oh dear … them.' I hold my head in my hands, in mortification, at what I've just voiced. And wait.

A long pause. 'You speak of nothing, Poss, that I haven't sometimes felt myself.'

I gasp. Look up. The vicar smiles ruefully. I laugh in relief and babble in a rush that sometimes my faith feels like it has more to do with the earth and the sky and the land and I gesture to the wildness of the bush outside, unlike, unlike … I look at him, again, for permission, for reassurance. 'Am I speaking out of turn here, Vicar? Please tell me.'

The vicar shakes his head. 'Not at all. I welcome all manner of thoughts and perspectives, yes. Always have. Go on.'

I hesitate. 'It just feels so hard to reconcile, all this. And *your* faith, Vicar? Am I spouting nonsense here?'

He smiles shy through his hair that falls too long over his face and needs a cut. I almost brush it back behind his ears, to clearly see his face; he does so himself. He tells me he welcomes any kind of talk – deep, searching, doubtful – and never has it enough and misses it. The challenging kind.

'Well then, challenge me, Vicar. Do you ever feel, um, contrary?'

He looks at me, accepting the gauntlet; this feels like a dance of honesty. He describes a torment sometimes, a questioning.

'About what?'

Being here, he says, and that sometimes his church seems like a closed fist against this world and it does not sit quite right with him. That sometimes he feels there's more spirituality in the natives pushed to the margins than in ourselves, sometimes, and that even that sentence seems like blasphemy itself. The vicar ploughs on. 'It feels like there is something rich and deep and harmonious. With their land, that they seem so blended with. If that is the word.'

Silence. I stare at him, my head on one side, deep in thought. He says he has a dear friend, a native, who comes and sits with him sometimes at his little bush abode and he learns a lot. The man's language, for a start, and a glimpse into his soul, if he can dare put it like that. He's so blunt and brave and thinking, and quite possibly right.

The vicar says this strange island is deep in the natives' blood and they understand it in a way we settlers do not and he's seen them sometimes fall sick if they aren't close to their home, where they've lived their whole lives, as have their ancestors' ancestors. I think of the glade, of the two lonely deaths, and a little girl watching through the leaves. The vicar tells me the land seems almost like another person to them, protecting them.

'Like a mother?'

'Yes, perhaps,' and he's rambling now, lost in talk. 'They have a very rich spirituality, Poss ... it's nothing to do with mine, ours ... I can't begin to know it, but I do, I do respect it. Greatly. Yes. From the very little that I can glean of it. They feel very generous with ... with wanting me to divine something of it, Poss. I do think. And am grateful. Yes. But understand little. So little.'

He hesitates. Says, carefully, 'Sometimes the natives initially help the settlers but then ...'

'What?'

'It turns. Into something else. There is much distrust. From both sides.' He continues that maybe it all comes down to the greed and the ambition of the new arrivals, perhaps, the white men with their Christian faith – and this disturbs him greatly, he can't shake the knot of it. 'What we do.' As Christians. And that some of his countrymen justify their cruelty by saying their antagonists are not quite human but something else. And it's very hard to articulate this to anyone but it does not sit well in his heart.

He's extraordinary and I want to drink him up. When he speaks of spirituality and the bush it feels like no tempest could ever penetrate his inner pond of calm. I tell him gravely without looking at him that it feels like this land has some kind of a presence, sometimes, and it's as if I'm spilling a secret; I say that the high stone ridges near Willowbrae hum with a ... something. Other-worldly. Can't describe it.

'Yes, I feel that.' He says his church's buildings have been coracles of solace for him always, they quieten him with a great spiritual enveloping – but he gets it also from the bush. From his two-roomed cottage in the middle of nowhere under its vast ceiling of stars. 'Alone. Yes. Under my blanket of God that is my sky. My new sky. On this strange and magnificent island. Where I feel very alone, but for God.'

A glittery pause, where nothing and everything is said, where we both know but can't articulate anything. I imagine his cottage dwarfed by swathes of bush and a thin trail of smoke and a frugal kitchen because a letter told me this. My thudding, knowing heart. Yet I won't declare myself and the vicar blushes as if sensing this too, as if he's trod by mistake on my thoughts. 'Are you comfortable here, Poss?'

Am I? I can't jump ship yet. At that moment there's a knock on the door and I smile my thanks then hold my hands in fervent prayer, and when Mrs Craw enters loud and clattery with a fresh pot of tea she takes the bait and leaves me to my piety. I draw a cup of tea and the vicar doesn't even notice me placing the cup in his hand yet he drinks from it. He says his evenings out in the bush are clean, the shining hours, when he feels lit, as close to his dear calming God as he can get. Unlike town, where he feels agitated and awkward – lacking, somewhat – because he never knows what to say and it never comes out right: in the bush he feels nothing but gratitude at the wonder around him and is content. 'It's very beautiful,' he frowns, 'despite what is said.' He smiles that perhaps he would've been better as a monk because a vicar is far too public. For him.

I chuckle. Possibly, yes, I could see him as that and I tell him of my own heart-swelling gratitude when I'm basted in the woods, in the restless air. I tell him I sometimes find myself closing my eyes in unstoppable thanks, in the wild places, where the silence hums; under a full butter moon or with my face to a high sun. 'I love it all, all. Just want to drink the wild up. Never want to be anywhere else.'

The vicar murmurs in agreement and my hand slips without thinking over his and he looks down at it and loses his words as I barely hover a touch, in collusion; he goes on that there are mysterious places on this earth that concentrate your being, in some way, if you're still and quiet enough in them, places that distil your presence into something very small. 'When you're struck by ... what is it?'

'Awe? Reverence?'

'I think, yes.'

I squeeze his hand and the vicar looks down awkwardly as if he's never been touched and I draw my hand back. Apologise, and barely know what for. We sit in silence, not wanting this to end, whatever it is; the wash of the conversation is pluming through me and with all the grave thinking from it. Sometimes, the vicar says eventually, he feels silted up by the great challenge of merely existing, somewhat depleted, and he needs the cleanness of a religious way: a tuning fork, if you like, into calm. He laughs and says that he's afraid people aren't quite his calling and looks at me sheepishly as if he's never said anything like this in his life.

I smile, warming to this shy man. 'Who are the most religious people you know, Vicar?'

He thinks. 'Well, I'd say those that shine with love. And there's not many of them.'

'Well, *you* don't!' Oh, but he's hurt! 'I'm sorry,' I hurry.

He shakes his head. 'Marital love, n-no, Poss, you're right. I've never had that gift. But love of God, yes. And the land. The glorious, God-given wonder of this land. Yet not a person's love, no, n-not that.'

I tease that he's a man who seems very close to his God but it's as if the wild has vined its way into him somehow too, and my fingers wriggle towards him like looming tendrils. 'Yes?' He chuckles. 'So you've never married, Vicar?'

'N-n-no.' The remnant of some childhood stutter. 'I'm … n-n-not good with ladies.' His helpless smile. 'In fact when it comes to you confounding creatures, a friend writes my missives for me. Yet it never works. When they meet me. I'm not g-g-good at it. There's a school of thought that I should just marry a stranger and be done with it.' He looks at me. 'But I'm liking this approach less and less.' A pause. 'Now. As I learn the ways of the world.' A pause. 'Slowly.' He can't go on, he puts down his teacup.

I take a deep thinking breath. I must talk right now of the great unspokenness between us – or never. 'It's important to … to marry with love. Because there's a … holiness … to it. A sanctity. Which can only come from knowing someone well. Love needs to be brewed strong, like this pot of tea. You need to nurture it over months, years. Don't you think? It'd be a great cruelty and unfairness to do anything else. A grave injustice. If love is … holy. And it's our right, surely – *my* right, *your* right – to choose who we want to love. No one else's.'

He looks at me as if he's suddenly reading a map into my heart and he tells me, with a rasp to his voice, that indeed my argument is sound. 'Who are you, Poss? Really? I feel like you know. Actually. Exactly who you are.'

Silence. I wonder if I can trust him. It feels like I could but … but. I bite my lip. He's a good man yet I must be a locked chest before him and he mustn't be entrusted with the key under any circumstance.

I fidget from him, suddenly pony-restless in this pen of a house, looking out to the waiting wildness. 'The shining hours, yes. Out there, Vicar. In the bush. I know exactly what you mean. And I've enjoyed our talk very much.'

He clasps his hands in front of him and shakes them in fervent agreement, then he gets up, readying himself to go – 'Oh! Too soon!' I say – but asks if I can help him. He forgot, he's all in a muddle. He has a list. He draws out the piece of paper that he'd snatched back from me earlier. He was so agitated, yes.

He asks again if I can help him, it's one last thing, with some identification, briefly; if it isn't too hard, yes? 'It's why, actually, I'm here. I got distracted. Goodness.'

Says he has a list. Of – of the bodies, er, found. Only if I'm up to it. And he's sorry – not everyone has been located yet but there's hope, still. 'As Julian of Norwich said, "All shall be well and all shall be well and all manner of things shall be well"; so we must trust that, yes.' But some identities have been determined, by watches or embroidered names on clothes or faces people have recognised. 'A grim task.' The vicar trails off. He says the colony didn't even know what ship it had been when it first washed up; it was recognised from a name on a tripe crate. 'But there's still hope, Poss.'

Hope. For Jack, cusped on an ocean rock. For everyone I'd befriended on that trip. For my father's son. I want to gulp the vicar's list because my future lies with it and he hands it across as if he isn't doing the right thing but must. He tells me it's only partial, there's more work to be done and of course more survivors. My fist is balled at my solar plexus. Yes, of course.

I read. All the names, the too many names. That I knew from the journey and am winded by. Captain Grent. Pim the kitchen hand. The Kenton family of seven heading so excitedly into their bold new life. Jeremy, the giggly first mate. Tobias, the grizzly stonemason needed for all the new churches the colony might want. Young Dr Kirby. Oh, and oh. Yet no Jack, thank God not yet.

But Ambrose and Mariana. Their names at the bottom, bald before me.

So. This. They are vanished from my life and I feel as if I'm floating suddenly, that nothing is pinning me down anymore as I hold the list and reach out to a bureau to steady myself and declare in a deadened voice that, no, I'm sorry, this doesn't bring the memory of any name back and I feel soiled by the low lie of it. To this man. Of all people, this man.

'It doesn't jolt a single thing, Poss?'

Now is my chance to declare myself. 'No.' Yet my brother, gone. The only close relative I had left and the gulf feels cavernous despite our complicated love. My heart lurches. Gone. I'm freed of him now, and his wife, and all their manuals telling me to be what I'm not. Freed yet not. For there's guilt and also a strange, deep, complicated yearning here, even though I am loosed.

The vicar explains that the wreck has shaken the fledgling settlement to its core, because alongside the cabinloads of strangers were many locals returning to their colony. Convicts now sailing as free men and bringing their families back, a doctor sorely needed. Stonemason brothers, four seamstresses, nine governesses heading to new lives. A man who'd established an estate here; he was bringing out his orphaned sister who needed looking after. A pause. 'A sister, in fact, who was to be my, er, wife.' A pause. 'It was a charitable act.' A pause. 'I – I was led to believe I was helping relieve a difficult situation. Or, or perhaps not.' He looks directly at me. 'I grieve for the loss.'

'But how could you grieve if you never knew her?' I ask. 'How could you want a wife, sir, without ever meeting her? A woman, just like a man, needs freedom of choice. Which should be a basic right.' I think of my Palace of Fury that vined me up the moment Ambrose declared I was to be married to a man of his choice, whom I'd never met. Think of my new future decided by everyone else where I had few choices at all, with no money behind me and no one to fight for my needs, no one to listen or help.

I fling at the vicar that I'd only ever marry for love, which is impossible if you've never met. Unfair. And that I hate, *hate* unfairness more than anything. And every time I come across it there's an implosion in my heart, a tightening of rage, and I make it clear it courses through me now. That this vicar, so thoughtful in many respects, is remiss in this most of all: he has enabled this world, he hasn't considered deeply the consequences. 'We're all equal in God's eyes. It's the only way any human can have happiness, to not be … bound.'

His thinking silence. Pain in his eyes. He says, finally, that he's learning. That he enjoys my bluntness, believe it or not, for not enough people in his church are like this. I wilt into a smile at his openness. He wants me to know that I can always talk to him, any time, that he enjoys the tussle, and he'll be returning to his cottage with much to think about. And, oddly, nourished. By so much thought.

'Tussle?' I laugh. 'Hmmph. I'm used to it. Because the entire world thinks I'm wrong, Vicar, and it's always a tussle. With everything I do. With what I look like and what I talk about, with what I want. The world would change everything about me if it could, and I just want to find a place where I belong. And to live as fully as I can. But how? I don't know.'

'I – I – I would not dare … dream … of going there …'

Eye-deep. The vicar snaps himself to attention. 'Good grief, I might have ended up with someone like you. Imagine that.'

'Oh, I'd be appalling. You'd last ten minutes and then want to return me to the shop, quick smart, to get your money back.'

'Oh, I don't know. Poss. I'm all confusion here. I – I just wish …'

'What?'

But the vicar doesn't say; his awkwardness is closing over him like a shell, he's retreating into it. He doesn't varnish me with light like Tobyn; he's a man no woman would leap at, for his lack of confidence doesn't inspire confidence in anyone else. Yet he's a dear, good man. I take his big hands in my tiny ones and squeeze my gratitude through him. 'What's this for?' he asks, barely accepting it.

'For our talk. I've enjoyed it. Very much. Despite the circumstances. Thank you.' I squeeze his hands again. 'I mean it.'

'I know who you are, Poss.'

I am stopped. Speechless. The vicar says nothing more, gives me nothing more. I hope, I suspect, he won't reveal my identity, and besides he has no proof, it must be a hunch; but this feels like a powder keg suddenly between us.

Then he walks away abruptly without another word, as if the wildness has closed over him and claimed him once again and anything else is too hard, too much, and now he must retreat back into what comforts him the most.

His 'List of the Found' is crumpled and tossed on a table in something like defeat.

'Goodbye,' I call after him, but he doesn't look back, as if he hasn't heard, or can't.

As I watch my vicar depart on his grey horse, from the verandah by the front door, I hear footsteps behind me. Mr Craw.

'I'm off, Lex,' he yells towards the back of the house. 'I'll be home in time for lunch.'

'Do you have to?' comes the returning cry. 'Today of all days?'

'I need to get out,' Mr Craw says. 'Clear my thoughts. Work out what to do next.'

Next? I cross my arms and hug my shoulders deep in thought.

Turn. Mr Craw is almost at the front door, his footfall distracted by his thinking. 'Oh. Poss! I didn't see you there. The vicar's gone so quick?'

'He had to get away.' I smile tight.

'Odd man. Now, how are you feeling? Much improved?' The snap of his enquiry and the message conveyed is that soon his house guest could possibly be fit to leave, perhaps. 'Thank goodness you're out of those confounding clothes. Between Mouse's hair and your attire, God help us all. Willowbrae is falling apart.'

I stop smiling, snuffed.

'My guess is that you're quite well.' Mr Craw clenches both fists at his sides as if readying himself for a boxing match then strides off, taking the front stairs in one leap. Of course he'd like me gone. Me staying here is his wife's wish, and his youngest son's, but as soon as I'm better he wants me turfed out.

I can't find the woman of the house anywhere, perhaps she's retired to bed; the doors at the back of the house are resolutely shut. All the menfolk must have headed for the bush and Mouse must be with Flea in the kitchen. The big house feels cool and silent and waiting.

Now is my chance.

IN WHICH A PRIVACY
IS TRANSGRESSED

The aim, to look around. In secret. To get more of a sense of this family, of this place. A row of closed doors leads down the hallway that's lined with Craw men. I mustn't chance upon Mrs Craw. She's somewhere at the back of the house, the area that's darkest and quietest.

Mouse's room is probably closest to mine. I check and yes. It's Mammy-neat. A boy haven of toy soldiers and teddies and books, so many books: on fairy tales and magic and pirates and phantoms, all manner of imaginary kingdoms that fill up his life. A Bible is next to the bed, a high fort for two rows of tiny soldiers. Apart from that it looks untouched.

A floorboard shifts outside. There's the familiar jangle of keys on Mrs Craw's chatelaine; she's moving about the hallway, coming close to this room. Need to work fast. I dash out of the French doors onto the verandah then into the room next door. Tobyn's, it's obvious. An ancient military jacket hangs near an unmade bed and aside from a mess of clothes the bedroom looks anonymous, as if he doesn't often frequent this space; he goes to town a lot. A Bible is also next to the bed and it too looks untouched. Virgil's room next, but where?

A clatter at the back of the house, something solid is dropped. I still, hold my breath. Will have to be quick. So. The room next to Tobyn's. It must be. I gently open the door and yes, yes. Step inside. Shut the door carefully behind me. Again, the restless chatelaine; Mrs Craw walking up the corridor. The blood thuds in my ears, heat sprints over my skin. The footsteps slow near the front of the house, and stop. I exhale and look around.

Like Tobyn's, this room has the look of a space never bothered by anyone but its owner; they each must be responsible for their room's cleanliness. Which affords them privacy and the sloppiness of an unmade bed and also in this space a volcano of clothes piled by the bed and scattered shoes and toppling books and papers and dust, a mess years in the making. On a pedestal is an opened Bible, yet it's far from the main oddity of the room.

Virgil collects. Objects cram every surface. Slivers of leaves as long as forearms. Shells like fingernails. Cicada husks. Dusty seed pods of brutal spikiness. Discarded snake skins. Shiny beetle carapaces. Small slabs of sandstone are stacked in a corner, smoothed as if waiting for an inscription, like a frozen pond ready for skates.

I spin, gulping the wonder. I'm trespassing on a hidden world. Chiselling tools line a windowsill alongside a calligraphy book. By a window there's a small easel with layers of paper pegged to it. The footsteps again down the corridor. Trembling, I lift the blank outer sheet on the easel, fast. There's a drawing of a spotted shell like a many-legged creature. Underneath, a fish with a unicorn's horn. Underneath, a seed pod like an old man consumed by his beard. Underneath, a splotched egg. And underneath many blank sheets, right at the bottom, hidden away on a dirt-smeared sheet, is a woman. Her face. Naked chest. Tender breasts.

I gasp. Blush. This feels intimate, like I've trodden on someone's heart. Like I'm witnessing something, a deep connection between two people, that isn't my right to know. It's some transaction between art and sitter captured in charcoal and it's built on intimacy and trust.

I peer, close. The woman has four strands of shells with black ones interspersed. *The* woman? The mother wrapped around her baby? No. Yes. But in the sketch she's smiling, right at the artist. Comfortable and playful, loose and light. *Her.*

They *knew* each other. Well. A relationship. No. Surely. But the shock of her breasts, close, too close. It would have to be extremely secret, more so even than the hiddenness of my name. I imagine Mrs Craw knowing. This. It can't happen. No. Mrs Craw with her stiff cuffs and severe hair, her community standing and her ebony cross. *There's no finer woman, no finer family. You're in good hands, lass.* But her beloved son. With a native. And their baby? No. Such an illustrious family. And surely not Virgil, of the godly name and pale indoor skin, destined for the priesthood or piano? Yet the woman's teasing smile is captured, as are her warm eyes, her trust. And Virgil's black fingertips, of course: the charcoal that made the drawing. But a baby. Could she be Virgil's? No, no. *Yes.* And the other girl, watching by the tree, how does she fit into all of this? Is she connected to Virgil? To my rescuer?

I am walloped by the thinking. All of it. Virgil at the grave, inscrutable, the handkerchief at his mouth. There'd be people here who wouldn't want this getting out under any circumstances, who'd need it stopped. Was the child a Craw, was the woman a threat? I've seen the explosive clench in some men back home, seen a wife struck in quick anger who never got up, seen others sent off to the County Women's Asylum as if it was somehow their fault.

A man's boots. Bounding up the stairs to the verandah. Striding with purpose down the hallway. I squeeze into Virgil's cupboard and breathe in deep the smell of sweat and muskiness: he doesn't wash as much as he should. My fist clutches the cloth at my chest, willing my thudding heart slowed.

The footsteps pass, go to the back of the house then up to the front again. A door opens. Virgil enquires if his mammy needs anything; he's heading out again, he's forgotten something. The footsteps come back up the hall and the door to his room is flung open. 'Please don't get a coat,' I pray. 'God spare me.' The footsteps don't come my way. I press my eye to the cupboard's keyhole: Virgil is trying to open a tiny drawer in the cluttered, shell-crammed desk. It's stuck. A key is jiggled and finally the drawer is opened and something is taken out. Red, small. What?

He has his back to me. The key locks the drawer again, it's fiddly, and it's placed in his pocket alongside the unknown thing from the drawer, then hurriedly Virgil slips out. 'I'm heading off, Mammy.' He closes the bedroom door.

'I love you, Virgil,' Mrs Craw yells out, in what feels like a challenge.

I slip away too as soon as silence takes over the house. I run through the French doors into a gulp of replenishing air, far away from the claustrophobia of Willowbrae. I run straight to the bush and hold my forehead to some cool bark and think, and think.

Did someone find out about Virgil and the woman? I picture Mrs Craw's shame, her trauma and fear over all of it, picture the volcanic disruption this would bring to the big house. It would destroy the Craws' reputation. Out here, Ambrose told me, even marrying an ex-convict is frowned upon.

Or maybe someone else found out and spared Mrs Craw the horror of knowing. Maybe someone else got in first. To protect this entire estate.

A cacophony of thinking, too much.

QUESTIONS, QUESTIONS

A late lunch of damper and cold cuts. We eat mostly in silence. Mouse is not with us, yet no one comments on his absence. Flea flicks a smile at me, as if to convey to keep my spirits up, keep strong. Mr Craw's frown is casting a heavy weight in the room; something is swamping his mind. My curiosity can't contain itself. I swirl the spoon in the sugar bowl, wondering how to approach the bodies in the glade and Virgil's connection and what anyone knows about anything here. 'Sir, who exactly are those people in the glade?'

Mr Craw looks up from his plate.

'Sorry, sorry. But where do you think they came from? It all feels so … sad.'

He winces as if my voice is too loud for this confined space, too loud for this house. Tobyn leans forward to explain to me that there are no answers to these questions. I look again at Mr Craw and sense that he's the type of man Pa warned me against, who doesn't like young ladies loud and unleashed. Hairs sprout strongly from the man's nostrils and ears and it's like his stillness is masking some volcanic inner force and he's very controlled, and quiet, yet everything feels suddenly precarious.

'Virgil, what do *you* think happened to them?' My flourish accidentally knocks over my glass. 'Ahh, sorry, I'm always doing this. Silly me.'

Mr Craw's hand slaps the dining table and we all jump. 'This is rather challenging,' he says forcefully. 'And where is the blasted child that began all this nonsense?' He glances around, yet no one can help him with Mouse's whereabouts. 'Bring me that boy. I need to cut the wretched hair on him. Once and for all. Trousers on girls, long hair on boys. The whole world is going to ruin here.'

'What? Callum!' Mrs Craw cries.

'He's not a girl, madam.'

His wife glances at me. Frowns. 'Cal, please. We have guests.'

The man shoots his arm out at Flea without looking at him. 'Scissors. Now. I've been embarrassed enough in my own house this morning. The guest in trousers, what was all that about? I thought we'd had a sleepless night to stop it, madam. Lord knows what everyone thinks of this madhouse.'

'Callum.'

'It has to stop. All of it.'

The convict leaves the room silently through the door to the kitchen; Mrs Craw gasps as if personally wounded then calls her youngest son as if summoning him to the table yet also beseeching him to run far from this.

'I must have my house in order.' Mr Craw stands, screeching and scraping his chair as he moves. Looks at me. 'And, oh, I can give you some stories, girl.'

'Callum. You are being watched. Your food awaits.' His wife's warning and admonishment work, and the man sits, furious, as if the caution about being watched is the only way to stop a volcanic snap. Silence like a shroud hangs over everyone as Flea enters again and sets the scissors on the sideboard. I catch a movement beyond the doorway, in the hall. Mouse? Flea walks around the table, passing the doorway and I think I see a gesture, a clean and secret flick of a finger. Go. If Mouse is there, he doesn't enter.

'Our father likes to be in control, Poss,' Tobyn explains. 'And with this incident in the bush he's not. And it grieves him.'

I pocket my man's rescuing smile and blush at the stomach-dip that occurs whenever he speaks; yet he must not distract me now, for Mr Craw had been on the verge of saying something but then it was lost. My leg jiggles uncontrollably. I'm all rangy energy, wanting understanding. 'Control, Tobyn?' I ask. 'Control of what?'

'Tobyn, that would be our mammy who loves her containment,' Virgil says quietly from a corner of the table, gnawing at a blackened finger with a mop of hair over his face. 'You've got the wrong end of the stick. As usual. You're not here enough to know anything.' He's not looking at anyone. A closed book, and Tobyn is too ridiculously open. He pokes out his tongue at his brother; Virgil looks up and blinks slowly as if his sibling isn't worth it. 'Nothing to see here, little boy,' he adds quietly.

Mrs Craw's fingers dig into her temples as if trying to press something inside her head into obeyance, to stop it worming out. I ask if she's alright. She nods abruptly.

'So, Poss, how were you raised? Do tell.' Tobyn cuts the air with his sly knife. 'Come on, amuse us, we need some distraction.' His withholding watchfulness feels like a weapon and I suspect this entire conversation is about something else, that I'm some plaything to distract them from a flint that will set them all alight.

I say that I recall something of a father but nothing of a mother and Virgil looks at his father and exclaims too loudly, 'That explains it then,' and they laugh at some private joke. Tobyn smiles and shakes his head and his mother looks up, bewildered, and joins in with the laughing as if she doesn't quite know what it's about, as if all the worms in her head need containing and she's only focused on that.

Yet my loneliness. All of a sudden. The great yowl of it, here, among them all. At becoming the butt of their collective mock. Something has shifted and they're turning in on themselves, shutting me out. And I'm so far away from anyone else, from rescue or help. I redden.

'Too hot?' Virgil asks. 'Not the weather for you?'

But Tobyn's roguish and rescuing grin flashes across the table, one side up, one side down, like a puppy lolloping into sight, his grin that says we're both stranded on the outer with this. I smile in relief at him, arrowed. 'Where have the people from yesterday been buried? I'd like to take them some flowers.'

'Maybe they haven't,' Tobyn says.

I frown. 'But those people from the glade need a burial. Don't they? Tobyn?' A pause. 'Virgil?' Because I cannot let this lie. Because I've chosen the fighter's path. Because I had a friend called Bec who was loud and stubborn and magnificent, with a fierce intelligence and an insistent voice, and she became pregnant by Knockleby's vicar and of course he'd never leave his wife and of course he wouldn't provide for her and of course he denied any knowledge of her child, of the shame of it. Bec's father said his daughter would be sent to the asylum as punishment for the mortification she'd brought upon their family, and her baby would be taken from her. We knew the asylum rumours: stories of freezing baths and vaginal enemas, blood lettings and water tipped over women's heads. So Bec ran away, to save herself, to find a new life; and she ended up dead, lying with her newborn son under a shroud of frost.

Pa insisted on a proper Christian burial for them, paying for it anonymously. 'Because that's what good, feeling people do, Tommy Tom. And we must never be talked out of that. It gives you a quietness of the soul. As the great Juvenal said, "If you want a tranquil life, then pray to be good."'

So I will not be veered now; my father wouldn't allow it. Nor Bec. 'That woman and her baby, they need to be buried. Laid to rest. Blessed.'

Mr Craw's sharp intake of breath. His wife looks at me and says, 'Yes, actually, they do need a burial, don't they? Callum? Deep under the earth. Gone.' Mrs Craw asks where the mother and child are now and says she could supervise, yet her voice is wobbling into someone else as she speaks, it's slipping from its constraints, and none of the menfolk are responding, as if too weary of the familiar tone of this. 'They deserve a burial. So they're gone. Callum. For good.' Mrs Craw looks straight at her husband now meticulously cutting too much of the ham.

I tell her I'll lay flowers on a grave if she'll let me – just as I did with Bec and her baby, the only one left who did it. 'Because they're a mother and a baby, and we're good Christian people around this table. Aren't we? It's what we do.' Yet as I speak I wonder if that is what is required, actually, of a native mourning ritual. I have no idea.

'Leave it,' Mr Craw says. 'They're not human. Not us.'

A vivid silence. I breathe shallow. Turn to Flea bringing in a dish of potatoes. 'What do *you* think happened out there in the bush?'

Flea stops and shakes his head as if he doesn't know what I'm talking about. He silently sets the pot on the table and leaves and Mr Craw explains with very pointed enunciation that as a convict almost at the end of his sentence Flea doesn't need his nerves frayed by a silly goose with silly ideas in her head, when a snake bite or lightning were the most likely cause of death. 'So stop it. Just stop. For all our sakes.'

Tobyn looks at me, into me. I feel like a spring coiled ready for release. He winks. His father catches it. Mr Craw's cutlery drops onto his plate in crisp dismissal like a judge's gavel bringing proceedings to a halt. As if he's just seen a future he does not want, as if he cannot control anything anymore in his house. 'Where is that blasted boy? That hair, I swear that hair.'

As if he has to take out his lack of control on something.

And Mouse is it.

WHAT FATHERS DO

A scene of strop and shout. Mr Craw is dragging Mouse to the verandah by the ear and the boy is protesting – 'No, Papa, no' – as is his mother, begging her husband to stop. Her tightly bound hair is shockingly loose, as if her whole world is unravelling here – 'Callum, please' – yet he's ignoring her and the sense of order that holds his house together is flexing, creaking, fracturing like the *Finbar* against rocks and all hell is breaking loose.

'He's a boy, woman, a *boy*. How many times do I have to tell you? He needs to grow up. Boys with long hair, girls with trousers, I won't have it. He's a freak. You're all freaks. Flea. Scissors.'

The little boy yowls in pain. And it's a child and it's deeply unfair. 'No,' Mouse whimpers, and cries in bewilderment. 'Poss! Help me!'

Mrs Craw catches my eye before her husband does and beckons me to disappear, to get far away from this for my own sake. And in that moment, staring at the monstrous spitting bull of a man snipping and snapping and flinging hair before us all, I realise in a flutter of a shiver that I too am vulnerable here, prey to this man's anger, his heavy hand, his impotence. My questions have turned him into someone else and it feels like nothing will stop him right now, and I have contributed to it.

Mouse sees me and cries out.

Mr Craw turns. 'Well, well. Here she is. The girl who began it all.' He slices off another tendril of his boy's golden hair and his mother clutches her head and wails as if it were her own locks being butchered, and she can't bear it.

'Stop! Please!' I stride forward without thinking. I have to do this.

'Go away, girl.' The man is holding the scissors in one hand and his son in the other and speaking as if he doesn't quite trust himself or what he might do next.

I tell him to let Mouse go, the boy is good and has done nothing wrong, he doesn't deserve this.

'Flea,' he barks then turns to the son and cuts another lock and flings the hair like a pale whip across the lawn as Flea comes up swiftly and quietly and with an iron firmness forces me away with no talk and I cannot break his grip and I know the bruises will be blossoming on my arms yet I do not cry out, I do not.

Flea tells me to stay in my room. As he leaves I ask him if he knows where my knife is, but he just throws his hands in the air as if he has no idea and to leave him right out of this. So. Not on my side at all.

As the tide of the day ebbs into darkness Mrs Craw brings a light supper on a tray and the woman's hair is still loose and her face is reddened but she will not talk, she's a closed book. 'Are you alright, ma'am?' No response. 'How's our dear little Mouse?' No response.

And as Mrs Craw leaves I notice her apron is undone at the back as if her entire existence is unravelling yet she hasn't noticed, neither her hair nor her clothes, as if something else entirely is taking over her thoughts.

WHAT THE NIGHT BRINGS IN

Night settles in and licks its wounds. A tap on my door. Mouse's face is blotchy from crying and his head is tufted in ugly clumps. He holds out the scissors and asks me to fix it because his mammy can't bring herself to touch it, she's been crying too much. I smooth out the jagged snips as much as I can. Then to nudge a laugh I cut off a lock of my own stubborn curls with a flourish. 'We're even.'

Mouse gasps. 'Again!'

I comply and his giggle is back, just like that. I snip off another lock. Then without looking at anything but my boy I hold out handfuls of my hair and snip another lock and another until the bed is littered with curly fronds like wood shavings and Mouse looks at them and laughs, in delight, and tumbles into my arms unlocked, quietly soaking it all up with a nourishing pliancy that's repairing the giver as much as the receiver. We hold in the darkness, and hold, two shorn lambs, until I nudge Mouse awake and tell him gently to go back to his bed before he falls deeply asleep and someone finds out.

He gets up and sleepily walks out, a fist of my hair in his hand. 'I love you so much, Possy!'

How could I ever abandon that?

In Which the Dark Is Dived Into

Late. Restless dozing is harangued by the wind and a distant wailing seamed through it – sky or treetops, human or ghost, I don't know what, but Willowbrae's secrets are trapping me in wakefulness. I fling the curtains wide and open the French doors to feel the sky. Have never been afraid of the night. I breathe in deep its intoxicating smell and run across the lawn into the fringes of the bush. Stop. Wonder where the mother and her baby are now. Shiver.

A twig crack. 'Who's there?' A rustle but no one declares themselves. I spin. Something fleet of foot retreats in a rush of leaves. Animal? Human? I head further into the bush, to the noise, but then think better of it and turn back. It'd be so easy to get lost in this.

I think back to the night of my rescue, to the man I lay next to under a pelt of soft rain, flat on my back on our mattress of rock. A man whose back I licked. Licked. Look around. Is he back? But there are no blacks left, Mrs Craw said it the other day at lunch. *Why are they here, Callum? Do something*, she hissed. *Be a man for once.*

Another twig crack, further off. 'Hello?' My fingers hover in memory at my lips: of the secret rescue, the shine of it. He shouldn't be here if it's him. It must have been dangerous for him to be so close to Willowbrae when he laid me down on the verandah, so risky to have deposited me here. To venture into this world with the dogs about, and Mr Craw and Virgil, and guns and axes, and a convict built for violence who says nothing yet watches everything, clenched.

So. I was dropped on the big house's doorstep at enormous risk, or I would have died on that sea-battered rock.

I walk strong towards the twig crack. 'Thank you,' I say loud into the dark, but there's nothing, he's gone. If he was ever here in the first place.

HAVING IT OUT

I walk around the side of the house, hoping to slip inside with no one seeing me. But Virgil is here, alone on the verandah, tucked into a corner with his boots propped on the extendable arms of a low-slung chair. His legs are forced wide into a V-shape, and a pipe is cradled between blackened fingertips.

He looks at me sideways as if he's been cornered and does not shift his legs as I walk past and wish him an awkward good evening and continue on. He says good evening in return then acidly asks to my departing back if I'm always in the habit of getting about in my nightclothes – and where did I learn such a thing.

I stop. I pause. Turn to him. 'What's going on here, Virgil?' I wait. 'Really?' Because it feels like there are layers and layers of things going on here and I want to peel away at Willowbrae's secrets like the bark on the Ripping Tree until a bare core of truth and honesty is exposed, and nothing else is left. 'Come on, Virgil, you can tell me.'

The man draws slowly on his pipe then laughs softly with dirt in it and tells me this isn't the house for me, especially with a haircut like that, and the sooner I leave the better. 'You need to be in town, Poss. Resting up. You've had a big knock to your head. Out here is too wild. Too remote.'

'Those poor bodies, Virgil. Out there, all alone in the bush. No one to love them.' I think of the portrait of the woman in the glade, lovingly rendered in its charcoal. The careful strokes. I think of Bec's glitteringly lonely death.

Virgil smacks the glowing embers from his pipe into the palm of his bare hand and winces and says nothing, as if welcoming the hurt. The glow of the ash is cartwheeled into the black. I move away, but stumble on the uneven sandstone of the verandah. The man offers no help or comfort, he's closed in on himself as he packs some new tobacco into his pipe. 'What's your real name, Poss?'

'I'm going to bed, Virgil. I'm tired. Good night.'

'Maybe this isn't the best place for a young lass who might have a few secrets tucked away herself.' It's jabbed at my back. 'And who's got a brand new haircut that Mammy really isn't going to like. Did you think about that?'

This entire day now feels like a fist in my mouth, stopping me up; like a dead bird, a mouthful of flesh and feathers. I stride past Virgil without looking at him and he smiles oddly then stops abruptly as if life has suddenly caught up with him and there's nothing left to do now but drag on his pipe, which he lights and keenly draws on, sucking the life out of it in despair, or something else.

The only thing that drops me into slumber is the thought of my rescuer – his calm and strong walking and the generosity in it, the mattress of rock and the pelt of rain and the wonder of all that – and I finally, finally sleep.

THE FOURTH DAY

THE DAY OF REST

The morning feels scrubbed and soothed by early rain. The air smells cool and damp and the earth has opened up as if breathing in a great benediction. What day is it? I count back. My head still hurts; I'm unsure of the sequence of time and the jumble of all that's happened. It must be Sunday, yes. So, church, perhaps. With the vicar quite possibly, the shy one who thinks deeply and hesitates, and my heart dips at the thought of his quiet audacity, the lovely cool draught of it.

Breakfast. Everyone feels reined in, tight and stiff. I ask if it will be the same vicar as the one who visited yesterday. Mr Craw says no. He muses over why the man entered the church in the first place. 'He doesn't have the constitution for it. For people. Or appearing in public. Poor sod.'

'So I gathered.'

I've tucked bits of my hair under a hat that Mrs Craw has left out for me so none of them know of its newness yet. Except for Mouse and Virgil, and both of them are quiet. Mrs Craw asks why I've got my hat on already. I say I'm eager to try it, to get out, to see the world beyond Willowbrae.

'There's not very much out there,' Tobyn says and laughs.

Church is a long carriage ride away, Mrs Craw says. I'm guessing that someone with the wrong kind of God in them might well be delivering the sermon. I've seen enough of it over the years, so often when my father and I went, which was infrequently: Christmas Day and funerals and the like. But again and again I saw men of the cloth who seemed oddly bored or uninvolved and I never understood. Why do this if you do not feel somehow righted by it, lit?

Now that I know my vicar won't be there, I ask Mr Craw what he'd think of a guest who stayed home alone at the big house, who went for a walk by themselves instead of going to church. Is it ever done?

'Are you mad, girl?' He raises a stern eyebrow. 'It's just Flea left behind, to guard the house. A convict. We are one of the leading families of the district. We always attend church; it would be remiss of us not to. In fact, an impertinence even to consider it. Wilfulness. Disobedience.'

Yet my instincts tell me I might be safer with Flea than some of the others here, and almost blurt this out but stop myself. I'm learning. His rage could lead to anything in this house.

'No church for my little Possum? Is this a sudden attack of the vapours?' Tobyn hovers his hand near my forehead; I bat him away. 'You don't want us to think you weak-minded, do you? Our mighty mermaid in her scandalous trousers. Sorry, *my* trousers. That you keep forgetting not to wear. Repeat, mine. Keep going this way, Miss Poss, and you might end up at the Asylum of Industry.'

'What is that, exactly?'

'It's a female factory in town, where badly behaved women are sent. It's just ready and waiting for anyone considered ... feeble-minded.'

Right. So. I'll not be giving them any excuse then. I'll get to this church in quiet obedience because not attending risks accusations of Godlessness and Stubbornness. A neighbour in Knockleby, Lizzie Fry, was sent to the local asylum after repeated refusals to attend sermons. 'I was assaulted on a pew,' she told me. 'I can't bear to go near that place again.' So she was discarded in stone and I heard whispers of her fate. That the women lay on straw not mattresses. That babies were jammed head to toe in cots, their white coverings black with fleas. That the inmates' job was to procure oakum, which meant endlessly unpicking old ropes for plugging ships' holes. And that if you were disobedient you'd get an iron collar around your neck that was so heavy it could break your collarbone. Lizzie was charged with hysteria, the most perfect lunacy because it wasn't up to you to decide if you had it or not – so you could be cured of it, or not.

'I'll get Lizzie out. This is so unfair!' I cried to my father, but he responded with a sigh.

'Always choose a fighter's path, Tommy Tom – but perhaps find other ways with this one. Because with this situation you'll never win, you can't.' And he was right, for when I raised it with the local vicar and mayor I was ignored; they didn't want to know.

'A little flushed, Poss?' Virgil persists at the table. 'Are we taking a turn, perhaps?' I glare at him. 'You've got your hat on very early this morning, I see.'

'I like to be prepared, Virgil. For church. Or anything else that I come across at Willowbrae.' He retreats into his shell. And no, I'll not be risking staying at home. 'And I'll happily go to church because I'm feeling fine. Absolutely fine.'

'I'm so glad you'll be with us, Poss.' Mrs Craw is a picture of propriety in her fussy grey silk. 'God would be appalled at anything else.'

Tobyn grins at me in a challenge that's beyond the looking of anyone else. My stomach dips; I smile secrets back at him. Which are caught. By his mother. Who narrows her eyes, who does not like it one bit. Then with a voice that gives us both nothing, the matriarch of the house announces that Tobyn should take the pony trap to church. 'By yourself.' The rest of the family will take the carriage and Virgil the spare horse. And that Tobyn should, perhaps, prepare for leaving Willowbrae soon. It's time he thought about heading off. Into town. 'Where your proper world awaits you.'

I glance at him, my wings folding over me at his mother's voice, at her shut-down of us both. A fist presses into my tightening heart. Because I understand, of course. I'm the girl with a voice and I persist too loudly with it. And to be considered as an acceptable companion for Mrs Craw's son I'd need a name for a start. A history. A background. A class. Because scandal is what this woman fears the most. My wings droop.

IN WHICH GOD'S HOUSE IS PRESENTED

The road to the church is rutted, it dips and drops and precariously lifts. Boulders and branches bar the way and progress is laborious – not enough people use this track and when we finally arrive I feel clotted by weariness and dust.

The church is plain. A simple rectangle so it can be used for other purposes, Tobyn tells me, as a community hall, a school house, a meeting place. I run my fingers along the building's red bricks; some have strange indentations and I ask what they are. Tobyn explains that the bricks have the signatures of their convict makers dug into them: knuckly finger marks, rough letters and arrows, diamonds and hearts. The building isn't skirted with graves like in England; there aren't enough people for that. And there's no stained glass. Plain glass panes are cheaper and there doesn't seem to be a call for grandiose beauty in these parts. Everything is functional, simple. The pews are enclosed by wooden gates that keep the gentry removed from the great unwashed who sit up the back in watched rows. The Craws have a high-walled pew like a pen at the front.

The vicar seems to be thinking more of his waiting roast than the words of the Lord. He's a plum pudding of a man with reddened nose and cheeks who rushes through the homily with unseemly haste, as if too aware that this building is stifling and he wants everyone out before someone faints or he can't abide the smell of so many sweaty bodies close. Christianity doesn't feel quite sturdy enough in this humble brick box surrounded by bush; faith doesn't feel quite seamed into this earth. It's a fearful little building. Fortressing itself. Against what?

Afterwards the flock lingers outside on stubbly dirt. A genial phalanx of mainly men in Sunday best still manage to look dusty and creased. The insistent land has wormed its way into every corner of their lives, including the holiest.

Yet right into me: curiosity, whispers, glances. I try for composure, can't; a blush assaults and I fidget in Mrs Craw's scratchy dress. Something has hardened with all the family here, they won't quite envelop me. I feel a vast aloneness; I'm separate, observed. I look for Tobyn's reassurance but he's nowhere to be found.

'Oy. Are you recovered?' The question is flung across the dirt by a man in a hat pockmarked with sweaty holes. It sets them all off, the voices suddenly clamour.

'Do you have a name yet?'

'We're impatient, lass.'

'Can you remember anything?'

'There were some convicts on the ship. You one of them?'

'Is Callum looking after you?'

'Not likely in these parts!'

Through the laughter I sense a chance. To stop this nonsense once and for all, to disrupt and challenge and turn the questions upon themselves, despite the voice in my head warning me off, the little voice I so often ignore that says, *Behave, girl, hold your tongue, stay quiet.* Mouse is by the horses, cupping their soft mouths and feeling their snuffly trusting silk as he feeds them grass. I tip back my head and pull the trigger. 'I found two people. In the bush. Near Willowbrae.' Confused looks. Confused silence. 'Natives. Dead.' Mouse's grass flutters away. 'It doesn't seem right.'

The man in the hat chuckles. 'Well, Cal's doing something right.'

It relaxes them all. A man kicks the dust. 'So they're back.'

A wealthy-looking individual laughs. 'Better stock up on the strychnine.'

'We don't need the Governor knowing that.'

'Don't let young Virgil find out.' Laughter after that one.

I look around, not sure where Virgil is but know that he's somehow apart here, from all of them.

'Thanks to poison and the gun we've seen to problems like this, lass.'

'And we'll see to it again.'

'Amen to that.'

'Good riddance.'

'There'll be no evidence.'

The wealthy gentleman turns from me, they all do, with indifference, laughing it off.

I stand before the men with fists clenched and eyes smarting. What would Pa do now? *Always do the right thing,* he said once, *which is not necessarily the crowd thing. Find the courage to do it and alone if you must.* So. I persist. 'It was a mother and her baby,' I say. Because unfairness always flares something in me and outrage over a dead woman and her child won't loosen its grip; they're dug into me. Thinking of my Bec, and of Lizzie, yet no one seems to want to listen or care. 'We should find out what went on. So it doesn't happen again.'

Dismissive laughter and brush-offs: that it must have been an accident, that it's the way animals die out bush; leave them to it, lassie, forget it. The men turn to more important things: the salvaging of the *Finbar* wreck and sheep prices and crop losses.

'I just want someone to care about this!'

Mr Craw has been talking to the vicar; he brusques over and asks what's going on, while rubbing his finger on his waistcoat. He's told. He declares it's time, perhaps, for me to think about heading into town. To recover. If I'm not comfortable with what goes on all the time in these parts.

'What goes on?'

'Native business. A funeral ritual perhaps. It means nothing, Poss. As I've said so before. We leave them to it.' He seizes me strong by the elbow as if to propel me towards his carriage; there'll be no wrenching from his grip. Tips his hat to the men, the twitch in his cheek dancing back.

'So will you be staying with the Craws then?' someone yells out.

'It's the bush, lass, forget it.'

'Maybe the doctor needs to attend?' The wealthy looking man taps his head. There are looks, murmurs.

'Yes. She suffered a blow to the head,' Mr Craw says. 'Her recovery will take some time – if at all.' He glances at me with raised eyebrows and I step back like a wild pony trapped, but he has me in a tight grip and despite my protest he will not release me.

Virgil appears and says loudly and slowly that perhaps I should go off with one of these good folk, to town, to be questioned about everything I know of the wreck and to recover in peace. And I have no belongings of course, so there's no need to go back to Willowbrae – I can just leave so his family can get on with their quiet lives.

'Quiet lives?' I look across at Mouse.

'Perhaps it's for the best, Poss. Now.' Virgil is quietly threatening.

Mr Craw still has me in his tight grip; I cannot step away from the cloak of their enveloping will.

'You mean … leave Willowbrae? Just like that. Without saying goodbye to it?' I lick my lips. Nothing is resolved, it's all too soon, my heart thuds. There's the woman and her baby, how they died; there's a little boy who needs protecting from his father; there's an eyelid kiss. I glance across at Mrs Craw. 'Ma'am?' She rolls her lips in tight, can't quite let go of this yet, of her living doll and the idea of it.

I think of my father. *You must light your own kerosene lamp in the dark.* These men here have brewed a world where some people are deemed more human than others, and it doesn't feel right or fair, and I'm not sure they are, actually, more civilised than others. I gaze at Mouse's bludgeoned hair. The boy is utterly still by his horses, his hands cupped around a soft muzzle, listening intently. 'Please can I stay, ma'am? I'm not quite better yet.' Mrs Craw is stopped, no help. I turn to my little ally. 'Mouse, I was asked to be your governess once – and gladly I'll do it. Because you need a friend at home, don't you?' Silence. 'Do you still want me?' Silence. 'Mousey?' My voice wobbles.

Mouse walks across and holds out his hand with no talk and I extend my palm and clutch his little fist tight.

'Brother-boy,' I whisper fiercely and he squeezes back and I tickle his palm, in relief, in our secret handshake, our pact of friendship: I'm not abandoning him yet.

'Sister-girl.'

We're in this together and I just want to hold Mouse in my arms in that moment, and hold him, and I do.

Mrs Craw raises her hands in surrender at the sight. 'So be it, Callum.' Her husband nods, clenched. Doesn't like it one bit but will go along with it. In public.

I go to climb into the carriage, but Tobyn rushes past in his lighter trap and brings his horses to a crisp halt. 'Come on, Poss, jump in! Father, I'm relieving you of this one for now,' and before Mr or Mrs Craw can protest he's grabbed my hand and is pulling me to him and telling his parents he'll see them back at the house and to not worry, he's giving them a gift, taking me off their hands for the return journey.

Mr Craw takes the driver's seat of the slower carriage, rubbing his hand furiously on the edge of his coat; his wife shakes her head in annoyance; Virgil hauls himself heavily onto the spare horse.

I look back to Mouse, stricken and stopped as he stands there with a realisation on his face. Of a future, alongside us both, where he's shut out. 'She's *mine*,' the little boy accuses his brother.

I say to them that I'm everybody's friend, there's no 'side' to this.

'You're mine more than his, Poss,' Mouse challenges. 'I

named you. I got you out of that greedy bed. We've got our handshake, remember.'

A helpless grimace but I'm swept along by Tobyn's determination, all surrender suddenly and cusped on the brink of his adult world.

Mr Craw cracks his whip and his horses start in fright. Mouse twists around to stare at us until a bend in the road means we lose sight of the carriage.

'I need to keep a better eye on you,' Tobyn smiles, examining me with amusement. 'The things that happen when I go off for one single minute.'

'Tobyn!'

I feel like he's rolling me in his paws.

And I'm limp with it.

THE CHANCE

Tobyn shows off his skills with the horses, thundering them home, accompanied by my laughing as I hang on for dear life. My hat flies off. 'Your hair! Stop addling me, Poss. Mammy will not be amused. Did you think of that?'

'I love it like this!' I hold up my hands and butt the breeze.

'That's the spirit!'

We arrive back at Willowbrae long before the others. Tobyn indicates to Flea to take care of the horses as he steers me towards the house with a firm hand at my waist. I'm like a horse in mid shiver, shaking off a fly. I tell myself to be wary, to keep my wits about me but can't, quite, right now. Tobyn has a radiant certainty to him.

'Where are you taking me?'

'Wait and see, Miss Impatient.'

'Can I trust you?'

'Absolutely not.'

I can't help but laugh at this boy-man's beautifully loose grin and his confidence; no one most likely has ever held him in check. He grabs my hand and leads me on and we clatter into Willowbrae's hall and Tobyn kicks the front door shut. 'Girls aren't meant to wear boys' clothes. Or have haircuts like this.

It's very distracting.' He extends his arms on either side of me as I lean against the wall to catch my breath. I say nothing. Shunt away. Laughing, he shunts also. I duck under his arm to escape; he tries to catch me, can't, I'm too quick. I wander down the hallway with my hands clasped behind my back, feeling him close behind me, thinking of a kiss on an eyelid and a sprawl on the grass. My stomach dips. I try to concentrate. Alongside all the portraits of the grand whatevers is a painting of the big house, becalmed.

'We're the envy of the colony,' Tobyn murmurs too close. 'But we're very, very selective about who gets to see inside us. It's not everyone.'

I brush him off, flicking my hand dismissively; he grasps it, I pull away. 'Sir, know your place!' I laugh in mock shock.

We have the run of the house; I poke my head into various rooms, rangy with fidget, with desire and teasing and a wanting to know more. Every one of the rooms waits for air and laughter and light amid its oppressive wallpaper and damask curtains that shut out the sun; every one of the rooms has its Bible prominently placed, as if in watch.

'You're an inscrutable little brumby, aren't you?' Tobyn muses behind me.

A sheening of sweat. Tobyn slips silkily in front of a door I'm about to open. 'Uh! Not that one. It's father's study – and you do not need to see that.'

'Maybe I do.'

'No. Most definitely not.'

'Just a peek, Tobyn, come on.' Because this room might tell me things I need to know. 'Or are you scared of him too?'

'Stop it, Poss. And remember, I'm always your ally here. I'm on your side.'

'Why are you saying that?'

'I just – I don't know.'

Tobyn's eyes are green flecked with gold. I'm right up close, can't control my breathing.

'If you're an ally then tell me this. Did someone bury the poor mother and baby?'

'What? I told you. Just leave it.'

I grab the doorknob.

'Why do you care so much?' Tobyn holds my arm tight.

I yank it away, suspecting I'm now wearing his thumb marks, green and yellow blooms. 'I care, Tobyn, because I've been taught to. And I have a heart.'

He nods and grins, apologising if he's hurt my arm. I forgive him and breathe him in like a first drag from my father's pipe and my insides peel away, all appetite. He could be my downfall, and I knew it from the first moment of meeting him. But no, I mustn't be distracted here. My hand tightens on the doorknob and I turn it and Tobyn's fist closes over mine in a wilful stopping and for a moment I yield and I feel loose and light and dangerous. But no, too much to find out here. I turn the doorknob sharply. 'What does Mouse mean by … supply?'

'What?'

'He slipped it out once. It was to do with your father. Come on. You said you're on my side. Are you man, Tobyn … or mouse?' He viciously swipes my hand away but I grab the knob again and push at his chest.

'Right, little Miss. Let me give you supply. Maybe then you'll understand how things work around here. So I can have my other Poss back. The nice one. She needs to come back.' Tobyn flings open the door and I almost fall inside.

But no further. Look at Tobyn. He shrugs. 'So. Supply. You asked for it.'

I can barely enter the room.

What is this house?

THE ROOM AT THE BACK

Where to begin?

It is a busy workroom. A mahogany desk as deep as it is long has a throne-like chair behind it, intricately carved with eagle's claws as arms. The back of it looms tall and the sharp-taloned claws have been smoothed into shininess – by being gripped, often; by being clenched, quite possibly; by holding a fury down.

'The Chair,' I whisper. The chair, at last. I imagine a terrified Mouse facing this. *No, please, not the Chair.* I imagine the imposing figure of the seated father deep in frown. This room is the court of punishment, of course, and Mouse is familiar with it. And terrified of it. Mr Craw presides from this room, correcting any deviation from the path that will lead every member of his family to salvation and glory. A Bible rests on a thick golden stand of the kind you'd find in a church. The walls are wood-panelled and crammed with framed land grants and bucolic Scottish scenes of glens and lochs. This is the hub of the estate. Except for the main feature, and here I step back, and back. For stacked in corners and neat on shelves and in perfect lines along windowsills and paraded along the very front of the desk is the main and overwhelming shock of this room.

Bones.

I clutch the cloth at my chest. This is a storage room of some sort. There are spears — tipped with bone? — three- or four-pronged; axes and wooden dishes; arrowheads and string bags; but bones, mainly bones. Too many bones. Bones. That were people once, not animals, and I know this because there are skulls among them and in fact part of one is being used as a depository for pen nibs on Mr Craw's desk; it's a jaw bone that would be right at Mouse's eye-level when he's summoned to this space. That little boy. Here. So. This, all this, is 'supply'.

'No.' I retreat, my hand over my mouth. Bump into Tobyn by the door without even realising it; a crisis of touch. Sharply I pull away. That he exists in this family so sunnily, that he smiles so widely and untroubled amid this, that he can sleep soundly in this house. I can't stop shaking my head because this trophy room crammed with its objects, from the natives I presume, feels too close to plunder. It presents itself as a hunting lodge in the Scottish isles and is a triumph of collecting, but this is humans not animals — *humans* — and it's at the very heart of this illustrious estate. And an innocent little boy dwells in the middle of it. Is forced into this space. A little boy who's been exhibiting flashes of strangeness ever since I've arrived.

He can't have them, Mouse had cried at the glade, *they're not his to have*. And now I know exactly what my little friend meant and I want to vomit, need to get out of this world.

Tobyn stirs behind me. Reaches out for my shoulder. I hold him back with the flat of my hand, feel his heartbeat under my fingers. 'Are these what I think they are?' My voice is low, firm. He replies yes. He says there's a war going on, there are obstructions to be cleared, and when his father arrived he found a useful sideline in – 'How can I describe it?' he says and hesitates – 'procurement.'

I am very still as I let Tobyn speak, and speak, while my hand at his heart tightens into a fist, and drops. It's a small but lucrative business, a sideline, just that. He asks me if I've heard of the science of phrenology. I have not.

'It's the study of the mind, Poss. Of the native as a living link to earliest man. Imagine that. It's extraordinary, all the research into stone-age man. And these people out here are really close to it.'

I cannot speak. Tobyn moves to the desk and holds up the bones of a tiny finger curled like an ivory fishing hook. I gasp, thinking of a dear little back tucked into her mother's protective embrace. What did that woman know about the horrors that lay ahead for them? What was she shielding her child from?

'Poss. You alright?' Tobyn reaches out the finger skeleton and brushes my sleeve. I stiffen. 'It's just what's done over here,' he says and shrugs. 'Universities and museums in Britain and Germany pay good money for this. It's the origin of man, Poss, and it's right in front of us. There's an extraordinary scientific opportunity right on our doorstep. And my father's not the only one doing it. It's helping the world of science to understand.'

'Understand what?' I rasp.

'Them. Us.' Tobyn picks up a string bag threaded through with fluffs of feathers that's lying like a pelt over a chair. He explains that it's called a dilly bag and it's filled with ochre and the skin of dead relatives and it's extraordinary what these people do and how they live, their rituals, their beliefs. 'If we choose to look. If we're curious.'

'Dead relatives? Where does your father ... where does he ...?'

'Get it all?'

I nod, curt.

'Everywhere – if you know where to look.' Tobyn enthuses that these people are the missing link to the prehistoric, to animals and native fauna and it's important research. Some of the bones have writing on them, labels – G10, G11, F31 – like there's a meticulous scientific basis to it. I shut my eyes. But it's people. *People.* It's a child like the baby girl with the necklace in the bush.

And Mouse knows all of this about his father and his house. *Don't let him have them!* I think of his wide-eyed stillness, like he knows too much and can't fathom it, like he's in perpetual shock at what is done in his home.

Tobyn babbles on that the blacks are all going to die out anyway and this is a service, what his father's doing here, it's preservation for science and history and posterity. They're doing good, the Craws, helping with scientific endeavour. 'So those two in the bush, Poss, they're nothing in the grand scheme of things.' He flicks his palm in an offhand manner.

'Do you not think if you destroy a soul that you might be ghosted by it forever?' I murmur softly, slowly. 'And that you'll never be able to break free of what you did? That you'll be haunted by your actions for the rest of your life?'

Tobyn raises an eyebrow in refute. 'They're not people!' His hand brushes mine; I flip it off, repulsed. 'Look. I don't like it either,' he whispers, drawing me in tight.

I pull back. No, Tobyn, absolutely not. Now.

'This is what my father does, Poss. But we don't have to think about it if we don't want to. It doesn't concern us. And if you need it put out of your mind, well, maybe I can help. Because here we are. Just us. Alone. Finally.'

I stay my course, reeling, stay my course, when I just want to run away from this cursed house, run into the bush and far beyond it. As if sensing he's losing me in this moment Tobyn kisses me, suddenly, shocking my mouth into life with an invasive tongue; he's all enquiry and urgency and propulsion into a future I do not want. I'm all revulsion at this man, this house, at what they do so blithely and coldly and destructively and I don't want a bar of it. What world is this?

'Tobyn, no, what are you doing?' I push at him in disgust, need to get clean.

His face clouds, he's furious. 'Why not, Poss? It's what you want, isn't it?'

What? *What?* Does Tobyn really think I've come to this room of death and tears and trauma and bones, with all its implied violence, just to be alone. With him. To do … what? I break from him and run out of this addling space, slam the door shut on its restless spirits. And on him. Need to gulp fresh air, to get away from this horrendous place. I run down the hallway into the brutal bash of the light and dash past Mr Craw striding up the garden path and almost knock him down.

'Are you mad?' he calls out, but I do not answer, cannot speak nor refute his question and then I find my voice and yell impetuously, 'It's not *me* who's mad,' and regret it.

'What happened to your hair, girl?'

But I will not answer that, to him especially I will not answer.

'You look like something the dogs have dragged in from the bush.'

I turn and lash the full force of my fury at him. 'I'm not the one who's uncivilised here.'

Get out, get out, get out.

In Which an Invitation Appears Under the Door

I dive into my room. To think, pace, to work out what to do. Can't run away, everywhere is too far; the bush would claim me. The day staggers on. I don't feel completely fixed. Just want to scrub this house off. I pull a blanket over my head, humming my anguish into my fist. It now feels like the walls of this estate are closing in on me and I'm so tired and my head still hurts. I slip into an uneasy sleep.

A soft tap through my slumber, on my bedroom door. A note in childish handwriting is slipped under it.

Come to the kichen RITE NOW. Lesson One …
of the AMAZING EXTRORDINRY Mouse Esq Cookry
and Culnry Scool
Speshaltis: biscitts and damper (the speshal bred of this place.)

Mouse. I really don't want to see any of them right now but he needs me, the poor pet, stranded in this family, in this place. I steel myself. Brush myself down, tidy my room and make my bed for Mrs Craw then head out with a deep sigh. My little Mouse needs to be enveloped in a hug and told he's alright, that, yes, he's my number one friend and, yes, he did get in there first. I have to rescue him as well as myself, I must. A shrill from some kind of insect accompanies my walk to the kitchen; it feels like there are thousands of the creatures, a high wall of them pressing in. The noise rises and then falls then stops, as one, as crisp as an orchestra. As if the insects are all watching what I'll do next.

Mouse is alone, making pebble-boulders out of dough.

I force a smile and hug him too quickly then throw a dough ball in the air and attempt to catch it in my mouth; Mouse gleefully follows suit. We both miss and fold the balls back into the batch. My hands are shaking but I try to hide it. Where to begin here? Mouse is his old chatty self, doing what he loves best, explaining his flour-and-water bread that he makes a lot and you can actually eat it and it tastes alright while I'm reeling with knowing too much; I can't shut my mind off. My boy slips a mound onto the fire to bloom. He's practised, handles the heat easily; he must have spent a lot of time watching someone else and has made this room more his world than an adult's. For him, food is love. He tells me he loves experimenting with his baking, gathering people close, to be noticed, and he's worked out that food is the best way to do it.

A fly buzzes, trapped in an opened bottle of cider, and a line of industrious ants march up a wall to a honey pot. Mouse explains that the blue and white striped jar is one of the few possessions of his grandmother that survived the long journey from Scotland. I attempt to brush the ants away but Mouse tells me it's no use. 'They're everywhere, Poss, they've invaded us.' He says the bush teaches him so much when it comes to cooking.

'You wrap food in a ripping tree's bark and then bury it in some coals, and it comes out flavoured by the land.'

'How do you know that, Mouse?'

'I dunno. Everyone does, I think.'

I bend down to him and look straight into his eyes. I will rescue this boy, in some way; I will quarantine his innocence if I can. 'Mouse, tell me, are you alright … here?'

'What? Yes. I suppose.' He looks at me, puzzled.

I smile, bite my lip; he seems fine. He must be used to Mr Craw's extremes. As I contemplate the industrious ants marching to their faraway pot, Mouse babbles on about lanterns in the dark to lure the fish and lines made out of dried possum gut but I'm not listening enough, too lost in swirling thoughts.

A flour bomb hits me in the head. 'Ow!' Another slams in a cloud in my face. 'Hey! What?' The little scamp is determined to have my full attention. A pale anointing of powder is suddenly dancing through the air and colonising every surface of the kitchen, a hob is covered in paste, a meat safe is dusted with flour, heavy black pots are rendered a snowy white; a cackling, whirling devil child has taken over the space. 'Stop it, Mouse!'

But it's no good. The Cookr'y School demands my undivided attention and the boy's suddenly got the anger in him. He grabs the honeypot and elaborately lifts it to his lips to make me notice his naughtiness. I pull it away; Mouse snatches it back. It drops to the ground and smashes. Amid all the mess of what Mouse has done in this room.

Because I hadn't noticed him enough. Hadn't given him the gift of attention. What he craves the most. To be loved, looked at, listened to – and by his mammy most of all. Because she's good at withholding. She's a master manipulator in this house. I pick up a shard. 'Your mammy is going to be so furious.'

His dawning. The precious jug. He steps back, changed in an instant. 'Poss. Help me. C-c-clean everything with me. Please.' He's pleading for help with his mother's fury, a fix to her piracy of silence or worse.

'She'll hate this, Mouse. Unless …'

My little mate is crying. He's so afraid, of both his parents. I drop to the floor and start picking up the pieces. I'll do this, for him, in a trade-off for some answers at last. I accidentally slice my finger on a shard and press the cut to my mouth.

'Are you alright?'

'Yes. But tell me, Mousey, why didn't you want your father to know about the bodies at the Ripping Tree?'

Churning silence, he can't bring himself to say.

'Come on, I'm your friend. If you tell me, I'll say to your mammy that the pot was all my fault.' He looks up at me. 'Do you know something, Mouse, that maybe, um, you shouldn't?'

'If you promise you won't leave me, I'll tell you a secret.'

'About?'

'What Papa does. When no one's around.'

My thudding heart, my rasp. 'Which is?'

But he can't say, he can't.

'Is this about the … the bodies. By the Ripping Tree?'

The boy can't look at me, he's feeling his way. 'You can't talk about it to anyone, Poss.'

I say that he can always trust me and I'm very, very good at secrets, the best. But he's clogged. I squeeze his hand, there's our tickle too. A start, a stop, and then an embarrassed rush of a gabbling about his father supplying those big places back in Britain — museums — with things, that they might want. That they pay for. 'Big Rivers or something at some place called Oxford, and one in London too. Father supplies them.'

I can't bear to ask him with what, to go any further. It's too cruel for a little boy to know this. I tuck Mouse's hair behind his ears and whisper that I'll always be his friend, that I'm here to help him.

Then he whispers, barely there, 'It's the teeth.'

'The teeth?' I collect more of the pottery shards, my blood a dull thud in my ears. 'What do you mean, darling? I don't understand.'

Mouse drops beside me and tries to help as I sweep up bits of shardy ceramic with the heel of a hand, nick my skin, don't care. Mouse blurts out that the little girl had special teeth, magic teeth, and he's talking, babbling, like there's too much in his head.

'What? Mouse, who had special teeth?'

The little boy is clogged, his mind racing into punishment. 'That girl, Poss. The little baby. At the Ripping Tree. Who looked … um … asleep.'

'You *knew* her?'

Silence. Mouse hands a shard to me. 'I used to play with her sister. Sometimes. Not really. Well, sort of. Oh! But she wasn't meant to be there! None of them were. They came too close!' Mouse's hands twist his hair, his mind a cram of wrong, his words barely able to come out.

I smell smoke. The damper is burning and I rush to grab the loaf. Mouse is right behind me as I open the oven door and he yanks the bread out but exclaims sharply at the hotness of the loaf and drops it. I grab his singed fingers and put them in the cavern of my mouth and keep them there, and keep them there, holding, soothing, quieting, my heart racing with everything that's gone on.

I tap a finger on his nose. 'It's alright, Captain Mouse. Whatever you say. Just tell me what you know.' The little boy smiles back in wonder for I've returned his fingers intact with the gift of loyalty and forgiveness. 'This is our secret, Mousey. No one else will know.' Treading on eggshells here. The little boy suddenly holds me tight as if he's cramming all his bewilderment into me: at adults and what they do and all the secrets he has to hold in his head. 'So who was that girl in the bushes, my Captain? The one staring.' Mock casual, and ever so tender, but with a shiver as I think back to that first moment of seeing the bodies. What was Mouse's reaction exactly? All I can remember is a stick, dully bashing ferns, and a question to the girl: *What are you doing here?* But I didn't realise at the time they might actually know each other. And then she vanished.

'She was my friend, Poss. Before you. She wasn't imaginary but Mammy wouldn't believe that. She thinks a lot of things are in my head. She's always saying it. The toddler was Poiyir. Her big sister is Tinkin. Their mammy is Warai.'

'Warai.' I think of the tenderness in a hidden sketch. 'What a beautiful name.'

'And Mammy thought I was so desperate for friends that I just magicked them from nowhere – but I didn't, I didn't. And it's why she wants you here, Poss. Because you're a real live friend for me. A proper one at last. A distraction from all the silly things in my head. She thinks you'll grow me up but I don't want to be grown up, I don't, not like them. It's too awful. What grownups do, Poss!'

I hold his scrunched-up face in the cup of my palms and kiss his tears away – 'I know, I know' – as my mind flits, trying to piece the mess of Mouse's world together. I gently stroke my agitated boy. 'But what do you mean, exactly, by the teeth?' Trying to gently, so gently, lure more talk. 'Darling, what is it with the teeth?' I can sense a withdrawing tightening its clench as Mouse realises, perhaps, he's said too much. He's stepping back, slipping from me.

I reach forward. Hold the boy's dear, burdened little body sister-tight. Marinating him in love, cracking him with kindness. 'It's alright. I love you and I'll always protect you. I'll get us out of here if I have to. Ssssshh.'

The boy softens, surrenders, as his body yields into my enveloping blanket. 'She's got magic teeth, Poss. One row and then the other, right behind it. Like a shark's. I saw it when she ate my biscuits and laughed. And it was so odd and strange, and, and …'

I squeeze Mouse's shoulders; he's clamming up, I'm losing him. 'What? I'm on your side, darling. The teeth were what?'

He says something in the softest whisper; I lean forward to catch it. 'Valuable,' he repeats.

I let go.

'For all those places that Pa sends things to.'

Valuable for a collector. Of course.

'Did you tell your father about them, Mouse?'

The dread, suddenly, as a likely scenario unfolds before me, but it's all too much for Mouse, too overwhelming, and he turns with hands waving across his head as if batting away an imaginary fly and runs weeping from the kitchen, weeping from all the complications of his Willowbrae life. I've lost him, but it's enough for now and I let my little friend go, and I sit against the wall with my hands dangling from my knees and head bowed.

So. That's why my boy was so terrified by the prospect of his father finding where the bodies were. Because of a set of singular teeth. On one side of Willowbrae's world is a punitive patriarch who presides over his estate from a throne in a terrifying room of bones, and on the other is a little girl with a special set of teeth, in a tiny skull, that will one day end up in a lecture hall in London. A little girl with a curl of hair like a shell behind her ear. Whom Mouse knew.

Who he also knew was more valuable to his father dead than alive. A child who had ended up wrapped in her mother's fierce protectiveness, as if Warai had realised the world of the candle-skinned people was too horrifically much. And Mouse didn't want his father getting to the two of them. To their bones. *He can't have them. They're not his to have.*

My dawning horror. Of my own role in all this. That I've betrayed Mouse, and Tinkin, by unwittingly leading the entire Craw family to the child with the collectible mouth. Whose skull had to be procured before her baby teeth fell out and her uniqueness vanished. I led the entire family to a native presence once again on their land, when they thought them all gone. I led the entire family to a possible funeral ritual I knew nothing about and insisted on a burial and Christian blessing when I had no idea if it was wanted. All because I didn't listen enough. To a little boy. When he cried out in anguish at the dining table, *No, Poss, don't!*

But of course I had to speak out. Unthinkingly, mulishly, speak out. And muck everything up. Which has resulted in all of this.

I curl into the ground and squeeze my fists into my eyes. Not listening enough and stubbornness and hot headedness were imperfections Ambrose was always accusing me of. And now, and now.

What to do next. In the flour-dusted kitchen I pick up the remaining ceramic shards and place them in a pile, barely noticing the blood from my clenched hands. Then I head to my room.

The only sanctuary left.

A VIOLATION

Someone's been in it. My bed sheets are scattered with a furious violence and I can barely bring myself to step across the threshold into the sullied place. The bed's canopy is partly torn down and Faith's wooden doll has its clothes ripped clean off and my crushed nightgown lies among enraged sheets. The French doors bang: that's how the perpetrator must have got in and left. Whoever it was. But I know who, too well, perhaps.

I shut and lock the French doors and turn back to the mess. Should I tell someone? Don't know who. Who to trust? Someone needs to know. Someone wants me gone. The bed sheets look like someone has lain in them. Slept in them. I cry out urgently to the woman who is as close to a mother, possibly, as I'm ever going to get; Mrs Craw comes running.

She spins, her hands helpless at her head. 'Was it a fox, an opossum, a ghost?' What is she saying? Would she guess, possibly, that perhaps it was Tobyn; she saw her son's glance at me before church, our smile of secrets; would she guess at a sudden change in him?

'A ghost. Really, Mrs Craw?'

'Did you do this, Poss?'

'What?'

'Do it yourself? To churn things up.' The air is loaded between us. 'And, Lord, your hair!'

'Pardon?'

'Your hair. What happened? What have you done to it?' Mrs Craw holds a limp end and whimpers in sorrow at the sight. 'No, child, no.'

'Please, ma'am. I did it to help Mouse, in solidarity. But my room. My room!' Together we turn to look at it – at my bed and nightgown all jumbled up, and Faith's doll, her naked doll, discarded on the floor.

'No,' Mrs Craw cries.

'There's so much fury in it. Who could have done this?'

Mrs Craw pauses as if struck by the sudden knowing of exactly what her son is capable of; perhaps she saw me storm out of the house earlier, pushing past her husband on the garden path. Then she puts brisk hands to her hips and declares that the two of us will just have to see to this, immediately. As the women of the house. And with that a fury of domesticity is unleashed. She collects fresh sheets from the cupboard, switching instantly to the woman who needs every inch of her world under control, who needs to clamp down whatever's been unleashed. 'Don't think about it too much, Poss. We will never know who did it.' She looks at me in a cold challenge. 'No one else need know, mind.'

'But why?'

Mrs Craw flings out the sheets from their firm folding. Her briskness is her answer; she won't be going into it. I gather up the rumpled linen. She soothes and straightens, fiddles and folds, then sweeps up the nightgown and rolls it tight in old sheets.

Wordlessly she strides out of the room and returns with another nightgown and holds it up, declaring it's as ill-fitting as the last but will do. Then she propels me before the looking glass and smooths my hair with no tenderness, yanking strands into obedience and licking fingers to stick the hair down and tucking stray curls behind my ears. I squirm but am held tight. It's as if I've somehow caused the chaos myself. Mrs Craw flattens my hair into some kind of permanence, digging a pin into my forehead and not apologising.

'Ow! Ma'am. Please.'

She says nothing. Squeezes my shoulders in quick farewell then tells me this situation will never happen again, she'll make sure of it. And in a flurry of bundled sheets she's gone. I run to the French doors and look across to the bush.

Willowbrae's walls are closing in on me.

In Which the Beauty of Respair
Is Considered

Have to get away, to the sanctuary of the bush, its solace. Pa once taught me an old Celtic phrase – 'the thin places' – to describe those little pockets of the natural world that feel closer to the mysterious energy that drives all the earth. He said the thin places arrest you with their strange power, and the Ripping Tree glade, despite all the trauma it's seen, feels like one of them. I want to be stilled by it, healed, and learn more about it. And I need some fresh air because a headache is toying with my temples.

Willowbrae now feels like a trap, as if there's an ivory comb here, pulling hard on all my nerves. I want to flush myself clean, far away from this claustrophobic, secret-soaked house. Want to search for Tinkin and Mouse and want to somehow *respair*, amid everything. It's another old word Pa loved: a fresh recovery after despair.

I slip into the repairing air. Flit through the island's spikes and snags as fast as I can in Mrs Craw's heavy skirts. There's no softness to this land. Prickly slivers coat my clothes; little black sticks of annoyance, a thumbnail's length, hook greedily onto the cloth. The native flowers are tough to pull from the earth but after much effort I gather together a shardy bouquet of sharp tips and bleached colour and hold it to my chest like a bride heading into her quiet little death. Run on.

The leaves in their swan pattern are still there, just, but it looks as if someone has kicked at them in spite. The glade still contains its protective energy and I take a deep breath, and still. Settle the bouquet tenderly on the wing. Sit back. Look around. No one here, no one close. Loneliness stretches its claws in me; I'm hugely alone here, and in the world. Who can help me now? If I leave Willowbrae I'll be penniless, with nowhere to go and only the clothes on my back.

I skim fingertips over the soil but everything that could tell a story is long gone. Flop to my belly and wing my arms wide, pushing my fingers through the strange earth baked in its sunshine. Will I be swallowed by this soil eventually, will this country enfold my bones in death? This alien earth. I rest my cheek to the coolness and squeeze my eyes shut on a prickle of tears that will not under any circumstances come out. Home. It's gone. I ram my hands through the soil and once again feel like the wild-child of cut-off trousers and brambles and brook, the girl who never quite grew up. I won't inhale the lovely smell of home ever again. Or crunch through the resistance of snow. Or breathe in Knockleby's wetness after rain when the soil opens out to receive its benediction. The craving for it all feels like a sickness in me now, arrowing me across the earth to my squat little teapot of a house. That someone else owns now, because of Ambrose's debts. My place of belonging where I was at vivid rest. I'll never see it again, and I don't know how to go on.

A twig crack.

My face pops up like a lizard's. 'Hello?' Another snap, a rustle. 'Who's there?' My heart beats fast. 'Tinkin? Hello?' But is it? Do I have her name right? I prop my chin on the knuckles of both hands. 'Tinkin? Don't be afraid.'

The little girl steps from behind the Ripping Tree. Her blonde-tipped hair hangs loose and she wears a necklace of black and white shells just like her mother and sister did and her little body is as brawny as a boy's, all muscle and sinew: a warrior's, wary and ready. For what? We stare at each other.

I flicker a grin. 'I was hoping you'd come back.'

Tinkin doesn't smile. As if she can't quite let go, yet, still not sure if she should absolutely trust. My head stays propped, lizard alert.

'Don't go,' I whisper, and I place my fist again on my heart and smile, hesitant.

Tinkin comes up close, then closer, all the time edgy for flight. Her alert brown eyes are reading me, searching for some kind of trust, tossing up, yes or no. I don't move. But my speaking eyes, my relief that we're doing this: something terrible has happened to this little girl and also to myself and there's a connection over that if nothing else.

Tinkin drops to the ground in front of me, her belly in the dirt just like mine. My smile, sun-wide. So. Face to face, two lizards at last. Tinkin giggles and it's like a hat flying off to the sky for us both. 'Where you from?'

I exclaim warmly at her English and she shrugs and asks again where I'm from and I explain it's a place called Knockleby, far across the globe, and point a big way away and the girl mirrors my actions and we both laugh.

'What's your name?' I ask and when the girl says, 'Tinkin,' I nod yes, of course, I knew. 'How?' A frown, her head cocks. Smart one this one, intelligence radiates from her. I explain that the little boy Mouse told me and I mime his height and his stare and Tinkin looks at me in wonder as if she's drinking my intruder's mind up. I ask what happened here, does she know, pointing to the violated wing, and the girl looks at me quizzically as if weighing up what to say and whether to trust me with the truth or not.

'I love this place,' I say carefully, 'this ... little chapel. Almost.' Because it somehow feels like that.

Tinkin murmurs something about her mother – the land was her mother or her mother had been in this land – and I nod, grave, then hold my forehead between a thumb and forefinger and wince. Tinkin reaches out in concern. 'Are you hurting?'

She leaps up to the Ripping Tree and strips off some young leaves from its tips. Chews them then offers the wet wad to me, pointing to my head then my lips. 'To help you. Help.'

I take the saliva-soaked mass and put it in my mouth and chew on the tough tartness and feel suddenly heady and released and laugh. 'It works! Your mother taught you this?'

But Tinkin is poised, she's now listening to something else. It's as if a cloud has crossed over the sun and the world in an instant has dulled. She swiftly looks behind her, gasps and runs off.

'Oh!'

She's vanished. I've heard nothing.

'Tinkin?'

There's a rustle like a wild beast in return, scurrying off in fright. Then I hear it too.

A heavy, irreverent footfall, headed to this place.

I AM SWALLOWED

'Oh, *you*!'

Tobyn crashes in to the glade. He tears off a palm frond, laughing and mock-anointing me and tickling my neck. Which I do not want. Do not like. And why is he here? Did he follow me? 'So here you are, little girl lost.'

'Yes.'

'You ran away from me. And girls like you are not meant to run away, Miss Poss.'

I don't like Tobyn's voice, his new tone, as if there's unfinished business from the study that he needs to tidy up. He's too big and loud and wrong for the energy of this place. I scowl. I don't want his cluttery, hovery insistence right now; Tobyn is suddenly the happiness stalker when all I want is Tinkin back. Why is he here? He has no need of this. What does he want, from me, from this place? I back away, cup my hand at my mouth and spit out Tinkin's wad then discreetly discard it.

Tobyn moves closer.

'What are you doing here?' I ask, coldness in my voice.

He laughs, tells me he's trying to find his disobedient house guest, the one who slips away at odd moments and wears trousers and talks too much. So why am *I* here?

I take a deep breath. Tell him very slowly that I've come to the glade to try and work out what happened, once and for all – and to find some peace in this place. Tobyn sighs like I'm a child and explains that some things aren't meant to be found out; the dead woman, the mother, might have been rejected by her people, had I thought of that? She might have had nowhere to turn to, no land to go back to and no home that was truly hers. His voice is curdling into petulance and spite. 'Good riddance, I say. It might have been too complicated for her any other way.'

'Good riddance? She was a mother, Tobyn. A beautiful young woman with a baby and, quite possibly, other children. Maybe. And perhaps she was desperately homesick and … alone, and all you can say is good riddance?' I step back in disgust. He moves forward. This is some game to him, he wants something; oh God, he's not letting me go. 'I need to leave now,' I say.

'What?'

'Get away. From the lot of you. Leave. Willowbrae. Virgil told me to go and I refused. But you know what, he was right.'

'Oh no, we're not having that,' he teases, moving closer still. A chill. This man is tracking me. He's not letting up. He's breathing heavily. There is a smell coming off him, of anticipation, sweat, want. His fingers loosen his neckerchief as if this is the start of something and he is preparing himself and I'm not going to like it. The shallow flit of my breath. I snatch his palm frond and fling it at him and he grabs at me but I twist from his grasp and run. Run. Run. Crashing through the bush.

'Poss! Wait!'

I'm having none of it, sick of him, scared of him, wanting no more of his posturing and his talk; sick of the secrets of this house. I splash through the shallows, not even bothering to lift my skirt, making sure I don't take Mouse's track because I don't want Tobyn anywhere near me. Good riddance indeed and he'll be sorry for it.

But then. I'm alone. Too quick. I'm suddenly swallowed up by too much that looks the same as a minute ago, but isn't, or is, and I'm now walking in circles, or am I? The bush rings with a taunting. The hairs at the back of my neck spring to attention at each new rustle of nothing or everything and I can't read any of it. Tobyn's cries of 'Possy, wait, you silly' grow fainter and I refuse to call out, don't want his triumphant mock as he rescues me. 'What did I tell you, Poss? I know best. Don't I? Repeat: Tobyn the best, knows best.' No, I do not like his new way of talking, it's dipping into ugliness. I think back to the mess of my sheets and the snatched kiss in the study, the uninvited tongue pushing into my mouth and the smell of want; I don't like any of this and am afraid and alone.

A twig cracks, close. I stop. Walk faster, further away into the bush and further, moving as far as I can from Tobyn's voice. Spin. Nothing is familiar now and I can't see far enough ahead through the spindly scrappy trunks that in volume appear oddly dense. The sun is directly overhead so I don't know what direction is west, what direction is anything. I walk on and on.

Heat is a wall that now holds me trapped in slowness. I've lost sight of water and the direction of the big house. A bird screeches too close. My nerves are on edge and the blood pumps too loud in my neck – *boom-boom boom-boom* – and it feels like a strange presence is following, watching, most wilfully not helping and not declaring itself. Footsteps. Branches cracking.

A crackle of movement. Someone is taunting or tracking me or worse. The whole world of Willowbrae is no longer about sanctuary but survival, yes, and I grab a fallen branch.

'Who's there?' I hold it aloft. 'Hello?' It's my deepest voice but there's only silence back. Of course. 'Declare yourself.'

Silence. Goading or teasing or something else entirely and I will not show fear, I'll not.

I walk on then stop at an overhanging rock and try to sharpen the branch on the stone; I glance up to a native panorama of fish and stingrays stretching the length of the cave's roof. Heat presses its thumbs into me; a slick of hair is a sliver in my eye; a slip of sweat rolls down my chest. A giant lizard cocks its head then shoots up a trunk, all front leg propulsion and slippery strength and I will not, will not, be afraid of it.

In my exhaustion I'm now stumbling, running, stopping, but it's just more endless trees and more as the sun arrows cruelly down. Everything looks different but the same and I think I see Tobyn – tall, languid, mocking, leaning on a trunk – and wipe sweat from my eyes. Oh! No. A wall of trees. Another. He's here, he's close. Tobyn's laugh? Is he teasing or worse? Is he waiting for my exhaustion before pouncing?

Ragged breathing. Rocks that were there a few minutes ago are now back, and back. How? No water close, no bay, no house. The sun beats down. Wolf Girl is gone, defeated. I'm beyond tired now and ragingly thirsty and spent. Is he gone? Am I alone? Is that worse?

Slowly I peel some bark from a ripping tree that's like a creamy doll's blanket and sit down on it, too tired, too tired to fight anymore. Another twig cracks. A rustle of a scurry. It feels human. Again. Too tired to sit up, to investigate. I ball myself onto my side and shut my eyes to see Jack's sweet face and the piece of deck that saved me and the water, so much water, and then jerk awake.

Boots. Legs. Tobyn looking at me close. I shrink from him, terrified, pressing my knuckles hard into my cheeks.

'Willowbrae isn't quite ready to let you go just yet, my little Poss.' And he smiles at me. What does he want? But then something unseen catches Tobyn's attention and he turns, spooked, and sprints off.

Just like that. Like he shouldn't be here, like he's afraid of the consequences; he's been caught.

Oh! What just happened? Did I just dream all that?

I rub my face and stumble into a sit. Have to get back. I've missed lunch, it's late, the day is fading. What direction, where to begin? A flit of a shadow, tall, ahead; a smaller one, child height. I follow, trusting, can never quite catch up. Is this real? Am I awake? I trail after the ghostly weaving through trees until I see water and make out Mouse's goat path and with a pluming relief am on my way back.

To dubious civilisation, to torment. And resolve.

I need to get out of here. To rescue myself. From Willowbrae and its secrets and its ugliness. No one will do it for me. So. I'll have to light my own lantern in the dark. But how?

INSTRUCTION

Back at the house. Everyone too everywhere. Was Tobyn really going to harm me, or was it just his odd sense of play? I look around at the contained world of Willowbrae, its beautifully swept floors and firm sheets and waiting Bibles, with everything so calm and ordered and in its place. Am I being too sensitive here? Making mountains out of molehills? Mrs Craw meets me in the corridor and senses my agitation. She suggests I take a moment, in the library, all by myself. 'It'll do you good.'

I sit, shivering in the quiet space. But, oh! I hear whispering in the corridor and Mrs Craw comes in and shuts the door firmly behind her, not quite done with me yet. She sits herself in silence on the chaise longue across from me; she's allowed to, of course. She shuts her eyes with her palms crossed over her chest as if rehearsing for death, or gathering herself, then opens her eyes and looks at me. I sit up straight and try to smile, my legs still shaking under my skirt.

She suddenly springs up. Climbs a ladder. Plucks some books off a top shelf and settles them next to me, patting them fondly like pets. 'You never had a mammy, did you?' Her finger taps a manual just like the ones Mariana used to have.

I shake my head tightly. 'No. I think I'm allergic to these kinds of books.'

'Oh. And may I ask why?'

'Because they're always explaining to me how I'm wrong. Very, very wrong.'

Mrs Craw smiles serenely and reads a title aloud. '*Private Lectures on Perfect Women*. Then there's *The Woman Beautiful*. Well, I don't need any help in that department.' She laughs at her little joke; I do not. 'You, on the other hand ...' We exchange glances. I can't read her. Is she smiling at me? With me? 'How about *Female Beauty, as Improved by Regimen, Cleanliness and Dress*.' Mrs Craw hands me the book with a little thrust of fierceness through her smile; it reminds me of her tightness when she saw Tobyn's glance to me before church. She's all ... clench.

'Is there a problem, ma'am? I'm not so good with things like this.' I place the volume on the seat beside me. Tell her my mother died when I was a baby and Pa had made it up from that point. But never with these kinds of books.

Mrs Craw looks as if she is about to ask me something then frowns at the tome discarded and taps me on the shoulder, a touch too hard. 'Well, I might be able to help you then.' She commands me to sit up straight – 'Posture, posture' – and moves behind me and runs her fingers through my hair, massaging it in little tugs. 'Relax.' Which I can't, quite, of course. 'I might be able to help you, Poss. Because you really don't know how to give yourself a haircut, do you? Hmm?'

I say nothing. So that is what this is about. Mrs Craw says nothing either as she works me into a stupor with the lull of her fingers. Maybe I'm getting off lightly here so I'm not going to push it. I close my eyes and surrender to the maternal fingers fluid over my scalp. She leans in and whispers that we need to have a little chat at some point. Of the womanly kind. She speaks as if the very walls and the books are listening in and she doesn't want them to hear.

'What do you mean, ma'am?'

Mrs Craw's fingers dig into my scalp, ever so slightly, and stay there. 'Have your friends arrived yet? Do you need any … help?'

'My what?'

'Friends. The curse of Eve. Your monthlies.'

'Oh! Yes. Goodness. It's fine, Mrs Craw. Fine. But not here, I mean, they haven't come here. And I might be gone by the time they do.' What a thing to be talking about. I nudge away and cross my arms.

She asks if my 'friends' began at a young age and I hurry out a no, no.

'I'm relieved. A girl who develops too soon apparently has a feeble middle life.'

'Oh. Yes.' I glance at the stack of manuals now by my side. Pa recruited a farmhouse neighbour to tell me about 'women's matters', which she did, with apologies that she was too old for all that now, she only knew of cows and the like.

'Is your blood of … bright colour, Poss?'

I'm mortified. 'Goodness. What? Yes, no, I don't know. All colours, if you must know. I think.'

Mrs Craw tells me that an author she likes very much, the good Dr Chevasse, recommends that all menses blood be as bright as a cut finger. 'Many fevers come from anything different, Poss. Shakes, night horrors, sleeping at odd hours, frights.'

'What are you —'

'Nothing. Just asking.'

'I'm fine, ma'am. Please.'

Mrs Craw pinches my hair in little tufts, not quite affectionately. 'How to tame you, Poss. Hmm? This wilful, impetuous, blundering little head of yours. That blurts out too much. In public.' A pause. 'As well as private.' A sigh. 'No one's ever taught you how to converse in a genteel way, have they? You're very difficult to … control.' Her hands wrap around my hair and tighten; it hurts. 'For instance, this impossible hair. Faith had beautiful hair. It was so easy to manage.'

'I cut my hair to make your youngest child feel a bit better. It was impetuous and stupid, I know. I'm sorry.' I need Mrs Craw to loosen her grip. My hands cover hers but no relief is forthcoming; it's as if she's disappeared into the caves of her complex head.

'You must never speak of what you see in this place.' Mrs Craw's voice hardens. 'In public. Among others.' Her grip tightens, and tightens. I stifle a cry of pain. 'You're our guest here, Poss. And we do things our way at Willowbrae. And it works. Our way. Understood?' The last word is hissed. Her index fingers dig into my scalp and there's suddenly something utterly unmaternal about them.

I cry out in pain. Her fingers release me. 'Maybe I should think about leaving soon, ma'am.'

'No, oh no.' Her voice switches in an instant to the woman who just wanted a daughter to doll up. She bustles about the room, straightening book spines already straight and swiping invisible dust while telling me I could use nothing for my monthly unwellness, if I want, but there's also sheep's wool at Willowbrae, fluffy side up. Or a clout.

'A what, ma'am?'

'A cloth triangle. Secured by a belt. And I've got a ragbag of bits and bobs if you ever want to delve into that. Or raw cotton, which you can fashion into a wad and, er, insert.' Mrs Craw trails out. I say nothing. 'Or the baby's swaddling cloth.' She moves away. A quietness blooms between us, a silence of too much.

'Ma'am?' I enquire softly but get nothing back.

'I still have them. Just in case. I'm not … old. Yet.' Despite everything that's ruptured between us I stretch out my hand to her – she seems so brittle and breakable all of a sudden. 'Just leave my boy alone,' she whispers fierce, batting my hand away. 'For his sake. For ours. You have to be teachable, Poss. Do as we say, because this house, this life, demands it. Do. As. We. Say.'

I step back. Nod.

'I want you to stay with me but I just, we just —' Mrs Craw balls her fist at her mouth. She hurriedly leaves the room, her hand at her lips as if she knows something I don't and she's going to be sick. I look at her, bewildered. What is she trying to tell me?

So. I'm now stranded in this room with the books that insist on telling me what I must be like. And I have no heart for any of it. I hold my palm to the memory of Mrs Craw's touch, the caress like a trickle of cool water cutting through my thirstiness. Until it turned into something else. Yet the touch was so lovely until that moment: the physicality of it, the connecting. Her cruel art is to offer a little affection and then remove it, to plunge the recipient into a cold, cold place. And to maintain power at all costs.

DARK TALK

Night feels as open as a book. I withdraw from the bustle of the house, needing my own nest of quiet. I wonder where Virgil is, what he's doing; he's taken tea somewhere else and no one queries it. 'That's our Virgil.' Mrs Craw shrugs at the brittle dinner table where no one talks much. 'We never ask.' Tobyn winks at me, back to a semblance of his playful self.

But aswirl.

Later in the thick of the night there's a tapping on my window like a close branch in a frisky wind. I wake with a start from a shredded sleep, wish I had my knife that everyone still denies knowing anything about. When I go to the window, nothing's there, of course, no tree. Am I mad? Is my head still storm-wrecked? There's never been a branch close. Is it Tinkin? I open the French doors. 'Hello?' No answer, just wind-talk. No stick close.

So. Someone wants to spook me from this house or send me mad with it. Who would want me gone the most? Tinkin with her silent feet, or my native rescuer who whispers through all my nights, or the many ghosts of Willowbrae who've been pushed from their land yet haunt it still? Is the knocking someone tormented and angry and indignant – and white? Or a black man?

I stride outside, searching for my rescuer under a bright coin of a moon and wondering what exactly he had to do with this house. Was he attached somehow to Warai and Poiyir? He's here, I can feel it, in the hairs standing to attention on my skin. Yet no one makes their presence felt. A mourning sound is wrapped far away within the wings of the wind; it's a human cry yet not, rising in pitch then dropping to nothing and again rising, but I don't know if it's real or a night trick. I make sure I don't stray from any goat path.

Chili, Parsley and Sage don't bark. Of course. A night trick perhaps, or someone has silenced them or slipped beyond their knowing. I'm so confused; everything is poised, everything uncertain. I walk beyond the lawn and into the trees, stare into the silvered bush and turn, breathing quick. And turn. A whisper of a something in the alive quiet. I am very still. Is it Tinkin? It's her, surely, but she's not coming forward. 'Hello?' Softly I call into the night air. 'Tinkin?' A waiting silence.

'What your name?' A challenging rush of a child's voice.

'Tinkin, is that you?'

'Yes. What your name?'

I feel no need for withholding with her, no need for secrecy or lies, we must start clean with this.

'Tom,' I tell her strong.

Tinkin repeats, 'Dom.'

'It's short for T—' I'm just about to declare my proper name, the hated Thomasina, when she sees something behind me and runs off. No. I flit a turn. Flea is approaching. 'Oh!' I exclaim.

He has a look on his face that wants to haul me immediately home. What's he heard, or seen? He wasn't that close. I babble a panicky hello and blurt that I love the bush and can't keep out of it, that it's a lovely night, that the forest here is all so spiky and strange, unlike home. 'You frightened me, Flea! Sneaking up like that. You could've knocked. Ha!'

The man asks why I'm out here in the middle of the night. Like he knows something. About how I got to Willowbrae perhaps, or who I'm searching for. I bat him off, yet he's heard something suddenly, far away in the wind, and he holds his face to it and listens. 'We need to get back to the house.'

'I – really? I love being in the bush!'

'Let's go.'

No arguing. As we head back to Willowbrae I ask about the native people of the area. Flea says nothing, just swigs from a small silver bottle that he takes from a trouser pocket. I ask for a go too – 'to calm me down' – but Flea smiles and holds his bottle high. 'Not on your life, lass.'

'What happened to them?'

'Persistent, aren't you? And I hate a talker. Better to watch, take note.'

'It's just so I can understand, Flea.'

He sighs. Another swig. Tells me slowly that when Mr Craw moved into this area there was co-operation among everyone, a civilised sense of kindness, if you like. Curiosity on both parts. The natives helped the new settler, showed him medicine and pathways through the bush and where the water was and how tea could be made from the paperbark trees – those trees with them layers to them.

'Oh yes! The ripping trees. I love them.'

'"Ripping trees"? You make me laugh. Endless entertainment, from my perspective.'

'Really? Come on then, just a little swig. Pa used to let me.'

'No. You've got to keep your wits about you here, lass.'

'Why?'

Flea doesn't say, he just draws strong on his bottle. Tells me that when the rest of Mr Craw's family came, after the big house was finally built, there was a change. The boss got protective, possibly because his wife demanded it. He closed in, hardened. Decided something had to be done about the natives – 'They were vermin, pests.'

'What horrible words.'

'It's the way of this island. You better get used to it.'

Willowbrae in all its moonlit beauty floats serenely ahead of us; Flea sighs. 'Enough for one night. It's the story of every settler in this land. Come on, let's get you to bed.' And despite all my questions Flea snaps that the natives were driven from their land a long time ago and it's late and there shouldn't be any left.

'Shouldn't?'

Flea shakes his head. He says this land is infected with a great sadness, like, well, like he can feel it through his feet, and it has contaminated everyone in this place. 'In fact, the missus reckons Willowbrae has been haunted ever since.'

'It wouldn't surprise me, you know. I've heard strange thumps and knocks. Odd birds. Dead rats. All manner of things, Flea.'

'Curious things happen here, lass. Horses are let loose. Things go missing. Chooks disappear. Dogs don't bark when they should. Rain falls from a cloudless sky. A white kangaroo watches from the bush. And there are wailing noises on the wind at night, which is why I'm rounding you up now. It's like nature is somehow in cahoots with everything that goes on around here. A child dies on a family picnic, a snake bites a dog on the mouth – and Mrs Craw lives in terror of it all. Her nerves are shot.'

'What happened, Flea?'

'To the missus?'

'The natives.'

'You're a child,' Flea says, 'and these things are for adults.' He's had enough of the talk and propels me, determined, to the house. 'I see everything here, lass, but say nothing. It's not my place to – and you should learn from that. It's our job to be grateful, just that. Give the Craws no cause for concern.'

'Grateful?'

'You're alive. You've got a roof over your head.'

I ask again about the natives in the glade and Flea says to forget it, really, it wasn't anybody's business and probably happened just as the family said. 'A lightning strike, a snake bite, some kind of ceremony. Who knows.'

'Are they gone for good around here?' My eyes search the bush.

'Who knows.'

A prickle insists its way up my spine. Is that a shadow, child height, behind a ripping tree? Is Tinkin close? I call out hello and Flea barks that it's no one, a night trick, and pulls me firmly to the house like I'm a freshly caught child escaped from a workhouse. He says it's dangerous at night, in the bush, and yet again the hairs stand to attention on my arms. Someone is watching, I can feel it.

A soft crack as we leave the shelter of the trees, as if the hidden person is wanting to follow but not, as if they're thinking about it but can't make the leap. My hand trails behind me, waving softly in a way Flea can't see; then it opens out flat as if in readiness for a holding. A crack of a twig and something scurries off.

'Possums,' Flea chuckles. 'Pests.'

I'm marched to the parlour with an insistent grip. Mrs Craw is darning under a dim light, frowning and squinting too close to her cloth. A handkerchief spotted with blood is over her fingertip. Flea tells her about finding me outside in my nightgown, deep in the bush. 'It's madness, ma'am,' he says with his hand locked on my upper arm so I can't escape. I'm open-mouthed at the ease of the turning, so quick.

The two adults speak with a familiar shorthand as if I'm not there. I cock my head. So. They're used to working close. Flea has a frightening physicality packed into him, yet Mrs Craw seems to look beyond it, she seems fused to her manservant with an iron trust. Flea instructs her to lock me inside, for my own sake, and keep the key close to her chest, just as I feel the wailing on the wind increase in intensity.

'What's she been doing out there, Flea?'

'Wandering about. She needs to obey the rules of this house, ma'am.'

'Indeed.' Mrs Craw looks pointedly at me.

'Oh, I've been telling her. We don't know what's out there, do we?'

'Good man.' She leads me off to my room; I follow her offended back as she moans she has a headache coming on and it's just been made worse. A worm is turning. What have I done? What are they afraid of outside that I'll find out about, or be lost among?

'Cover yourself,' Mrs Craw commands as she opens the bedroom door and thrusts me inside. I look down at my ill-fitting nightgown and gasp, at the scandal of it, and in front of a convict no less. Oh! The gown's owner is wider and shorter than me and my calves and collarbone are exposed and I've been wandering loose and almost unclothed in the bush, which means unhinged quite possibly. Yet here I am. Wild-haired and bare-footed and almost naked in the dark, an insult to all the people of this fine estate. And Flea hadn't mentioned it.

'I said cover yourself, Poss,' Mrs Craw repeats in disgust. 'Your – your wantonness.'

She closes the door, and I hear a key turn in the lock.

Quite someone else.

IN WHICH A GIFT APPEARS

A tapping on the glass of the French doors just as I'm falling into sleep. It's softer this time, different. I sweep the sheets aside and run to the door, eager to see who it might be. Mrs Craw forgot to lock these doors – as if she couldn't comprehend why someone would want to go Outside.

But there's no one there. Of course.

I glance down. On the sandstone is a tiny gift of an object. Carefully I pick it up.

It's a nest. As intricate as a human vessel, made with much care and thought. It's shaped from clay and twigs, and the fluff of feathers has been threaded through it like tiny pillows of maternal love. I've seen it before. It's the same one, I'm sure, as the one on the ground from that first visit to the Ripping Tree. I hide it quickly in the bottom drawer of the bureau so Mrs Craw doesn't see it and ask about it. Or Mouse.

My little sister-girl has been here and I smile in great chuff; Tinkin has given me a gift. The only possession in the world I now own. I open the drawer again just to gaze at it in wonder and then softly shut the nest away and look out to the moon-flooded bush, my heart soaring.

Tinkin is nearby and the dogs haven't barked; she's elusively close and canny with it. I want to reach out to her, talk to her, understand something of her strange other-world and her grief. And I feel sure that shy child doesn't want me here and is trying somehow to signal it; she wants me away from the big house and is afraid for me. Perhaps yes. Or am I going mad with this? My head still hurts. I press the heel of my palm into my temple. Willowbrae is no longer a sanctuary, and there's a room of horrors at its core. Who have these people become? I need to find my way out of this.

The bones, the restless bones, they won't let up. Beyond the shipwreck, beyond the wailing on the ocean, I'm thinking of the bones in Mr Craw's study. The so many skulls. The children, warriors, elders, mothers. I try to fall into sleep but feel too close to all the lonely bones, so near, at the end of the corridor, all the unresting bones in this immaculate house that is mighty Britain yet not. Beautiful, immaculate Willowbrae: such a serene little piece of the mother country – and so adrift.

Get out, get out. But how?

THE FIFTH DAY

IN WHICH TEACHABILITY IS CONSIDERED

A knock on my door and the key turns, on a day that already feels like it's firmed into brightness. I stir in the stewy sheets; have slept late after a scrappy night in which a branch knocked again and again against the glass, but I was so desperate for sleep I couldn't rise to it. 'Take me,' I murmured eventually, in exhaustion, 'I can't do this anymore.' Then I coiled like an ammonite before falling into restless oblivion.

But now I have a visitor. There's only one person in the world I now trust and I spring up in relief; oh, for it to be him, please God. My soul-rescuer.

'Is it the vicar?'

'Yes. And I shall accompany you. The entire time.' Mrs Craw strides into the room with her fifth-best dress that's been adjusted crudely and she combs my hair with vigorous strokes, fussing curls flat with the heels of her palms that become increasingly agitated throughout. 'You're not the child I ordered, are you? Nothing can be contained, can it? Which is becoming a problem.'

'I don't know what —'

'Oh, be quiet.'

But my unruly hair refuses to obey. Harder Mrs Craw smooths, and harder, dragging the brush through my knots.

I will not cry out, will not give her that. I stare at the painting of the little girl in all her finery; it's like she's now taunting me over what I will become. Mrs Craw swiftly applies a heavy wax to dampen my tamed hair down; her cuffs are slightly dirty and there's the faint smell of sweat on her and her hair is springing loose. She seems frayed, unravelling. It feels as if something's coming to a head here and it's my fate to be the butt of it and there's no way out. 'We *will* get this right, girl.'

Once again I'm transformed under her fussy fingers. She straightens my skirt and strokes back my hair, and again strokes back my hair. She stands aside and surveys the new doll coming to life before her, all the while ignoring my squirm and scratch at the silk. I'm jittery, nervy, an arrow poised in its bow. When the fussing hands finally release me, I draw in a deep, slow breath, held in by the stiff decorum of my dress, and try to stop all my fidgeting, and walk slowly out to the room where my visitor awaits.

Mrs Craw's blunt hiss follows me. 'Remember, Poss, teachable. It'll be worth your while to try it.'

A Dilemma of Choice

'It's you. Back.'

'I am, Poss. Yes. Indeed. Back.'

I ponder this man in twitchy silence. This vicar who's like a long cool drink on a solid day of heat. Who's standing by a Bible on a high, sloping display table. He has mud spatters across his clothes and little twigs in his hair as if he's travelled fast across country to get here and the wild is growing over him and he doesn't care, he wants it. He looms into a greeting and pulls back blushing, which makes me redden too in companionship.

So. Two prisons await. The prison of Willowbrae with a woman who wants a daughter I can never be and a first-born son whose attention has curdled, and the prison of a marriage, which would require me to be submissive and obedient and somehow smaller despite this man's promise. And while the big house offers me an occupation and a roof over my head – an escape into a new life – is the price too high to pay?

Choice.

The vicar tells me, stumbling, that he wants to keep an eye on me, he hasn't been able to keep me from his head, and I jump in over his shy, stumbly words in rescue. 'I'm glad I've been too much in your head, Vicar,' I say and laugh, 'because you've been in mine too.' Without thinking, I roll up my sleeves that were so carefully straightened only moments before and Mrs Craw right behind me tuts; I roll the cloth back down again, wincing. The vicar notices, frowns slightly. Mrs Craw falls into silence.

The vicar begins to say something but stops as if not trusting himself and turns to Mrs Craw in confusion. 'You've been having some trouble with the natives, ma'am. So – so I hear. Yes?'

'Oh. Natives.'

'That passed. In the bush. I heard of the talk in the churchyard.'

'No trouble, Vicar. It was quite some distance away. But, yes, they're back.'

Mrs Craw's face has slid into tiredness as if it can no longer perk itself into anything else. 'Natural deaths, Vicar. Poss doesn't see things quite as we do. Yet.' She gives a small smile of complicity. 'She has much to learn.'

The vicar looks at me and asks, halting, if we can possibly continue the conversation in private, perhaps, only if I want to – and I go to jump in with a yes, yes, but Mrs Craw snaps a no.

'Our guest is delicate. Still. Her head, Vicar. The blow. And things don't seem to be improving. I need to watch over her at all times.'

I bite my lip, look down, mustn't make a scene, am chafing at the bit in my silk-stiffened stillness. I crave in this moment some replenishing talk with this man I know will roam through religion and nature and the sky and the people of this island and the beautiful, rescuing sanctity of love, perhaps, as a haven, a harbour to rest from the toss of the world; for this vicar is not what I'd thought.

Mrs Craw trills a hard laugh. 'Our confused little mermaid says things are happening here, Vicar, or so I've heard. She thinks that our place might be haunted. Poltergeists! I mean really. Her head's agitated with all manner of things.'

A tightness like a stone is now resting on my chest. 'You're making it sound as if I'm mad, ma'am.'

'You suffered a blow. You're not well.'

I still at the abrupt hardness in her tone. A new Mrs Craw entirely is turning a coldness into distance and is happy now to publicly display it. As if she doesn't want me upending her careful world in any way, as if I've somehow transformed from a help into a hindrance. 'I'm fine, ma'am. Really. My head is fixed.'

The older woman raises her eyebrows and tugs at her cuffs. I thank the vicar for coming so far and checking on me and he nods and asks if I'm enjoying Willowbrae and I gabble on about the beauty of this land and he says a lot of people don't see it, actually; they say it isn't proper colours and that it's ugly, the trees are spindly and scrappy. He says that Joseph Banks himself described it as resembling the back of a lean cow, with shrubby long hair and its rocks as scraggy hips.

'No, no! I don't see it as that at all.'

'There can be a great beauty to it, Poss. Yes.'

'If you just open your eyes to it!' I glance at Mrs Craw whose lips are rolled in like she doesn't quite trust what might be blurted out next.

The vicar looks at me, as if what he wants to say next is difficult. 'I think we could have been friends under different circumstances, Poss.' A pause. 'Yes. Fine ones. In fact.' His voice falters.

'I just want to go home,' I stumble out, brimmed. 'To where I feel safe. Held. By … by …'

'You're safe here, child,' Mrs Craw admonishes.

The vicar nods, he understands me. He talks of his home too, of his shepherd family and the wild slopes in Cumbria that they tend. He talks of heft, as it's known with sheep, a homing instinct that continually brings them back to their place of belonging. 'Just like us. To belonging. We all need it.' But he says that belonging for him means here now and perhaps I just need to learn this world, to let it seep into my heart. And it could.

'My home will always be where I grew up, Vicar.'

'And that is?' he gently asks.

We stop. A crowded silence. So, to a gap in the conversation, to leap in with – what? – nothing and everything and Mrs Craw is watching close. The vicar stumbles on, asking who I am, really; can I remember my name? Now?

'No,' Mrs Craw snaps. 'Apologies, but we'll let that lie. For now. I need to work on her some more. She is not fixed.' The woman looks at her watch. I bite my lip.

The vicar tells us in a rush that it feels to him as if I'm on the cusp of something now, poised, passing from one life into another and it's exciting and terrifying and wondrous all at once in terms of what I might do next. 'Yes?'

My heart is galloping in my chest because I want to declare everything before him suddenly, the whole burdened lot, yet my name is a secret in my heart locked. And Mrs Craw is close. Do I blurt out that I might want to go into town right now? That I'm becoming afraid here? That at night I find it hard to fall into sleep because of the horrors in my head and a room of bones in this house and a son who taunts me, whom I no longer quite trust? I start to articulate my unease but hear Mouse playing on the lawn with the dogs and stop myself. Can't leave him alone here. He needs me. And Tinkin is out there somewhere and it's all too complicated; it feels too easy and cowardly to just abandon them both, so, no, I must stay, warily and restlessly and somehow bravely. For now. Because God spared me and I have an obligation to make the most of this new life, in courage and gratitude and generosity and grace. Somehow. So. Choice. And I need to hide from my future a little longer. 'I'm sorry, Vicar.'

Is this right? Is it?

The vicar is concerned: do I need any help? Mrs Craw says crisply that I have everything I need. Do I? Grieving can be a great blow to the mind, the vicar says; it can turn you into someone else, someone dangerous to others – and to yourself. I want to yield in that moment, to collapse into him with the great weight of the past days, the bash of it all. He reaches out to hold me but not, me to lean into him but not. We both know what's required next and everything is on alert as both our futures could go this way or that. Yet we say nothing. Choice.

'Poss is still recovering,' Mrs Craw crashes in. 'It's been a difficult time for her. She needs her rest.'

Yes, says the vicar, he must be off. Shortly. To his home in the bush, his humble home.

I scratch at the silk of my dress.

'Do you enjoy it out there, Vicar?' our hostess asks.

He tells us it feels close to the earth and that's a good thing, for him, in the bush, among the great towering trees; it feels like his cathedral, yes. The vicar looks straight at me and I gaze back at this man, so awkward and grave and clumsy and right. How on earth did we come to this? Everything is alive, ready, lit.

The vicar says he will return. Now is my chance to speak out, to disrupt, but I think of Mouse and Tinkin again and I am stopped up. Can't. The vicar smiles, right into me, it hurts.

'Can I call on you? If ever I need it, Vicar?'

'It goes without saying. I – I care for you. Poss.'

'Thank you.'

A speaking pause with everything and nothing in it. 'Likewise.' Why does he bring me to this tear-prick? I tip my face back in a rescuing blink.

Mrs Craw rushes the vicar to the door, telling him that, yes, their little mermaid needs another few days of rest and he needn't visit again for a good while, it's not required, the child needs her health restored, and quiet. 'Her nerves …'

'What?' I ask.

'Visits are proving disruptive,' she says and glares at me, willing me into silence.

'They are not!'

'Your head, Poss. The blow. I need to call in Mr Craw. Right now. Quick. Good day, Vicar.'

'Take care, Poss. Unless you want me to stay?'

'Callum!' Mrs Craw calls out.

'Do you need me, Poss? Tell me if you do.'

I go to say that perhaps I do, actually, yes, but Mrs Craw talks over me. 'Of course she doesn't, Vicar. Thank you. My husband is on his way now to see you out.' And in that wild moment I think of blurting out everything, of seizing the vicar's rescue.

But what kind of rescue would it be? A compromised one, with possibly a name slipped out as its spoils. And Tinkin is still out there and Mouse is distraught and a room of bones still exists and will be further filled up. And if I declare everything right now in front of Mrs Craw I might be packed off to the women's Asylum of Industry and that will be that, I'll be vanished. Encased forever in a wall of stone. I haven't forgotten her husband's volcanic temper or her son's surprising spite, and Mr Craw and Tobyn are on their way, I can hear their footfalls. 'I'll be fine, Vicar. By myself. For now. Just ... don't forget me.'

'How could I?'

'I'll manage here. I'm tough.' But I don't feel it right now. Have I just let go of my one good shot at escape? Is saying nothing a cowardice or a strength? I'm all adrift, yet I must stay on the fighter's path, must continue to stride along it. Even if I suspect I can't.

Thunder rumbles in the distance; the sky is clearing its throat. The air feels loaded as the vicar walks into it without looking back.

I call out to him, needing his face once more; I ask his name since he knows mine. He turns, hesitates. 'Jemuel. Or simply ... Jem. But, Jemuel. Yes.' He speaks with faltering eyes, an unbearable intimacy, as if I've almost unclothed him, and I roll the name Jemuel in my mouth and again say it firmer and pronounce it a good name and that I could grow used to it.

'As I could yours.'

He leaves quick, without another word, the air unsettled between us.

SCRAPS

After the vicar leaves, Mrs Craw releases me. I dive into the alive air to find Mouse but he's nowhere in sight. Stride across the lawn tetchy and nervy like a colt new to its bridle. My boy's vanished. I catch Flea fattening a scrapheap near the kitchen with vegetable bits and old bottles. 'Can I help?' Silence. 'Flea?' Silence. 'Please.' I'm told no, finally, that it's too messy a task for a lass like myself. Dark-blue bottles of mysterious opacity are nudged under the pile; his actions are furtive, he's trying to hide them from me. I've come at the wrong moment. 'What are you doing?'

Flea sighs and explains that it's all to be burnt off when the days get cooler.

'But why did you put those bottles in there?'

'So the dogs don't get to 'em.' Flea's voice is reluctant, like an old log at a fire's end; it's crackling and cindered and not wanting this.

'What's in the bottles?'

'Don't you worry about that, lass. A kitchen's got many things not meant for children.'

'I'm not a child!'

'More child than adult. And why would you be hurrying yourself into anything grown up? It's all downhill from there.'

'I can't wait to be grown up.'

'In this land? God help you, child.'

'I'm ready for whatever is ahead, Mr Flea. Don't worry. I can take it.'

Flea laughs and tells me he'll be enjoying the ride. From a distance.

'Where's the mouse of the house?'

'Now, *he's* the boss of the house, Miss Poss. But I've no idea where he is. And at least he's got a proper one now.'

'A proper what?'

'Friend.'

'Aren't you his friend?'

'The likes of me isn't allowed the joy of that.'

'So you won't be staying here afterwards? When you're free?'

'I'll be straight off. As quick as I can get.'

Flea says no more on the subject, just urges me to get back inside. Insists I follow him to the kitchen. He has some calves' feet stewing and is making jellies for dessert and he could do with some help, of the tasting variety. I stand my ground, sensing that his reluctance to answer me means there's some mystery to his actions at the scrapheap. 'But the bottles, Flea?' Firm.

'It's nothing to bother your pretty little head about.'

A flare of frustration. I stalk off to the bush. Flea strides alongside me and rounds me off. 'It's dangerous out here. A young girl like you. Come on, inside. My jellies need a taster and you're it.' I shake him off. This man will give me nothing of use; he's too closed and blunt and practised and after last night there's not much trust. Flea holds my arm and is vicious with it.

'I'm trying to protect you, but you won't have it, will you? This is no place to be alone.'

I can no longer disobey, there are jellies to taste. I look back in yearning at the waiting bush.

Something cracks, soft, close. I trail out my hand to it. A bird screeches into the baked blue as if in alarm as I'm swept inside to the kitchen. As soon as I decently can, I run out.

To find Mouse and anything else that might be waiting for me.

A TALE OF LONG AGO

Virgil is with the dogs. He's rolling his face through Sage's fur and holding her ears like handles as the dog licks him in slobbery wallops.

'Barkingham Palace,' I murmur. 'Clever name, isn't it?' The man stills as if invisible hackles are rising at the sound of my voice; everything about him is closed off. Thunder murmurs far away, a faint rumble of it. 'It's ingenious, Virgil. Coming from Tobyn. Who doesn't always strike me as … clever.'

'My brother will tell you anything that he wants. I named this.'

I pause, softened. 'I'm sorry, Virgil. I didn't know.'

Virgil will not show his face nor turn to me. I hesitate. Now is the time to leap in with everything I know and I'm never stuck for words, yet I don't understand this stranger at all, want to say something but can't. I take a deep breath because I need to know this. 'Virgil, was that baby yours?'

The man is stopped, every pore of his being absorbing this question. He grips his dog as if she's the last thing he has to hold onto in this place. Sage quietens. The sky murmurs far away, sullen. 'What?'

'The baby. The poor dead one. Are … are you the father?'

Virgil twists Sage's ear and the dog yelps.

'I'm so sorry. Virgil. If she's … was … yours.'

'Why on earth would you think that?'

I look away, towards the big house, floating so serenely on its lawn. A relationship between Virgil and a native would be almost unthinkable within such a family. Unthinkable for a son of the upstanding and deeply religious Mr Craw. Unthinkable for the son of Mrs Craw with her ebony cross and stiff, displeased back at anything seamed too deeply into this earth. I move right up close to Virgil, whisper-close. 'I saw the drawing. In your room.' He looks up sharp. 'I'm sorry, but I … looked. I just needed to find out … what's going on.' The man holds his hand to his mouth as if quelling sickness; he turns away, shuts me off.

The wind is flurrying up. Virgil now holds his forehead to his dog and grips her ears firm. She whines, but his holding doesn't let up. He's slipped into a world of his own.

The dawning. Did *he* do something to Warai and Poiyir? I look wildly around in the restless air. No one else is in sight, anything could happen alone with this man. He's holding something in, furiously, and we're so far away from neighbours and authorities and help of any kind in this extravagantly isolated place. I think of Mr Craw's mulish violence and Tobyn's change from flirt to aggressor: the impulsive anger that could also, possibly, be in the clotted son. Yet I don't cry out. I just take a deep breath, I carry on. Trusting. Feeling my way, with the tenderness of Virgil's drawing in my head. 'It doesn't seem fair, Virgil. Or right. What goes on here. And I don't even know why I'm saying this – I just feel it. In my chest. It … hurts. To think about it. What might have happened. To them.'

Virgil stands. His fists are clenched as if willing himself not to say or do something that I will not like and he might regret. 'You know nothing about anything. Stay away from us. All of us. Please.'

Dust from the wind smacks us in the face. I lean closer, whisper. 'You knew her. I can tell from her look, in the drawing.' I blush, for I'm not meant to know of such things let alone voice them, am not meant to be able to interpret that boldness, yet it's an intimacy I wanted to stroke. 'You're a beautiful artist,' I add, connecting and soft. 'Tender.'

'I knew you were trouble, girl, from that first morning you landed among us. I knew it would end badly. For all of us.'

I tell Virgil, my voice raw, that I have seen his father's study and I know what happens at this estate and before he can respond I ask again if the baby is his and in his cracking, shaking silence I want to hold him and cry, with him. Because it's like we're two unanchored and vulnerable souls here, alone and reeling and lost. And strangely twinned, as if we're both trapped in a place we shouldn't be.

'What if she was mine, Poss?' Virgil's voice has grief and anger and pride in it. 'What could I do?' His hand covers his eyes and he's now turned from me as if he can't bear it. 'You're in over your head.'

'What? Virgil, why?'

'Get away from me. Before you regret it – and I do too.' Virgil's hands drop to expose a face razed with grief. It feels shockingly intimate, as if I'm witnessing a door flying open into a soul. This is a person who's been going through his own particular hell and right under everyone's noses. I've never seen a man cry; it transforms him. It is shocking to witness, this peeling away of all the complex adult layers to expose the soul of a broken boy. Virgil sobs. Holds out a hand to a tree to steady himself. Wipes a finger across his nose trying to stem the tide, but it's no use. I hold both his shoulders; the connection makes him tremble even more.

'What happened?' I ask it soft, but he says to stop it, please, to just go, leave, as if I'm too close to something here but he will not say what, he'll never say it.

'Go. From all of us. And never say anything about this. For your own sake and mine, Poss. Please. Mine.'

I hover my hand gently over Virgil's arm. He tosses me off. Right up close, too close, I can smell the eggs and steak from breakfast and something else musky underneath. He needs a shave and to have himself sorted, it's been a while; he's neglecting his toilet, unravelling here like everyone else. 'I'd like to help you, Virgil. Help them.'

'Since you came everything's gone wrong.' He takes a deep breath, tips back his head, steadies himself. 'And I've got some questions for you too, actually.' As if Virgil's desperate for deflection, to throw the light onto someone else.

'Like what?'

'Like how did you get here? Really. Delivered right to our doorstep ...'

My back is now against the trunk of a great, wide tree; he is close. We speak in stabs of whispers as if the sky is listening in and rumbling its disapproval. I go to push him away; Virgil won't budge. 'Someone helped you, Poss. Who?' I bat off his close face; he clamps my chin. 'Tell me.'

I say that I'll inform his father of everything if he doesn't let me go, then leave him to deal with the mess. 'What does he know, Virgil? As much as me?' The man moves his bulk closer; everything in him is poised. But I push back. 'Why do people think the natives have gone? Why doesn't anyone expect them back?' I will him to astound me with the truth. 'What did you do to them, Virgil? What did you all do?'

'What did *I* do? Me. Ha.'

He propels me further into the bush, far from the ears and eyes of the big house, its tuts and taunts. Virgil stands in front of a ripping tree and leans on his arms that are crossed above his head, his face to the bark's softness and shielded from me.

Then he begins. Quietly. So quietly I have to slide into a sit to listen.

To a tale of a father welded to his family and the wishes of a querulous, demanding wife. A tale of a man who needed to rid his land of the blacks, the pests. Once and for all. Because the father had come to this fine coastal land and lived in a tent and had built a house with his churchgoing friends alongside him while his wife had stayed in town with their young sons and baby girl, their little Faith. Until the clearing business was done and they'd be safe. Yet they never were. Because the pesky blacks kept coming back. They fought for their ground, they taunted and haunted it and refused to give it up. But the big house was Mr Craw's. By right. He had a land grant from the Governor. So he decided to do something, once and for all. For his family, his sanity, his precious baby girl's safety. And for his wife.

'Are you ready, Poss? Don't you ever ask me again what I *did* to them. Because you know nothing about this island.'

Virgil breathes deep through his nostrils as if this account is being extracted from the rancid pit of his stomach and he can barely dig his words out. And so a tale begins of a day of happy, breezy blue. A Sunday, after church. His father in the thick of it, with his merry men, all on horseback and furious over their years of taunting and torment. So. A bit of Sunday afternoon sport. The tribe is rounded up. Men on horses, guns, whips. The tribe is driven over a steep plunging cliff, by the beach. By all the good men of the church.

'To their deaths?' I gasp.

Virgil nods.

'No. God.'

Some escape. They're shot. Then a baby is found. 'A tiny boy, on a coolaman. He's buried in the soil with his head above the ground.'

I'm now tight in a ball on the ground, covering my ears and groaning.

Virgil continues. 'A game is played.'

'What … game?'

It's barely voiced and Virgil exhales a deep breath, heavy breath as if he is infinitely old now and wearied by it. 'A game to … to … um, kick the baby's head off. Clean off. To win.'

I yowl into the ground like some wild thing. My fingers push through the soil. I want to cover myself with it and disappear entirely from this island, this cursed place. Yet Virgil goes on. That it's how things are done around here; it's all about secret codes and clearings and no one official is meant to know. 'It's what the natives have lived with for the last ten years or so.' A pause. 'As have we.' A pause. 'And some of us are going mad with it.'

I'm bent on the ground, scratching at the skin of my face as Virgil goes on, and on.

That it's called a 'Sunday shooting party' because expeditions like this often happen after church and no one finds out because these things are never found out or else the law would get involved and the men would be punished – 'and we can't have that'. So the shutters are drawn and it all slips off into rumour and folklore and forgetfulness and only those closest to what happened carry with them the truth of it. 'Like me. Us. Everyone here at Willowbrae. Who are stained by it. Each in our way. And it's untalked of, silenced, but it's deep inside our heads and we can't get rid of it.' Virgil finally looks at me. 'And that's why you shouldn't be among us. There are people of good conscience here, but this business isn't finished yet. And it'll never be finished while my family is on this land, and you don't want to be a part of it.'

Virgil walks away, hunched into his coat as if he's shrugging the entire world of Willowbrae off and leaving me to it.

Or not.

Repulsion

The sky hangs, pregnant, the world is waiting for relief. My fingernails are dirty from gripping the earth, my throat sore from yowling. I need love and warmth and connection, from my dear little Mouse most of all, need his childlike cleanness and innocence amid all this. I just want to burrow into the unsullied smell of his hair and the dip in the back of his neck and his still, yielding body that's almost porous with acceptance.

He's in the parlour, trying to get the attention of his mammy. She's deep in her sewing: a new dress for me, I suspect. Mrs Craw is attacking the cloth with a jabbing quickness as if she really doesn't want to be doing this but must, must. She scrabbles at the cross at her chest and mutters to herself, pressing the ebony against her forehead like she is trying to cool her fevered flesh. A strand of wilful hair has escaped and she doesn't brush it back.

'Leave me alone.' She frowns at her pestering boy. He wants her to taste a new dough concoction, a gloop of dubious lumpiness. 'Scat. You're worse than a fire that needs tending.' She needs the pesky encumbrance gone; he won't go. 'Get away. I need peace.' The little boy runs past me with a tear-crumpled face. Because of the weapon of love withheld. For a child, the most callous weapon of the lot.

Outside are a few spits of wet but the storm is dissipating and heading elsewhere after its sulky build-up; the world feels like it's waiting, parched, that it didn't get enough relief. I head after Mouse into the bush and find him on a low tongue of rock jutting into the harbour. Near the cliff. A shudder. It's so steep, the rocks below so viciously jagged, like they've been thrown from a great and furious height.

I sit beside Mouse and silently hold him, curving over him in a shield of solace. Need this. He surrenders without words, as if he loves nothing more than being cradled against an unknown dark, then licks me like a puppy in a grateful hello. 'You'll never leave me, will you, Possy?'

I inform him that I'm his big sister now and will always protect him because that's what big sisters are for.

He squeezes his glee into me. 'Protect me from what?'

I hesitate. What does he know of the horrors, so close? He knows of the room of bones if nothing else and that's horror enough.

I murmur vaguely, 'Everything, nothing, you're alright,' and Mouse is satisfied and wanders off and retrieves from between two boulders a fishing rod made from a stick, with a hook fashioned from a piece of abalone shell. The sun has come out fully now, the clouds have dispersed and the splodges of wet have almost completely disappeared from the rocks. Mouse perches on the edge of one and pats a seat next to him. The line's made of dried fish gut.

'I'm clever, Poss. Out bush. The cleverest.'

I stroke my boy's earlobe between two fingertips. 'Indeed you are, Captain.'

We sit in a repairing silence, listening to the lap of waves on water-softened stone. I softly sing:

But when I came here to survive,
With hey, ho, the wind and the rain,
By swaggering could I never thrive,
For the rain it raineth every day.

Mouse nudges me affectionately. '"With hey, ho, the wind and the rain." Yeah, right, that's really going to happen. The storm ran away!' I smile, he's right.

His line tugs. He draws in a flapping fish. 'What did I say? The best, Poss.' The gasping, panicking creature is too small. I urge him to toss it back.

'What? No.'

'Yes, Mousey. Come on.'

The boy bursts into tears, too quick; surely I'm not ganging up on him. I'm on his side, I insist. Mouse is inconsolable. He wants the fish dead and gutted by a knife but I won't let him, it needs to get back in the water. To grow. Mouse howls. I glance around as if in a crowded street, wondering who can hear; this feels like failure. He's so babyish and loud and unhinged all of a sudden and I can't stop him. Yet he has his whole life ahead of him to learn the rules of fishing, of when to hand back and when to take; to learn the rules of men, of when to destroy life and when to not. I scold that his mammy will want him to toss the fish back. That it's right.

'I'm always trying to do the right thing! I cook and clean, do the garden, try everything. It only ever makes her cross. She wanted a girl, not me. I'm never good enough for her. Ever. Ever.' He stamps his foot, his hands are clenched in anguish.

I clasp my little Mouse close and promise that he always has my love, as a sister, and it'll never be withdrawn. And as I speak I think back to the strop in the parlour and wonder if his mammy is fracturing in some new way, splintering right in front of us all. With something bottled up deep inside. She seemed so brittle as she stabbed her needle into its cloth and told her boy to scat. With something like hate.

IN WHICH A ROOM IS INVADED UNSEEN

We return hand in hand to the big house. The French doors to my room are swinging in the breeze and the curtain's waving an airy greeting. It isn't how I left them. *Again?* A hand is pressed to my racing chest. I look around. Feel something undeclared, watching. Virgil is hacking at dead roses over a garden wall and I yell across to him to accompany us to my room. 'Please.' To check it, as protection and witness, because someone has possibly been in it.

'What? Are you mad?'

'Please, Virgil. Just help me.'

He shrugs. 'Fine.'

'With pleasure, my crazy little Poss,' Tobyn says loudly over the top of his brother, walking into view from behind a ripping tree. I didn't realise he was also in the garden. Tobyn examines me playfully in the way that used to make my stomach dip. Comes up close. Our hands graze. I used to be too alive to that touch, spelled; now I snatch my hand away as if burnt. Virgil stays his course, perhaps sensing I do not want to be alone with Tobyn, and so I have all three Craw brothers accompanying me.

My eyes dart around the tiny space of my room, fingers travelling jumpily over the surfaces. Something feels rearranged, missing, but what? Mouse is fearful. I ask what's different, can he tell? He shrugs, afraid, he has no idea. Virgil is silent, watching us all.

'So what's going on here, Poss?' Tobyn stands back with his hands in his pockets. He remarks that the doors sometimes bang by themselves and maybe that's it, maybe I'm really going mad here. The wind's been up with the storm that wasn't, it could be that?

But of course. The painting. Of the little girl drowning in her finery. It's gone. Not even the hook that held it to the picture railing is left. Tobyn scoffs that it was never there, not in this room; Mouse can't remember; Virgil has no idea.

'Really? All of you?' The girl with the claustrophobic frills and her eyes just like Mouse's and her stare. I spin, laughing nervously. 'Is this house haunted? What's going on?'

'Absolutely nothing, according to us,' Tobyn says.

I rub the wall where the painting was, where the little girl stared at me day after day. She *was* there. 'Tell me I'm not mad. Someone. Please.'

'Ah, but if you lose your mind it means you fall in love with me. Which is exceedingly excellent in my book. So yes, most certainly you are going mad.' Tobyn laughs. 'Along with Mouse. You're both addled in the head, I think.' He rocks on his heels in merriment; I back away. Tobyn's charming ways feel so flippant and hollow now; something has soured. Mouse roars at him, beating at his stomach with tiny, ineffectual fists. 'Stop it, Tobyn! She's my friend not yours. Stay away from her.'

Mr Craw bursts into the bedroom. 'What is going on in here? Your mother has the headache! Why are all three of my sons in this bedroom?' He turns to me in fury. 'It's extreme impertinence. What, girl, are you bringing into my life?'

'Poss thinks she's losing her mind, Pa.' Tobyn smiles provocatively, challenging me to refute it. 'She invited us all here. She says things are going missing from her room and she wanted us to see for ourselves. I've been assuring her she's most certainly not mad, just … confused.' He raises his eyebrows at Virgil, who still says nothing. 'I've gently explained to our guest that the doors sometimes open of their own accord in this house.'

'Tobyn, Virgil, get back to the roses. Mouse, to your room.' Mr Craw turns to me with a face set in fury. 'Poss, the library, now.' His voice sounds wrong, it doesn't let me in. He rubs his finger furiously at his waistcoat's edge.

'But, sir, someone —'

He holds up his hand in a vast stop. Not here, not now. He's the embalmer of my curiosity, doggedly shutting me down, yet I hold my head high to him because now is my chance.

To have this out.

A NEW CHAIR

Mr Craw sits heavily at a desk in the library. Indicates the chair opposite him. I obey, arms crossed. I've witnessed the uncontrollable snap of his rage and it feels like his frustration and fury have stolen a good Christian man and warped him into someone else. I open my mouth to speak, but he holds up his hand as he leafs through some notes in a ledger as if anticipating everything I'll be saying and putting a stop to it. But I won't be stopped.

'I'm sorry for all the fuss I've created, sir. I began on the wrong foot. Right from the start, and regret it. But … it … what's out there … and —'

Mr Craw's fingers saw at the desk's edge as if his internal itch is slowly eating him from inside and will never be quelled, it's worming its way out. He looks across at the Bible on its golden plinth opened in readiness then closes his eyes as if shutting out not only his guest right now but his entire world. He opens a shallow drawer and extracts a pipe. Lights it like a man in a desert drawing in water and the smell is of my father and I close my eyes and think of him in that moment, of what he'd do next.

A barbed silence. 'How did you find us, Poss?' It seems we are now settling down to the nub of it, like two men in a pub as the whisky begins to bite.

'I – I don't remember, sir.'

Mr Craw says I must be protecting someone. 'You can't have arrived here by yourself.' His fingers drum the table in hard taps. I tell him that toughness is character and he says that gentleness and obedience can also be character and I flare that I don't admire those qualities so much. A raised eyebrow. 'Well, you should. Because I need some co-operation.' He shuts his eyes and keeps them shut as if he's energising himself by doing this. 'Right now.' He opens his eyes and points to my head, his finger wavering. 'The hair. The trousers. The public declarations. The persistence. All my boys in your bedroom. You're a troublemaker, Poss. You're becoming a problem.'

I gasp in refute. Am an open wound in that moment; everything hurts as I feel my Palace of Fury once again closing over me. 'I – I don't mean to be a problem, sir. I'm just trying to be my father's daughter, the daughter that he raised … to do what is right and necessary …' My words are fast, stumbly. 'And your son, Tobyn, he crowds me in, stalks me, agitates me.'

'You imagine things, child. Quite possibly make things up. I have seen nothing of what you talk of.'

'What?'

Mr Craw's high hand maintains its control. The man points to a homily on a plaque above the door: *Forget the Former Things; Do Not Dwell in the Past.* He leans in and tells me gently, so gently, that I have to move onward, with everything, I have to rest and repair myself – and forget the past. 'It's the only way to live a free life, Poss. It's what I practise all the time.' He leans back, sighs. 'You're too loud, girl, too big with your energy. Doggedness in a woman is most unbecoming. You take up too much space. In my house. And in my head.'

I retort that I was raised like this and know nothing else.

'Well, God help your family then, Poss. And by the way, who are they? Pray tell. Come on, out with it.'

I gasp. I've gone too far. Indicated to this man that I know who raised me, which means I may well know my real name. An internal buckling. I clamp a cry. The wild unfairness, the growing anger and I need to distract him with the unstoppable question rising in me. 'Were you involved in their deaths, Mr Craw? Did you do it?' The man looks at me in confusion as if knowing for the first time exactly what I could mean to his world. 'Is this what you do? To get your ... supply?' I grip the edges of my chair, waiting, yet the explosion does not come.

He tells me softly that I know nothing of the bush and get everything wrong and need to go elsewhere, very soon, for everything loud and unquiet in me is too ingrained now. 'You're a danger to us, Poss. To my family and livelihood. You could destroy me.' He nods as if only just realising it. 'You refuse to entertain doubt. Your mind is too swiftly made up. To the detriment of everyone. It's a humanising quality, you know. Doubt.'

I shut my eyes on him. Mr Craw is like hurting sand from the beach in high wind. With nothing now to lose I stand to take my leave but then a snap of revulsion takes over me and I tell him that the natives are people, not animals. With souls. And that St Paul's decree is neighbour must love neighbour, and where is his Christian charity now? 'Because you sell bones, sir. From dead people. That is your low and wicked trade. And you kill them, don't you? To get what you want.'

He crosses his arm at his chair. The fingers of his right hand are clamped under his armpit as if to still down the jump of them. He says nothing.

'Where is your God, sir? Where, in the pit of your soul, is God? You sully His good name. For me, and for all of us.'

Mr Craw shouts at me so loudly I jump, shouts that the natives are not neighbours and not even properly human; they're pre-religion. Primitives.

'Do you *need* their bones, Mr Craw, is it lucrative?' I pace the room, knowing I'm rushing headlong into disaster here but cannot stop my words as I hear my father's indignation rise in me and take over, and I'm told to get out yet do not, cannot, this has gone too far.

'You invade and disrupt, child – with absolutely no basis in fact – and by doing so you publicly threaten the very fabric of this house.'

I stop at the Bible on its golden plinth. Anger is coiled. I rest my hand on the book and tell Mr Craw, very calmly and very low, that a black man carried me to his doorstep. 'In an act of great charity, sir. And civility. And courage. Oh, I've heard what happened in these parts. Yet he returned. To make sure that I was safe. A stranger. And that, *that*, is Christian charity, sir. Everything that Jesus wanted us to be. Yet it's not your way, is it? With your … perversions.'

Mr Craw's fists smash upon on the desk. 'You're mad, child. Seeing things. It's a sign of hysteria – and that ridiculous insistence on men's clothes was only the start. There's no "black man" here or anywhere near Willowbrae. You had a blow to the head and need medical help.' Is he right? No, surely. 'You need a doctor. Immediately.'

'I swear on the Bible that it was a native man who rescued me.'

'Impossible. You're deranged.'

I place both hands flat on his Bible, willing him to reason.

'Get away from my precious book, heathen. I know there was no black man to save you.'

'How?'

'Because the dogs did not bark.'

IN WHICH CRACKS APPEAR

A stand-off of fury as the bell is rung for lunch. Mr Craw and I stare at each other across his desk. Mrs Craw puts her head around the door and beckons us to dine, without noticing the tension between us. Her cross hangs awry around her neck, the ebony chain is caught across her jacket as if the cross has recently been clutched then flung aside. Mr Craw stares at it, goes to say something and stops.

'What are you waiting for?' Mrs Craw cries out. We both dissolve into obedience and make our way out behind her rapidly disappearing back.

'I'm warning you,' Mr Craw whispers flintily into my ear, 'you be on your best behaviour. Don't go making any trouble.'

I nod as I walk up the corridor with Mr Craw crowding the space behind me and Mrs Craw oblivious ahead of us. She's changed her clothes and freshened her hair and is now a picture of maternal calm: her blue dress with yellow flower buds is freshly stiff as if holding her up; everything is in its place.

'Our guest seems very interested in the natives of this land,' Tobyn declares during lunch, to everyone and no one. His father glances at him, annoyed, now is not the time; his mother says nothing as if willing herself. Tobyn makes a casual comment about missing them, actually, their corroborees, bush medicine, chants. 'Sometimes, you know, I wish they were back.' He smiles directly at me, his knuckles balled under his chin.

I look at him with my head cocked; what's he playing at?

Mr Craw is watching us both. I look at his precious Tobyn, marvelling at his beauty, his scoffing ease; but whereas once it attracted me, it now repels me. He's the first-born son who knows exactly who he is in the world and always has. It all feels so confident and unclotted and clear and it's a firmness that will carry him through life. He's so lucky.

Virgil, on the other hand, is turned in on himself, biting his skin on the side of a blackened fingertip. His face is pasty and sweaty as opposed to Tobyn's smoothness. It's unfair that one sibling can be so blessed and the other so soured. But this one contains depths; he's the one to note. What does he know that the rest do not? And what does his father know? I watch them all.

'You want them back, Tobyn?' Virgil asks, hard. 'Need more girls in your life? Don't have enough?'

'Well, you, brother, certainly enjoyed them. When they were around.'

'Stop it!' Mrs Craw's voice cracks whip-quick across the table. She's exposed in that instant – not a drop of black blood will ever sully the fortress of this grand family name.

Tobyn explains to me that his darling mammy is always searching for perfection, in herself and family, and she'll punish any hint of failure because she can't tolerate it. But it's a perfection that no one can provide because no one is perfect, of course – he tips an imaginary hat to his brother – 'well, Virgil, possibly'. The brother goes very still with his palms flat on the table and waits.

Mrs Craw claps her hands to stop all this nonsense and in a rising inflection asks if her husband has secured the house, her voice slipping from her. He nods to confirm a ritual seemingly endured many times, yet his wife stands abruptly, not trusting him. She moves around the room like a penned dog, opening curtains and peeking out then abruptly pulling them shut, pushing in a stray chair and patting Mouse's hair then a lamp like there's no difference between them.

Her youngest is eye-deep in stare, just as when I first met him, looking at nothing but a point on the wall and lost to the lot of us. Is he in shock? I glance at all the Craws. It feels like some external pressure is closing in on the entire family and slowly crushing them, and they all know it.

I stand. Excuse myself. Mr Craw remonstrates, but I put an arm around his wife's jitteriness and tell her that everything is secure and fine and perhaps she should retire for the afternoon, I'll take her to her room, she needs it. The older woman looks at me as if no one's ever said this to her before and nods, yes, she does need it. I lead her out as the menfolk watch in silence. Once we have left the dining room the voices swell, in agitation, and the door is shut behind us and I can't make anything out.

In Mrs Craw's room, I help her to bed and she suddenly grips my arm and will not release it. 'I wish we'd known each other in another life, Poss. Edinburgh or somewhere. I miss it so much, you know.'

This contrary, complex woman suddenly seems like a child; her agitation is seeping into all corners of her life and aging her into vulnerability. And her menfolk don't seem to care. As if they're tired of all her flurries and turns and perhaps if they ignore them they'll eventually go away, surely, as they always do, all the strange and exhausting ways of women.

'I thought that you were a gift from God, Poss. That you'd been sent here to rescue me. But you wouldn't obey me, would you? Oh, I miss it so much. The soft light and soft rain and a life that's easy. Just … easy.' Mrs Craw wails then scrabbles in wonder at her sheets and declares they'll be good for some clothes and she'll stay up all night to sew them, yes, as she furiously tears at some cotton thread by her bedside, but I tell her in a calm voice it can wait, all of it, shh.

'No, it can't. We have to make this right.' She's furious at me but also at herself, as if having another female at Willowbrae has been a failure and she can't bear it, can't bear to lose another girl, another daughter.

I draw the curtains tight on her windows, but at the sight of Flea galloping from the house at great speed, I ask where he's going. Mrs Craw murmurs vaguely she has no idea. 'Men and their business. I don't know. Don't trouble yourself, girl.'

I shiver. 'This place is so … unquiet. There's something about it. Do you think it might be haunted?'

'Haunted. Oh, poppet.' Mrs Craw looks as if she can't bear to tell me the truth, to deal with any of it, and bats me away.

I head for my room. How long have I got here now? What am I going to do? I run my hands down the walls of the central corridor as if pushing it all away. Who'll give me solace? Anyone, in my canyon-vast loneliness? Who'll comfort me here when I most need it? Not Tobyn. He can no longer be trusted, he's someone who's always going to be about his own desires and needs and wants. And not Mouse, he's too young. Who can I turn to? The vicar, only him, and how ironic is that? I want the quiet between our souls that stilled each other down, want that good, calming man, but he isn't close enough.

I'm aware of every sound outside my room, every footstep; dread Mr Craw's heavy thud coming down the hall. Lie on my side on top of the bed. Feel like a dog turned in on itself in the grass, its back to a cold wind. It hurts to be in this place. And a headache is gathering at the corners of my forehead as if, like Mrs Craw, I'm being infected by it.

IN WHICH THE LONELINESS OF
THE OUTSIDER IS CONSIDERED

Later. Mr and Mrs Craw are in discussion in the hallway. I press my head against my bedroom door. 'But she's the girl I finally got.' A guttural wail rises from the matriarch and I open my door to see her folding over as if someone has punched her in the stomach and she crumples into a comma held up by the wall. She sees me and her face changes. 'Stop hovering,' she hisses. 'It's no good you being here. For you. For any of us.'

I shut my bedroom door. Outside the knowing.

'And don't go anywhere near my boys again!' The indignant yell is flung from the other side of the wood.

My future is closing over me like a blindfold here. I open the door again, fury rising like heat, and stride towards Mrs Craw. 'What — exactly — have I done wrong here, ma'am? Please tell me. So I know.'

Mr Craw turns to me. 'You need to recover. You're seeing things. Making them up now. Go back to your room and stay there. While we work out what to do with you.'

It's like the air has been snatched from my lungs; I try to breathe but can't draw in enough oxygen to fill my body up, can't catch a deep breath. I appeal to Mrs Craw but she holds up a palm against me and turns and stumbles down the hall. I stalk back to my room with the velocity of an arrow propelling me into a future unknown.

'Go to your room and stay there,' repeats Mr Craw, his palm clamped under his arm.

The door is closed behind me and locked. I pace the room, brain stolen by agitation. What to do? Can't run away into the forbidding bush with its ridges and valleys and cliffs and rocks; it would swallow me up and I'd die in the heat or fall from a precipice or be bitten by a snake. Can't head down the road to town because we're too far away; I'd die of hunger and thirst. I'm stuck. Trapped in a prison that hasn't quite declared itself but seems far, far worse right now than the prison I was going to be trapped in: the one called marriage to the man I didn't want.

I push away the manuals and can't bear to open the Bible by my bed. Draw the coverlet over my head. Every instinct tells me to get away, to run, but I don't know where.

COLLECTING

Later that afternoon, when the house is quiet, I go in search of Mouse. His retreat from the house feels too thorough. I wander restlessly in search of him outside, amid that wall of sound like an orchestra shrilling then abruptly stopping.

He's by the vegetable garden. Has just caught a cicada and holds out the insect's vibrating magnificence in the cage of his hands. 'It's a Black Prince, Possy! The best. It's for my collection.'

'Like the one in the library? On the table, under the glass. Is that yours?'

'It's Mammy's. We all collect for her.'

'Oh.'

He spans out a wing to show me its lead-light beauty and accidentally pulls the membrane off. 'Oops.' The insect is thrown away.

I step back, examining the pragmatic and unsentimental child of this land, hardened in the ways of the bush. 'There's plenty more where he came from, Possy. They're making that screeching sound and there's a lot of them.'

'Oh. I wondered what that was.' I trail after him as we search for more cicadas – 'Lead on, Captain Mouse' – and we chatter away, then I carefully slip into the conversation a question about whether he knows where the bodies of Tinkin's mother and sister are, whether he's afraid and whether, by chance, he ever wants to leave here.

Mouse tells me he knows nothing about anything. 'I'm being good, Possy. Now.'

I hold his arm. 'Do you ever want the glade thing to happen again, Mouse?'

No, he answers, no, with anguish. 'I just want everything to stop.' His plea is so quiet I barely catch it then he bashes at the bush with his stick in a furious manner. No, he doesn't know anything about anything and please, stop, please.

If only I could ease the path for my little friend but he won't say any more and so we head home, holding hands, silent and cicada-less. Mrs Craw calls from the verandah as we make our way up the lawn, asking where we've been. She's nervy, jittery. Mouse doesn't want to explain anything and I can feel in his reluctant hand that he's a volcano of suppressed anguish. What does he know?

Next to Mrs Craw is an enormous spider's web, golden tinged. At its centre rests a tiger-striped arachnid as big as a handspan with a belly like a chestnut about to crack and she catches my intrigue and sweeps the web away with a swift flap of her embroidery then turns and smiles at me, hard. 'Do not place any of your ideas in my little boy's head.' The voice is honeyed and calm, woman to woman, with a world of unspoken things beneath it.

'I wasn't. What?'

Mouse jerks his head and murmurs to his mother something about us wanting to find the bodies but then stops, abrupt, as if to divert the conversation. Mrs Craw propels herself forward with a cyclonic force and slaps her son hard across the face. 'I warned you.'

He's furious. 'I told Pa.' The shard of his words right back at her. 'Everything.'

His mother is stopped, a world of weight between them, then she takes her howling son by his ear. With no loosening of her grip she says to me in a studiously calm voice to get back to my room – 'and by God you stay there'. And she drags him away.

I lie on the bed with my hands over my ears as if the weight of this entire house is closing in on me like a great press of water in a drowning. Muffled voices, from Mouse's room, threats I can't make out. Poor little man. This day is soiled, this whole stay is. Willowbrae now feels like this malevolent beast squatting on alien soil, poised, waiting to crack open. It's such a strange, out-of-place building in this beautifully wild world, with a core of darkness just down the hallway.

Later a flushed Mrs Craw flurries into the room with a dinner tray and tells me to stay away from her boys and the rest of the house. I'm banned from it all now except for family meals and banned from every one of her boys including her husband. I go to laugh but stop myself. It's like she's cracking apart, going mad with it. But with what?

In my bedroom, alone again, the big house feels suddenly very quiet and dark. As if everyone has decamped from Willowbrae and I'm now left alone in a dwelling holding its breath. But for what? I open the door a few times but each time it's slammed shut on me, by Mr Craw, maintaining a watch outside my room.

At bedtime I hear an elaborate turn of the key in the lock.

A night of toss.

Too quiet, too quiet, all of it.

And then my fears take hold. That man could be capable of disappearing me. Have me lying dead in the bush. Am I mad to even think it? He could have me sprawled under a tree and looking peacefully asleep and no one would know what had happened; Mr Craw could tell the world their visitor known only as Poss had succumbed to the knock that had turned her head, a knock that everyone knew of; or she'd eaten wild berries or been bitten by a snake. Who knows? And it was regrettable of course but to be expected from someone like this, the girl with the wild hair who wore trousers and asked questions and didn't know her place. They'd all believe it. And my grave would be unmarked, for I never gave anyone a name, and that would be it: disappeared from this earth, as easy as that.

I cannot sleep.

THE SIXTH DAY

THE DECISION

Flea brings me my breakfast on a tray then comes back to collect it. When I go to leave the room with him he stops me; he tells me I'm required to stay here and go nowhere else and he gives me nothing more. So, the whole house is in collusion now. I spin from him in frustration and notice that the painting of the girl is mysteriously back. The wretched painting. How? By the time I turn to Flea to ask how it got here, he's vanished down the corridor and I'm left with the little girl trussed up as a bride staring at me with a challenging gaze, wherever I am in the room.

I throw my pillow at it. If I had my knife I'd quite possibly slash it.

Mrs Craw retrieves me for an early lunch. She directs my dressing, smooths my silk and straightens and fusses without a single word despite my attempts to draw her into talk, as if she hasn't heard me or doesn't quite trust herself.

Mouse is not with us, only Tobyn and Virgil; Flea nods to me as if he is relieved to see me. Mr Craw is curiously unlocked as he dabbles with his stingray, scraping it amiably around his plate. 'We call it skate in these parts.' I don't answer, trying to read the room. Can't, except it is obvious that everyone knows something I don't. Mr Craw chews loudly, enjoying it; his wife doesn't admonish him, even though I know she must hate the swish of other people's food in their mouths, the imperfection of it. Her husband is freshly scrubbed and released, as if some storm within him has passed. He stands abruptly. Walks to me and puts both hands lightly on my hair as if in a tender benediction.

'We're worried about you, little Poss.' His hands press in, ever so slightly. 'That blow to your head … we fear you may be seeing things. We watch you jumping at every small noise, running around in the bush in your night clothes, babbling about ghosts and black people, all manner of things that don't exist … and now, my wife says, there are irregular menses … it's all very concerning.'

I want to violently shrug him off. Hold myself very still. 'I'm fine, sir. Really.'

'It's not for you to decide.' Mr Craw's fingers tighten their clench as he tells me a doctor will soon be seeing me. Ah right, so that's it. 'We're worried about you, Poss, gravely.' And as he speaks his smooth words I feel as if my heart is being dragged into my belly.

'I do not need a doctor, sir. I'm fine. My sore head is fixed.' I pull at the lace at my neck, at Mrs Craw's tight little knots holding it secure. They're scratching me up; I feel hot, sweaty, constricted. I look at each of the Craws poised over their stingray and shark and oysters, their bounteous feast from the fat of this land. Mrs Craw is toying with her food, whether out of disdain for the local dishes or it's something else, I'm not sure. But it's a grand occasion for them today, from the tone of the food and clothes, as if they are celebrating something. Yet I don't know what. I look across at Mr Craw, now seated again, leaning expansively back in his seat.

'You know nothing of this island, Poss. Always read too much into everything.'

Quite a new man before me, unfurled in some kind of victory. Because a doctor has been arranged, to assess me, this afternoon in fact; it's a friend of Mr Craw's, a good man, and he should've done this earlier. 'My good doctor is arriving soon. Very soon.'

My skimming heartbeat, too fast. A doctor. I know what this could mean, where this could lead me, to a place walled by stone I may never get out of; and I turned down the vicar when he offered escape and now I am trapped, by all of these people, and I look in silence at this man in his supremacy and want to cry into his strong fatherly arms yet run screaming from them.

I turn to my once-ally, his eldest son, the man who kissed my eyelids only a few days ago; I swallow my pride, need him now. But he looks away, of course he does; there's the slap of his whole body as he turns. I glance to the other son, who once drew a woman with heart-cracking tenderness; perhaps he, now, is my only ally. 'Virgil?' It's hardly voiced, the word constricts in my throat. 'Virgil, please. This might, it might mean —' I can't even voice the horror of it.

But nothing.

'Virgil, what's happening?' I'm talking to him as if we're the only ones now in this constricting room.

He shakes his head to silence me, as if now is not the time, while Tobyn's beautiful lean finger runs along the length of the salt shaker, and runs along it. I stand up, trembling, and walk to them both. Crouch down to where Tobyn sits – it's unseemly,

I know, but I'm beyond caring what is right and what is not anymore and my face looks up to his, close, he can't avoid it. 'Tobyn? Please help me.' I shut my eyes on the memory of his lips long ago, the lips to my lids that rescued me once, but of course get nothing in return; this is who he is. Then I turn to Virgil, the one with the open heart, surely, who recognises the courage in difference and respects it. 'Don't leave me stranded here, Virgil. Please. I'm frightened. Where this might lead ...'

My heart, my heart. Waiting. One tiny word, any single word, will be a rescue, will mean someone is on my side still. That someone here has a conscience.

But nothing. They don't even look at me.

So. I feel viciously alone here now and the sensation has been increasing over the days as my entire future contracts. No one will help me and the good doctor is about to arrive. I stand, contained, and walk back to my seat, the humiliation burning through me. Am I that hard to love? My brother always told me so, yet I refused to believe it. But now. I feel wrong in every way, just as my brother and Mariana always made me feel wrong. And now Mr and Mrs Craw too, and Tobyn, and even Virgil, who was meant to be different.

I know now that in everyone cruelty is a mere flicker from kindness. I know now that I was to be the toffee swallowed whole and carelessly before Tobyn moved on. I know now what these brothers are most of all. Family men. They're protecting something here and protecting themselves.

'You think too much, Poss,' Tobyn tosses across as if in defence. 'Overthink. Swamp think. You'd have a much quieter life if you just calmed down. About everything.'

'What are you talking about, Tobyn?' I hold my head – please stop, just stop – I can barely push my voice out.

'We just want some peace and quiet around here, Poss,' Tobyn says. 'My father runs this house and my mother needs her calm.'

'Right. Of course. And, ma'am, where are you in all this?'

'A doctor needs to see you, Poss. It's for the best. For all of us.' Mrs Craw's voice sounds flat and tired and rehearsed. She tugs at her cuffs and straightens her already straight cross and I know now that her desire for order and neatness is like a sickness in her. She needs the medicine of looseness, of letting go, but she'll never find it in this place. The land won't let her and she knows it.

I excuse myself in a weight of thinking and float into the strange new now. Mrs Craw follows to make sure I'll head straight to my room no doubt and that I'll stay in it with the door locked. She lifts the key from her chatelaine in readiness.

'Don't even think of speaking, Poss,' Virgil throws at my departing back. 'They've won. Don't show them how much it hurts.' I look back. Right. Finally he talks. He looks straight at me as Mr Craw's hand tightens around his wrist to silence him then releases it when he's satisfied nothing more will be forthcoming. Then Virgil chews the skin from his nails as if he regrets speaking so nakedly. His father holds his hand gently and lures it away from his mouth and stills it palm down on the table and does not leave him.

And I have no one to still my hand. No one to put their arm around my shoulder, no one to hold me tight. I just want to dive into Mouse's room and burrow into his wriggly yielding warmth because it feels like he's drawing love into him with each person he holds, that he's hoarding it, the gift of attention; then I remember what he was like, in little moments, with the fish and the cicada. Like he was becoming someone else.

One of them.

In Which I Am Watched

Mr Craw's good doctor examines me in the parlour with its hard light. I stand stricken before this stranger, feeling too much but not showing it, holding my head high and not giving him anything of my wild racing heart. The doctor looks as if the sun has been squeezed from him long ago, as if he's been left on a windowsill to gather dust. He has no idea of the workings of someone like me.

As he speaks his smooth, too-ready words of diagnosis, I have a sensation of the ocean bearing down once again, of its great weight holding me under and I can't kick my way out of it, into the light, into life – and I suddenly start gulping in panicked breaths. Gasping for air that will not fill up my lungs.

The doctor stands back. Nods. Through heavily lidded eyes that don't quite look at me straight, he insists I am fragile, yes. 'Uneven menses?' The query is dry and disinterested but somehow grubbied. Some information has already been confided, I can tell, something has already been decided upon. I think back to the conversation in the library with Mrs Craw, when the colour of my blood was discussed in a prickle of discomfort; everything was for a reason, of course: the collector was collecting her evidence.

'I'm fine, Doctor.' Muted right back at him but with blinking eyes that are fighting their own battle against the raging unfairness of this. For my head is full right now of the Asylum of Industry in this colony, where all the uncontrollable women are sent, but wilful isn't necessarily mad, far from it. It means a woman who might just want to seize responsibility for her own life. To own it. By herself.

'I said, do you suffer from uneven menses?' Silence. 'Tenderness of the breasts?' Silence. 'Sensitivity to light? Sudden crying?' Silence. 'Uneven temper? Or, shall I say, wilful and disobedient muteness?' I respond with nothing to any of it because anything I say will incriminate. 'Classic signs, hmm,' the doctor says. 'Headaches most certainly. Excessive fondness for men's clothes. Cranial derangement, menstrual derangement, precocious puberty. Quite possibly a diseased uterus. Further tests would need to be conducted.' I bite down on my lip – where is this leading, all these weighted words? – but I will not cry. Furiously I tip back my face and wipe my eyes in a swipe as he writes and writes. 'Fragility and hysteria,' the doctor concludes, jabbing his fountain pen into the paper with a triumphant stab.

Strength is draining from me. It's actually happening, what I dread. I want to snatch the man's wretched notebook and rip out the page yet can't give him that ammunition; oh God, I must, must contain myself. I think of all the women who vanished into Knockleby's asylum, with its walls the colour of a sky in surge. Beth and Mary and Lizzie and Hetty. Their crimes: uneven menses and fret sickness and wilfulness and being too emotional and talking too much. And a chorus of Craws is now saying it's all in my mind – the murderous deaths and the rescue by a black man and imaginary friends in the bush – and now this doctor is officially confirming it. 'What are you writing?' I rasp at the sunless man but he holds his hand in an impatient stop. *Hysteria*, I note. Repeatedly scribbled down. The nothing word, the one size fits all word. 'I'm fine, Doctor. Really. This is all about something else.'

'It's not your choice, child.'

'They want me to think I'm mad but I'm not. Really. No. I may – they may think it. But no, no, they're making it up.'

'It's not your choice.'

Ah, choice – the prized word, my old friend – back. And the world closes over me as the doctor takes me to my bedroom with his firm hand clamped on my arm, as he tells me it's all decided and there'll be no escape.

'Ma'am,' I yell out wildly in the hallway, but there's no answer, the house rings with a listening silence. The doctor pushes me into my bedroom and shuts the door and orders me to change into my nightgown in front of him and I feel invaded by his eyes that do not move away from me but I have to do as he asks; he is breaking me. If I am pricked, a torrent, I fear, would pour out. He puts me to bed and instructs me to lie on my back with my arms on top of the sheets then he traps me tight within the binding cloth and orders me not to move. He takes the key to this room that Mrs Craw had at lunch and tips it to me and smiles. We both know what it means. 'Please help me, sir. Please. Don't do this.'

The doctor puts his paper-dry hand on my head and says I need rest to get better.

'How long?'

'That's for me to decide.'

I tell him I may well be sick, vomiting sick, and he calls for a bucket, which someone unseen leaves swiftly by the door. He checks that the French doors to the outside are secured and locks the door to the hallway as he departs, leaving me fluttery and panicky, a colt in a fresh pen, unable to escape. I shout in frustration and burst from his sheets and punch the wall crammed with its blousy chrysanthemums.

Mrs Craw calls from the hallway, 'Control yourself. Learn to be a lady. You need to be better. I've got just the thing for you.' She clatters away and I flop back against the pillow. Then Mrs Craw opens the door and hands six books across as if I'm now contagious with some unspeakable disease that must be quarantined from the rest of the house. 'Here,' she says, 'improve your mind as you rest.' She swiftly shuts the door and turns the key.

'Ma'am, don't you trust me?' I call hopelessly through the door.

'I'm under instructions,' Mrs Craw replies, giving me nothing. I flip idly through her various books, *A Manual of Medicine and Allied Nervous Diseases* among them, and look up the dread word.

The mental condition of a woman affected with hysteria is somewhat peculiar. The patient does not feel disposed to make the slightest effort to resist and yields to her emotions. She cares nothing for her duties. The patient laughs or cries immoderately without cause, has hallucinations; there is pain in the ovary; she is prone to headache. There is a peculiarity of the hysteric which is very characteristic of the complaint, namely, a hysterical patient

is afraid to go either to church or to any other place of worship.
If she should venture there she feels as if she should be smothered
or suffocated, or as though the roof was going to fall upon her.

Well, yes but no. And my bedroom door is locked. And the doors to outside are locked. I'm trapped. A fly hovers close and I'm stuck with its whine unless I flatten it, yet can't bring myself to. Hands slap at the wallpaper and rattle loose doorknobs but none yield; my legs kick walls and fingers scratch at the door. I scream through the wood as loud as I can, scream for anyone, but no one comes. The house is silent. The day yawns on. The manuals of womanhood are flung across the room. A tome smashes into Faith's doll, dislodging a traumatised eye. Good. So be it. I could never be that girl Mrs Craw wanted. I peer through the keyhole; the key is in the way.

The key. Mrs Craw left it there. If I could knock it out then slide it through the gap underneath the door … the large gap … big enough for fingers to reach. I scrabble at the table for a pencil and poke it through the keyhole. Knock out the key. Slip my hand under the door. Have it.

I'm out. Back on the fighter's path.

THE PATH

The parlour, I can hear them.

What to do? Run away? Into the bush I got traumatically lost in? Into the town I've never been to and don't know how to get to along winding bush roads with diverging paths? Or run to the Ripping Tree and Tinkin, who could possibly be there but perhaps not?

Or do I defend my sanity to the Craws? Yes. I have to break away from my future too set.

I stand tall in the doorway of the dining room as Mrs Craw pours her steamy tea. Flea catches my eye. Says nothing.

'I'm well,' I say. 'I don't need a doctor or confinement. The diagnosis is wrong. And you all know it.' I hear my voice as if at a distance, my voice sounding wondrously strong, steady and clear.

'How the blazes did you get out?' Mr Craw bangs a fist on the table. 'Minx!'

The doctor rises as all the Craws look at each other, checking who's with them or who not, who colluded or not.

'Will no one defend me here? Virgil?'

A spot at the bottom of his teacup holds his rapt attention. So. That is the measure of the man. What is he protecting? I'm brimmed with a wild alone here, no one will come to my rescue. Neither Virgil who knows too much, nor the little boy who began this, nor the man who kissed my eyelids once – and my fingertips find those very spots now and press, and press, until my eyes ache with starriness. As I stand before them all in their stranding silence.

'It's for the best, Poss,' Tobyn says finally, calmly, taking on the mantle of responsibility. 'For all of us.' His mother squeezes his forearm as if transmitting her strength and I know in that instant that someone has told Virgil and Tobyn something. But what?

'Who are you protecting? Did you kill them, Mr Craw?' I hear my voice rising. 'Was it to preserve the good name of your family? I know what you did to the baby. Long ago. Buried in the earth. Except for his head. His little head.' The man shuts his eyes, statue-still. 'I know what you are capable of, sir.'

His wife gasps. The doctor urges me to hold my wretched tongue, but I will not because I feel emboldened and reckless and wild among them now. They will all have to act or none.

Mr Craw stands and rubs his fingers along the edge of his waistcoat; his wife puts her hand over his, calming him into a stop; her other hand clutches her Mouse. He is utterly still and withdrawn from the lot of them, blocking the grownups out.

I stand before their great hedge of silence and repeat that I'm fine, in body as well as mind, and I know I'm fighting for my future here, my freedom, fighting for all my own choices in my life. Because if you have none you are a husk. 'Virgil, tell them what you know about the dead woman and her child.'

The man looks straight at me and answers bluntly that he is not on my side over this and I have no reason to think it. 'Stop, Poss. With everything. It's no use.'

Mr Craw stands, takes me firmly by the elbow. 'You can be a very trying girl.'

I retort that I'm just being honest. I tell the doctor that hysteria, with respect, sir, is a condition that can mean anything, it can be concocted for mere convenience. To get an inconvenient woman out of the way.

'Hold your tongue,' the doctor says, crashing down his teacup as Mr Craw holds both my arms in a steel clamp; the head of the house has had enough of this nonsense. He announces I'm to leave tomorrow and the Asylum of Industry will repair me and he does not know how long it will take. Days, months, years for all he cares.

'Till death if you must,' Mr Craw says, and I'll be cleansed of my sins most mercifully.

'Sins? What about yours, sir? Your sense of Christian charity? You sell human bones. You murder for them. Examine your Christian conscience, please.'

Mr Craw speaks very slowly and very quietly. 'You have no idea, child.'

I say please, listen to me, because I'm not hysterical or fragile and he knows it. He says that on the contrary I appeared at their front door semi-naked.

'Through no fault of my own, sir!'

'You insisted on wearing men's clothes,' he responds. 'You took them from our cupboards.'

'I did no such thing! I was given them.'

'You go around the house at night,' Mrs Craw adds, 'shamefully half-naked. You ask a servant for alcohol.'

I look at Flea. His back is turned to me as he arranges the food on a side table and most resolutely he will not meet my eyes. So, he betrays as easily as that, as does Mrs Craw, who says nothing more. I'm going under, the great weight of the water is pressing on my chest. I turn to my little mate. 'Mouse, you remember how you helped me with the boys' clothes. Yes?' He squeals, high-pitched and anguished and runs from the room, pushing past me as if he's drowning here too and has to be away from the stain of all of us.

'Do not drag my son into this. You've confused him enough.' Mr Craw twists the flesh on my arm. 'You spout untruths about my family in public and in a churchyard no less. The carriage will take you away first thing in the morning. You're a wild one. Unteachable. I should have recognised it from the start.' He turns to his oldest sons. 'Tobyn, Virgil, take our guest to her room immediately. And make sure she stays in it.'

The brothers nod to their father and herd me off, hemming me in and allowing no deviation from their path. A collusion of silence at all my questions. They're knitted now; there's not a single one of them who will come to my aid. There's not even an eye flick from Flea. So. Everyone. What fresh news binds them? Tobyn wrenches the key from my fingers. 'It's for the best. Our best. And your best.' As he pushes me into my room and shuts the door and locks it and pockets the key I'm sure.

I lie on the bed with my arms folded across my chest, shrunken and neat. A single tear runs silently back into the seashell pool of my ear. I now have only the fading light of this ebbing day and night left at Willowbrae – left of a free life – and there's a great and outrageous unfairness at the heart of this.

I huddle like a baby on my side and fall into sleep, dreaming of my mother wrapped around my heaving back, clamping me strong on a swan's wing oily and green-black. Behind us, back to back, is Warai holding her little Poiyir in a fierce maternal clamp. I wake with a start. I did them both wrong. Shouldn't have just assumed they needed removing and a Christian burial, that my way was good and proper and right; I never thought to ask Tinkin what she might actually want. My arms envelop my head and press tight. Everything has gone wrong, I'm always jumping in too quick. Yet no tears will be allowed out and I don't utter a sound, for no one will know, I will not give them this.

My soul.

Later, in the vivid alone, I find my voice:

A great while ago the world begun,
With hey, ho, the wind and the rain,
But that's all one, our play is done,
And I'll strive to please you every day.

I sing it over and over to the darkening wild, in a cadence of connection, for my Mouse. Pace the room and hold my cheek to the cold door and do it again, but my little Captain never comes, no one does, and there's no way out because I've tried every way out and the evening yawns on then shuts down into night.

I fall eventually into a squally sleep across the top of my quilt.

In Which I Am Rescued

I wake with a start. Someone's in the room. I shoot up. 'Oh!' Mouse. At the foot of the mattress. How? 'What are you doing here?' My whispering relief.

The boy holds the key high and announces he got it from Tobyn's pocket and isn't he the clever one. '"And I'll strive to please you every day",' he sings softly in return and I throw back my head and punch my fists to the ceiling and laugh in almost-silence at this little boy who can surprise me still.

Mouse whispers that he had to see me, he's worried about me. He's back in his doctor mode. He has an apple in his pocket in case his Possy is hungry and some lumpy biscuits wrapped in a linen cloth. He throws the apple across and I catch it in a snatch and eat in great ravenous bites. Mouse doesn't like me caged up, he doesn't understand why everyone has turned strange; he's losing a friend for no good reason and it isn't fair and he wants it to stop. 'They wouldn't let me talk, Poss. Mammy was squeezing my hand every time I tried, hurting me. Her fingernails were digging in.'

I draw my boy close. He smells of my childhood, of sweat and apples and trust. I hold my fingers over the bedroom key and gently squeeze. 'Let's get to the Ripping Tree,' I whisper to him, 'one last time. Come on. Before I die in this place, in my heart.' Because instinct is calling me back to it, I don't even know why, but I need to get there, right now. Is he out there, somewhere, my rescuer? He feels like hope, somehow, my last chance. 'One last adventure, Captain. Come on.' Moonlight has slipped its tongue into the room and is calling me out, away, calling us both.

Mouse hesitates. 'Go … now?'

I spin my little captain in a whirling dance and he giggles in a softening and I slip the key from him and hold it high. 'Oy! Give it back!' I hold him swiftly tight, pressing him to me to stop his talk and to leech his love from him and it's like holding a volcano with lava bubbling close; he too is brimmed with agitation on this night.

'Come on, Mousey, do this. Just for me. We won't be long.'

'The Ripping Tree's over, Poss. It's all been tidied up.'

'It won't let my mind rest.'

'You're going mad with it, everyone says so. It's all made up. Everything you say.'

'Come on, little friend. I need to find a way out of this.'

'This what?'

'Mess.' I want to scream at him: 'This is about my survival!' But do not – just tell him I can't love him forever unless he comes with me now, can't be his big sister if he scuppers this chance. 'It's what mates do, Mousey.' I tell him if he doesn't come now then I'll have to go it alone and never speak to him again because his parents won't let me; there'll be no goodbye and no visits and I'll never come back and he won't have a friend at Willowbrae. 'You'll be all alone. And – and, oh God … I need you to quieten the dogs. Mouse? Please.'

The boy's wide-open traumatised heart. I shut my eyes and hold the key out of his reach because this world of Willowbrae is a stone under my mattress robbing me of sleep and I have to do something, anything, to scrub it from my life, to survive this. 'Alright,' Mouse says finally, 'you win. One last time.'

I grin with relief. Shake his hand and tickle him in our secret signal and he answers in a clutch; yes, we both need this. I pull on my boots; Mouse already has his shoes on. I open the bedroom door and lock it once again and we creep through the sleeping house, stopping at every floorboard creak. Then we're out on the verandah, we're flying down the steps and sprinting across the lawn into the vast gulp of the night. Mouse flits ahead and soothes the dogs from their restlessness.

The moon has slipped from its cloud-clothes and it silvers the bush in almost-daylight. Mouse's feet are steady and swift; he knows the way through the thrilling dark. I'm suddenly aware of a presence, ghostly, right by us – it's there then not and it's enormously bush skilled and fast – on this side of us then on that, in front and then behind. Tinkin.

'Oh, *you!*'

She's weaving through the bush in parallel to us, flitting and softly singing her teasing, taunting talk, cutting Mouse off from me then dropping back then moving in front of us but never coming quite close enough, never enough to be touched.

'Come on, Poss,' Mouse urges and we push on, and on, the three of us in some unspoken collusion of childhood that I haven't quite broken from yet.

A branch cracks. In an instant Tinkin is vanished, just like that; she's gone and the singing stops. But Mouse is not afraid.

'She'll be back,' he murmurs, not breaking his step, 'she's always back.'

'Hello?'

I look behind and shiver a flinch but Mouse runs on and we get to the beach at last and the water is warm, warmer in the darkness, and the oysters scrape all over again and there's fresh blood on my knees but I don't stop to wipe it off, for this is my last chance.

To blindside my fate.

To tell the doctor and the world I'm not spouting hysteria but the truth. Because once again – just as before the *Finbar*'s journey to this place – men have imagined a life for me that completely disregards the life I've imagined for myself.

IN WHICH I AM NOT RESCUED

The glade is still, waiting. The Ripping Tree looms over the space and its great arms reach down and I rest my cheek on its cool, soft neck. What secrets does it hold deep within it, what has it witnessed? A frog croaks and something else chirrups in a rhythmical peace and it seems like the mysteries of the night are just beginning to declare themselves.

I feel strangely unalone here, with Mouse and the voices on the wind, distant chanting laments or perhaps not. The leaves have been scattered; the area feels untidy now, abandoned. Somewhere far away the wind-lament persists and I reach across to Mouse and he squeezes my hand and it feels like we're both in opposition to the world and know little of it.

'Mouse, I just need some peace of mind. What really happened here?' The boy drops his hand as if scalded, he tells me he doesn't want this. He's here to have one last adventure, just like before, when we were friends, only that. 'But I can't be your friend unless you come clean, Mousey. What does your family know? You're breaking the code. You're not being a proper mate.'

The piracy of withholding, and I hate myself for it, but I need some answers to prove I'm not going mad here; it's all about survival now. Mine, and I need any scrap I can get.

I know my words are working their way in because I can see how hard this is for Mouse, in the clot of his talking then not, in his starting up then not, as he finds his way around sentences which need to come out. He finally says that maybe I won't be his friend or anyone else's at Willowbrae if he tells me what he knows, so, actually, no, he can't, he won't do it. I grab his upper arms just as his father has done with me and dig my fingers in and hate myself for it. 'Ow! What are you doing, Poss?' The shock on his face at this fresh girl before him, at my new hardness.

'I'm leaving tomorrow, Mouse. And it's not my choice where I'm being sent. It's like a gaol. And I might never get out of it. I'll be vanished. So I have to puzzle it out, what to do. For me. And for us. So we can't have secrets between us and, actually, you might just float with relief after all the bottling up. It'll feel good to have it out.' My voice drops to a whisper. 'So please do this. For me.' I wrap my friend in my arms and breathe in the smell of his lovely hair. 'What happened out here? It's all about courage, my friend, and I know it's there deep inside you. Courage. Please.'

'No.' The little boy cries in confusion, he wants his old Poss back.

But I will not slip into my childhood self, that girl is gone; I have to save myself. I feel the cruelty of my brother, Ambrose, slipping into my voice as I squeeze Mouse harder in frustration then shake him and shake him to rattle the truth out. 'You're hiding something, I know. What's Virgil told you? What did you find out?'

He hesitates.

'Let him go!' Virgil rushes out from behind the Ripping Tree – ah, so he's been tailing us all along. 'Mouse, you don't have to say anything.'

Virgil's looking at me in horror, at how I'm holding Mouse, but I won't let go of my boy, I was so close, I won't, won't let go. Then Virgil forcefully severs me from his little brother and flings me away like a scrap of garbage. I scramble back but the man leaps at me – 'Leave the boy out of this' – and raises his hand to strike me hard on the mouth as if he wants to obliterate all my questions and accusations for good, to have me silenced, but at that moment a whirling sprite flies out of the bush and leaps onto Virgil's back to stop him, clawing and biting and pulling his hair and forcing him into a stunned halt.

'Tinkin!' Virgil and Mouse cry out and the man spins, trying to shake the girl off but it's only my arms, finally, around her waist – 'It's me, shh, it's alright' – that persuade her to loosen her grip.

A stand-off. All breathing heavily, all eyeing each other warily. Tinkin's fists are on her hips, I'm bent with my hands on my thighs. 'What … what is happening here?' I ask, placing a hand on Tinkin's back in thanks.

After a silence that's prickly with too much, Tinkin says, 'It's for him to speak. The one that done it.'

I slump to my knees. The one that done it. So. They're here, among us. But silence.

Tinkin says loudly that it's his braveness, if he's got it, and his choice, the one who done it, the one who must speak now. Yet again, silence. I turn to the man who followed us here, from his lookout on the verandah, I suspect. 'Virgil?' He says nothing, he just squats with his blackened fingers propping his head and his face turned from all three children before him whom he cannot look at now. 'Virgil.' But he's stopped.

My dawning.

'Mouse?' A sickened swallowing. 'You?'

Mouse is now breathing hard with his hands balled under his chin like he's run for his life for a very long distance and he's about to collapse from it. I hover a hand without touching his back, for I don't know what else to do, then we hold in a strange, prickly communing quiet as I try to transfer some kind of courage into him and it's this bewildered kindness that cracks him in the end; I can feel it softening through him like liquid honey down a starving throat. The vast relief of the truth finally out. 'Alright, Poss, alright.' He slams his eyes shut as if he can't bear to see it, all over again, to see it.

And so begins a tale. Of a little Aboriginal girl who is lost. Who can't leave her mother and her baby sister, who haunts this space. I look at Tinkin as Mouse speaks and she's keening softly and it feels like all the grieving of the world is in it. I go across and stand by her. Mouse says she's a cheeky one, just like him, always running away and coming back to the Ripping Tree, back and back to the secret glade that hums with its strange quiet.

'My place,' Tinkin interjects. 'Where I'm born.'

Mouse goes on. That her older brother was always trying to get her to return to their people but Tinkin couldn't leave the Ripping Tree, just as her mother couldn't, and she picks up here and says, 'Because I need it and it never goes away, that want.' And yes, of course, because the vicar has told me that connection to the land here is everything, that the land is like their mother and if they're not dwelling in it then they're sickened and lost and he's seen it with his own eyes with the friends he's made from this island that he shouldn't have, perhaps. But did.

'My brother found you. After the storm,' Tinkin says to me. 'Oh!'

'He's called Mirrung,' Mouse says. 'But you couldn't stay with him. He couldn't take you to his tribe cos you would have given them all away. So he took you to our house.'

Tinkin takes over. 'He wasn't going to leave you to die. Out here. But he couldn't take you with us. You belong to whitefellas. So he took you to big house, even but he wasn't allowed near it.'

'Our mermaid on the doorstep, Possy, remember?'

I nod, yes, I do, the mermaid who couldn't fix things up. 'And little Poiyir? And Warai?'

Tinkin softly keens, in anguish. This bit is so much harder. Mouse presses his stomach on either side as if he's trying to push the truth out after being clenched inside for so many days, rock-hard for so long; he pushes his flesh into hurt. Virgil shifts uncomfortably as if he wants all this stopped.

'Whatever you tell me, Mouse, I love you and I'm your big sister. And big sisters keep secrets and protect their little brothers. Right?'

'You promise.'

I stroke my finger along the length of his palm. Tinkin halts her keening and drops on her knees to the ground waiting for this too, willing him to speak the truth. The truth. With a deep, nervous sigh Mouse says that one day, on his adventures, Mouse found a friend. Just Tinkin, by herself, or she found him, he can't remember which.

'I found you.'

She ran away, Mouse says, but he was desperate for a playmate so he had to think of a way to bring her back. He reckoned that everyone loved sugar so he started experimenting by baking his special biscuits, his Mouse-made damper cakes, with lots of it. One morning he left a batch by the Ripping Tree, still warm. They were taken. It was a success. So he left some more, and then more, and one day Tinkin was there when Mouse was and shyly, slowly, they became friends. Mouse knew the Ripping Tree was the place Tinkin always wanted to be because she told him her mammy, Warai, used to bring her to this secret place. To teach her the lore of the tribe, the way of the women here.

But Mouse's mammy got curious about the biscuits being baked so often. Where were they going? To whom? He told her they were for his imaginary friends. She nodded and rolled her eyes, but one day when he was in the kitchen with her he slipped into explaining that you could cook fish by wrapping them in the skin from a paperbark, a ripping tree, and you could use a fishing line made from a possum's gut.

'How do you know that?' Mrs Craw asked.

Mouse replied in a flash that he'd been taught, in a tiny fire that made no smoke.

'Who showed you?'

'My imaginary friends,' Mouse replied.

'What imaginary friends?'

Mouse clammed up, felt sick, but his mammy wouldn't let up.

'I don't like you going into the bush,' she said, getting worked up, pacing the room and dropping her teacup. 'I don't like you going out there unsupervised,' she shouted.

'I didn't know, Mammy, I'm sorry.'

'I thought you were by the chicken shed or veggie plot. I never knew you went further than that.'

Mouse replied it was a mistake, he didn't know anything. It was all in his head, just that.

Mammy's knuckles squeezed into her temples, tight, like she was squeezing her brains out. She moaned. Grabbed her son. Dragged him to a ripping tree on the edge of the lawn with a bewildering hate. Peeled off some bark. Dragged him back and flung him into the kitchen like he was a piece of rag, and it hurt so much. 'Who do you love more,' she asked, 'me, or your imaginary friends? Show me what they've taught you. Wrap your food in their bark if you know so much, cook it well and good. Cook, boy, *cook*.' She was crazed. Broken. Screaming that paperbarks were not for civilisation, for civilised things, in a civilised world. 'Do you really have friends out bush?' she screamed. 'Tell me they're imaginary, that you've made them all up. My nerves can't take it.'

'I have made them up, Mammy, I have.'

'I can't bear you being out there, you know that. It'll tip me over the edge if the natives are back and you're playing around with them and bringing them close. I'll leave this place if you are, and it'll all be your fault. Alright? Because my nerves can't take it. You have. To make. Your imaginary friends. Go. If you love your mammy. So that everything is tidy and safe. How I like it. If you want your mammy's love. If you want her close. My nerves! If you love your mammy, you have to show your love. So vanish them. Forever, Mouse. Work it out. Be the man of this house like the rest of them never are. They never do what

I want, but you? Lift your head out of your blasted books and pirate ships and *do* something for once. Fix this. Make them go.'

Mouse was reeling, sobbing; he needed his mammy happy, needed to help her. But he had a germ of a solution. He knew the kitchen well, too well. Flea had mentioned all the things in storage and how he'd put some bottles on a high shelf out of harm's way, so Mouse could never play with them by mistake; it was something that was used a long time ago, before the blacks cottoned on. But Mouse got it, what was in those pretty blue bottles, *sick-nin* or something it was called. So. One day, all alone, Mouse put whatever it was into his biscuits. Just a little bit. To make the natives sick, that's all, to scare them off, and he baked his damper biscuits with their sugar in the paperbark in the kitchen coals. And he gave the biscuits to Tinkin. As his gift.

Tinkin goes very quiet at this point. Stands up straight. I put my hand on her back with a wildly thudding heart. Is Mouse ... is Mouse a murderer? He continues on. Tinkin always gave a biscuit to her mother first, who always tested it – the children had been instructed to do this. So that was his plan. The mammy would get sick and scared off and they'd all go away except for his Tinkin, who'd secretly find her way back because she was clever in the bush, much cleverer than him, and she'd never leave her place for good. And Mouse's mammy would be happy again and love him and see that he was the good man of the house that fixed everything up and kept Virgil away from what he loves but isn't meant to and everything would be alright.

'What Virgil loves ... but isn't meant to?'

'I saw him once, with Warai. And … and … Mammy could never know, she wouldn't cope. Her nerves. She'd drop dead just like that. Wouldn't she, Virgil?'

The man says nothing, just rolls in his lips, not looking at any of us. Mouse continues. So. He gave out the biscuits and the mother ate them as she was feeding her baby. But after a while it was wrong. Mouse had put too much of the bottle stuff in and it worked too well and suddenly too fast, and at this bit of the telling Tinkin starts keening again louder in a rhythmic chant, yet she takes over the account; she says that as her mama was suddenly falling, staggering, she fed her baby girl, lip to lip, the mashed-up biscuit then she put her baby to her breast to stop her crying and to protect her other daughter because the baby's screams would bring all the whitefellas close. And Warai told Tinkin to run and run and never look back, to never come to the Ripping Tree again, to leave them both. In *her* place. That she couldn't be away from. That always called her back. The place where she was born and where she'd grown up. Her sacred area and she had to be in it and she kept sneaking back because she was the keeper of its stories, over the years her own mother had made her this – and I have a flash of Tinkin in that moment as a holder of the secrets of Warai and of this sacred space.

Then the mama lay on the ground in agony around her baby because she knew her spirit couldn't rest until her body was home, and she was, at last, in a fierce arc around her little daughter, who couldn't survive without her because she was still on the breast and had swallowed some of the tainted milk before the poison had set in. And Tinkin cried that her mama was tired, so tired, that she'd seen so much in her life and she knew of the future that was ahead and there was no use fighting this anymore, she couldn't win. And she needed her other girl safe. From everything.

Then Tinkin stops her talk. The glade is very quiet, as if stunned into stillness. No one speaks any further, no one moves. Mouse slumps with his arms draped over his head as if shielding himself from the imaginary blows of them all.

So. He did it. My little mate. For his mammy. To make her stay. To prove himself to her. Because she never loved him enough. And Mouse found Poiyir and her mother by the Ripping Tree with their blackened lips. With me. When he thought they would have been gone by then; someone would have made them disappear but they hadn't. And he didn't know what to do, it had gone so horribly wrong, but there was a mermaid beside him and perhaps she was magical and could make everything right, fix his big awful mess. But I couldn't. And by showing me the bodies, he had made everything worse.

Mouse finally talks, a whisper, looking straight at Tinkin. 'I only meant to give them a fright. So they'd never come back. For Mammy. So she'd be pleased. I just wanted to fix things. I love fixing things.' To be noticed, yes, and Mouse is trapped and will always be trapped by this. He turns to me. 'Don't send me to gaol! Don't tell the Governor. I thought I was saving them.'

'Why?'

'If they left …' The little boy's gulping, sobbing talk. 'It would never happen to them. What happened to the others. And Tinkin's sister was just a baby. I'd heard what they did to a baby once and it might've happened to her. I just wanted them to go. To escape. To stop coming to this place.' Mouse whispers as if seeing it all before him. He's heard the stories and he says he knows it would only be a matter of time before his family rounded up the strays because that's what happens in these parts. He thought that making them sick to scare them off was an easier, gentler way, thought it was somehow right. 'Is this what good feels like?' The fixer, fixing things up, his very own way. 'If it is, I don't like it. What's happened. To all of us. Because of me.' Mouse's anguish and confusion and guilt.

I ask if anyone else knew.

'Virgil.' Mouse looks straight at his big brother, who lifts his head for the first time. 'Mammy once said you had a "thing" for the native girls, which made her mad, but you just liked them, didn't you, so I told you about my friend because you'd understand.' Virgil says nothing. 'You listen to them, don't you? You write their words in your little red notebook. And you want Poss gone away so she never spoils what we have. You didn't want her poking around. You said she could destroy our family if she knew, but you'd never do that, Poss, would you? You're my big sister. It was a mistake. Please, a mistake.'

His sister, I said it, yes. And the whole family knows about Mouse now, it was obvious from the lunch; they're all trying to protect him. Battening down the hatches to save the neglected little child in their midst.

From me.

From what I might find out. From what I might tell, because knowledge is a threat. I might spill the terrible secret involving my little brother-boy I somehow love yet can't but must, perhaps, among the mess of this.

THE SEVENTH DAY

THE COMMAND

I am lying on top of my bed with Mouse pressed into me, limpet-stuck. He can't sleep anywhere else, he's insisted, the night terrors are too much. His limbs are solid bands of warmth and trust as his rhythmic breathing presses into my back.

The bedroom door is open. Light is leaking into the night. I can feel from the house's hush that I'm the only one awake. Mouse will stir soon; he's always the first up no matter how late he's been to bed, his mother told me once in annoyance.

But how to proceed from this point? I haven't slept, again, and the tiredness is jagged through me. I must keep all my wits about me when I just want to plunge into rest, somehow, into deep, soft, enveloping oblivion. But what to do? There's the courage of Mouse in telling the truth, finally, of course, but over all of that is Tinkin and her brother and the knot of what's happened to them. Mouse has done something horrifically wrong in his twisted, innocent, child way, yet in the process of informing any of the powers that be on this island I'd be tearing my little boy apart. His family apart. Over the past few days their action has been love inside a sacrifice – and the sacrifice is me. Destroying Mouse was never what I had in mind, and I still need a way out.

He stirs. I flip to face his rosy cheeks and he smiles in his drowsiness and burrows closer and his long eyelashes flutter on my cheeks as I catch his sour morning breath. Tears prick, are held in. At the love, the release, the mess of this, at the horror that will be carried down through the years in Tinkin and in Mouse.

The boy wakes properly and sings in a whisper:

A great while ago the world begun,
And I'll strive to please you every day,
With hey, ho, the wind and the rain,
And the rain it raineth every day.

Then he slips out of bed and I ask for the key to the room and he takes it out of his pocket and holds it up high, away from me. What's he doing? A flutter of disquiet; not him too, please. 'I have to put it back, Poss, or Tobyn will find out.'

I bend my head sideways and stare at my boy, my new boy, with his calm and rational voice. Killer or innocent child? I nod reluctantly, right, then Mouse swiftly, too swiftly, closes his fingers over the key in something like ownership and shuts the bedroom door behind him and locks it.

I flop back on my pillow, glassy with tiredness. My body aches for rest from all of this. Uncertainty seeks the balm of knowing and I urgently need it. What will happen next?

I get up, make the bed, wash and dress slowly, scraping my fingers as a comb through my hair because that is how I'm used to doing it and then I slip on Tobyn's trousers under my skirts. It feels exhilarating to do this, a secret tonic of muscularity. I pull on the boots that have flitted me boldly through this strange bush. Feel sturdy, ready, earthed. Pull back the curtains as far as they'll go then lie on top of my neatly made bed and wait for the house to stir – the slanting sun through the French doors a golden blanket of heat that moves over my body in a slow caress, drawing me out.

When Mrs Craw brings in porridge on a tray I take a deep breath and ask her if she could possibly send in her husband, please, I need to talk to him. Because this is my fighter's path; I have a raging will to live a life that is my own, that will not be dictated by anyone else. The older woman looks at me dubiously and holds her cross between two praying palms and in return I bow my head piously and hold up my own praying palms. She is thwarting my destiny here, as she has constantly done, yet reluctantly, miraculously, she says alright, you win, just this once. 'But it's like you do as you please all the time, Poss,' she flings, 'and I really cannot abide that.'

In Which a Bargain Is Presented

Mr Craw knocks on the door but does not open it and he tells me that whatever I have to say can be spoken of like this, as if he can no longer bear to have his eyes sullied by the vexatious sight of me still in his house.

I nod, smile, shut my eyes, readying myself for what has to be said. I thank Mr Craw for granting me this audience and tell him quietly and with great steadiness that he cannot have me locked up.

'Really. Why?'

'Because I am not mad and you know it.'

'On the contrary, Poss, you have given us great cause for concern. We have collected a lot of evidence. We will not be swayed.'

A familiar flare of fury. I need to survive this. 'You cannot have me locked up, Mr Craw, because if you do, as much as I love Mouse, I'll tell people what he did. Because I know the truth. And I will declare it.'

Silence. A moment that could go either way. I imagine Mr Craw wrestling with his inner demons while rubbing his fingers helplessly on his waistcoat. This feels like a huge risk; I may never leave this room or house. 'You are a Christian man, sir. Please. Have mercy.'

The door slowly opens. Mr Craw steps inside and shuts it again and he sits at my desk with a great and weary heaviness. He sighs. Shakes his head. He tells me that everything I believe to be true about Willowbrae is hysteria, is imagined.

The magnificence of my fury. I stalk right up close to him. 'There is a sickness at the heart of this family, sir, that made Mouse do it. And I will tell everyone of it if I have to. And you cannot have people knowing, you cannot have your precious child compromised in such a way. Surely.' The great weight, heavy on my chest once again, is pressing me into breathlessness. 'So let me go. Please. Let me walk freely from this house and I promise you – on my father's grave I promise this – I will never speak of these matters again.'

There. It is done. Surely this will work. Mr Craw sits back and folds his arms. He starts laughing, softly, and it grows louder as he cocks his head, all the while looking at me as if I'm the funniest specimen he's ever come across; tears of laughter come from his eyes. The sting of his mock as I stand here, stranded.

'You understand nothing, do you, child? You stupid, foolish, little girl. We as a family will always draw behind Mouse to protect him. Even your precious Virgil. Oh, yes, it's been noted. Don't think he's on your side, minx. We as a family are strong and united in this.'

'I'll tell someone.'

'And who would you speak to?'

'It won't be hard.'

'Oh, won't it? A mere girl, flouncing up to the Governor of this colony and telling him what's what? Really. Even if you do manage to have it out with someone of high standing, no one will believe you. Or care.'

'What makes you so sure?'

'Because the good doctor and I may have spread it about that the sole survivor of the *Finbar* is sadly touched in the head, spouting nonsense as a result of her ordeal, quite difficult to save. Is nothing now but a hysterical, helpless, pitiful woman —'

I groan with fury, appealing to my father to be strong with me, somehow, to give me strength.

'The Asylum of Industry will set you to rights, I'm sure, or is it the Lunatic and Invalid Asylum you're heading to?' Mr Craw chuckles to himself. 'I can't quite recall what the good doctor said. And I don't know how long it will take for your rehabilitation, mind. Some women are in there forever. I've heard stories of the isolation cells for the most troublesome inmates. Now let's hope, Poss, you're not placed in one of those. It's all about obedience.'

'Stop it.'

'We could treat you at home, of course, but an institution is a far better solution. Because it offers rules, Poss, rules. Absolute conformity is insisted upon. And you should be welcoming a cure, actually.' This is the first time I've seen the man smile openly and it does not come easily to him; there's a little of Tobyn's cruelty to it. 'Freezing water over your head, the application of blisters to the sensitive areas; it's all for the best, child. Imagine being restored. Becoming that good, quiet, obedient specimen of girlhood at last.' As Mr Craw talks it's as if a hood is dropping over my life. 'I offer you my sincere thoughts and prayers for a swift recovery. I do hope, child. For your sake.'

I know what blisters are: the application of carbolic acid. I've heard the horror tales and I know of the white blankets black with fleas and the iron bindings for impertinence. I've heard it all.

Get out, girl, get out. But how?

A VISITOR

I glance across to the French doors, to the wildness beyond them that has cost the inhabitants of Willowbrae so much. Mr Craw has left my bedroom door open behind him and it's now or never, the terrors of the bush be damned amid this.

I sprint out of the room. Down the hallway. Mr Craw shouts after me. I run through the front door and across the lawn as both Tobyn and Virgil give chase. Just as I reach the ripping tree I first saw at this place, the one with the bark my rescuer clothed me with, Tobyn catches me; he wrenches my arm hard and cares little for it. 'Got you, you little rat.' He's breathing heavily, excited by the chase.

Just at that very moment a horse and rider come up the drive as the dogs wildly bark; the visitor cannot see me from the gravel. But it's the vicar, my vicar, my Jemuel. So. One last time he is here and I shut my eyes in unstoppable thanks. Yet Mr Craw is on the top steps of Willowbrae; he frantically motions to Tobyn and Virgil to get me around the side of the house, out of sight and silenced. A hand clamps across my mouth and I'm dragged away, vanished, as my tears of frustration spill over Tobyn's fingers.

I hear the crunch of gravel as the horse is halted, hear the vicar pat the steed's flank and say 'steady, girl' then dismount as the horse wheels. Hear my Jemuel ask after me, agitation in his voice. He stumbles out in his awkward way that he's visiting unannounced because he needs to see me, to check that everything is alright, he's worried yet scarcely knows why. 'Yes? Can I call on her? No?'

I tip back my head behind Tobyn's punishing hand and inhale deep. I feel like an open wound right now that can only be healed by the simplest of balms, the attention of someone who cares; and this dear saviour is asking after me, yet I cannot get to him. Furiously I wriggle but Tobyn is having none of it, he hurts me into stillness and clamps my cry; Virgil looking to the house and holding us both back, behind him; physical strength is the one thing I cannot beat.

'She's not well,' Mrs Craw says to the vicar with deep concern; so, she has joined her husband on the steps. 'It's her head. She can't see anyone right now. She's taken a turn for the worse. Anything will set her off and we can't risk it.'

'Oh. Well, I – I …'

Jemuel's at a loss. I can just picture him, awkward and stumbly and not knowing what to do next. I want to run to him and put my hand calm and steadying on his back. Tobyn tightens his grip over my mouth, I can scarcely breathe. I struggle and he holds me firmer; Virgil helps him. They are walling me tight.

'I might have some news,' Jemuel hesitates. 'Quite possibly.' I can hear in his voice the weighing up, the worth of it. 'I – I believe your charge to be one Thomasina Trelora, of Knockleby, Dorset. I have spent some time looking into matters, enquiring of people who may have some knowledge of the situation. I believe it so from the Dorset accent, and from what I've been told of the

Trelora girl: the hair, the voice, the curious and never-exhausted mind and, er, the stubbornness and strop.'

I smile bitterly through Tobyn's hard holding.

'A Trelora,' Mrs Craw says. 'Is anyone looking out for her here?'

'No, no indeed.' The vicar's voice catches in his throat. 'She's quite alone. An orphan, penniless. She was the sister of the poor deceased Ambrose Trelora, who went down with the *Finbar*, God rest his soul. He was her only close relative.'

Mrs Craw exclaims in mock shock; her husband says it will be a further blow for me that I may never recover from given the state of my mind. He explains that a carriage is soon to arrive to take me away, actually, for a medical assessment, that it's in my best interests. He is fulsomely stepping into the role of the caring patriarch and I slump amid the brotherly phalanx hemming me in. Mr Craw says with great concern that the sanitorium is to cure their poor guest, because of her blow to the head from the battering sea. 'We're concerned about her fragile mental state.' I shut my eyes, observing myself as if from a long way away through a window of thick alehouse glass; this can't be happening, yet it is. 'It will only take a few weeks or months, we're sure,' Mr Craw continues smoothly, 'then our dear young Poss will be free to take her place in society once again, rested and restored.' And all I can think of is my blazing Lizzie back home, who was never seen again.

'It's best to visit her when she's cured,' Mrs Craw jumps in, 'and she will be. The doctor will advise when that might be. We are determined, Vicar, to see her right.'

She invites her visitor inside but he says he won't stay, he must get back, yes, and I can feel the force of Jemuel's thinking, about so much; he's so wracked and uncertain and solicitous, yet he is the man who quietens my heart. He eventually mounts with a wheeze of his weight and says as an afterthought that as Ambrose has perished, it means, perhaps, that his fine grazing land some sixty miles north belongs to, well, who knows now who will care for it? Then he bids the Craws good day, as if he has spoken out of turn. 'Much to think about, yes, much.' Silence, then Jemuel adds, as if he can't quite pull himself away, 'I think Thomasina quite a – a singular woman. Fuelled by love, yes. She has taught me a great deal. How to live, in a sense.' Jemuel's voice is charged with yearn; it is a rope hauling me in. 'Tommy Tom. Her brother told me once that their father called her that. Something of a radical, I believe, their father. Their late father.' It's as if this man has aimed his soft voice directly into the bullseye of my home-sickened heart. 'Do take care of her.'

'Oh, we will,' the Craws warmly chorus.

'I do wish I could see her.'

'It would be absolutely the wrong thing right now,' Mr Craw says. 'She would fall into a relapse.'

'I see. Thank you.'

The vicar's horse clops slowly down the driveway and it is torment to hear him go, I am drowning here. The animated chatter of Mr and Mrs Craw about Ambrose's land batters into me. About who is there now to object if they run their own stock upon it. About it being unowned, undeclared for.

And goodness, it's clear, if I'm deemed mad then all rights to the property will fall away and the land can be used by another, a Mr Craw quite possibly, as an exceedingly fine secondary estate. So there's another advantage to having me disappear and their vanquishing feels complete and I wrestle mightily to free myself, to yell for help, but the brothers have me tight; I'm going under here, under.

The Willowbrae world closes over me and the great weight of its secrets presses upon my chest like the weight of water did once. Mrs Craw bustles close and Tobyn tells me it is time to go back to my room and as he hauls me inside his hand slips from my mouth and I cry, 'Virgil? Help me. Virgil!' But the man turns away and walks off to the kitchen and doesn't look back, ignoring Flea as he passes, who's standing in the doorway. I pivot to the old servant. He glances across at me with his careful silence and nothing in his eyes, practised. Mrs Craw soothes behind me then beside me that everything is for the best as I cry that Virgil knew the woman at the glade, that they were in love, but Mr Craw roars over me that this is exactly why I need to go away, to be medically assessed, to learn quietness and obedience and manners and my place.

Without any more words Mr and Mrs Craw and Tobyn wrest me to my room and at one point in the messy tussle I am thrown to the ground and as I bob up I glance across at the Bible; someone has placed Jack's knife under it, it is poking out, they have placed it back where it belongs and the others do not notice and I lurch my body over the tome and in the chaos of struggle and shrieks quickly slip the knife up my sleeve and suddenly docile I am held down in my bed and am trapped, am trapped. Then the Craws leave as one and lock the door behind them and I lie on the unwelcome bed like I'm auditioning for a coffin, restrained, stopped up, unable to slip the knife out and mouthing in an exhausted rasp, 'Help me, help me,' listening to a too-quiet house.

To the tick of the clock. To the dogs suddenly barking. To the carriage of the doctor on the gravel path.

To his heavy footfall on the steps of the mighty Willowbrae and to the steps of one other, brought along to help I suspect. To transport me to my rightful place.

But I am my father's daughter to the end, cussing and cursing and spitting at all their professed cures that I know will never make me right. Because I am right. I think of Tinkin's nest in the drawer of my bureau that I now cannot reach, her careful coracle of a gift made with twigs and clay and feathers threaded through it like tiny pillows of tenderness. I think of the way we shyly smiled secrets at each other to be held in the fists of our hearts, both so viciously alone and both wanting to astonish our lives, perhaps, with friendship, yet both thwarted by circumstance.

None of the Craws are there to see me taken out, none of them have the courage for that; they leave Flea, who will not look me in the eyes, and two strangers to do it. They come in, that phalanx of men, and they bind my hands and feet and of course my mouth so I am well and truly stopped.

The mad woman, silenced.

AFTERWORD

'So. Those were the words that roared,' our grandmother said quietly, shutting the book, 'and I was a different person then. And I've never used the name Poss since. It belongs to Willowbrae as it was, so there it will stay in the past. Your mother doesn't think I should speak of these things, because it was all too painful and she can't bear it, but the story needs to be told.'

We all clamoured for more. Wanted explanation and knowledge of everyone in the pages that she had brought back to life, wanted our grandmother's journey peeled back layer by layer. But she shook her head and her voice rang out clearly over all of us.

'This was written long ago, during a confinement I never spoke about. When I became little more than a rumour. Mad Tom, the only survivor of the *Finbar* wreck, driven to insanity by the trauma of it. Or some such rubbish.'

We exclaimed our indignation, for in the way of errant children we'd had little curiosity about much of her former life. She was just our magnificently singular, emphatic grandmother, nothing else.

Her hands smoothed over the words as if she was now softening them into sleep. 'The deeper I railed against the unfairness of it all,' she continued, 'the deeper I was entrenched. Because my voice was their evidence. And I was meant to remain in the asylum until I was quite, quite silenced. Oh yes.' She smiled over all our protests. 'Until I escaped. With the help of Jack's precious knife, which saved me more than once, and your grandfather, such a brave, good man. But that's all for another story, my lovelies, over many more evenings, and right now the hour is late.'

We protested mightily, but our grandmother would tell us nothing more of the knife for now; yet she did roll up a sleeve to show us a strange heavy scar on the flesh above her wrist. 'Where the irons bound me, many a long hour.' She gripped her hand in a flinch; it was as if the memory had singed her. 'This account was written in great secrecy, as an anchor, if you like, to sanity. Someone slipped me these pages to write upon in secret, piece by piece.' Who, who, we clamoured, but that, too, was for another time. 'I wrote for salve. Because the truth was locked in my heart and it could never be opened back then. Except in these pages. I was told to write out a truth I may not have been able to voice.' As our grandmother spoke her face glowed; in that moment she was quite magnificently fierce.

'So. These damning words have been hidden away for years, but it's time now, I think, as all the principal characters who lived in that cursed house are gone. Finally. And I'm the only one left. Most happily – if exhaustedly – with you lot.' We laughed, our mother especially, as if released. 'In fact, you're among the very first people to hear this,' our grandmother continued. 'I'm very old now and I've waited a long, long time to bring Willowbrae's true story into the light. Until all the Craws had departed this earth.'

How we begged for an account of what had happened to them. Come on! Please!

'Well, if you must. But quickly. Because our beds call us. Mr and Mrs Craw, well, they died from restless old age. Tobyn from a broken bottle to the throat, in The Currency Lass Inn, no less, and over a woman, of course. Little Mouse from a fishing accident at the harbour mouth, where he was swept from the rocks and swallowed by the sea when he'd barely made it into adulthood himself; poor, troubled Mouse, he never fully launched himself into life. For all his charm and vivacity he was quite callous and selfish, myopic, if you like, as if he was fatally infected by his living circumstances. Then there was Virgil, of course, the last of the lot. Who lived reclusively on his troubled land and had no children ... that anyone knew of ... he kept to himself. And after him, Willowbrae was sold, to an industrious ex-convict who made it great. And closed its eyelids upon its notorious past.'

Our grandmother smiled, stroking my earlobe. 'Let's just say my little tale is a history of a great colonial house that was burdened by a situation that was never resolved, and I fear all over this land will never be resolved. It is our great wound that needs suturing and it hasn't been yet and I fear, perhaps, it never will be, for we're not comfortable, still, with acknowledging it.' Her hands pressed down on the cover of the book, as if to suppress the agitation within it. 'We're not comfortable with exposing stories like this to the air and the sun and salt. And I cannot give you the native side of this tragedy, my loves, because I don't begin to know it, or them; I can't speak for them. But I respect them and acknowledge them and love them for the riches they bring to all of us, and I know we are remiss.'

We were all quiet, thinking of all we had learnt; our mother tenderly rubbed our grandmother's back as if acknowledging the corrective that had been carried out by bringing this restless tale into the light. It was time for bed at last. I took the tome gently from my grandmother and asked her the title.

'Oh, but there is none.'

There must be! Please! we exclaimed. She shot out a laugh that rang high to the ceiling then took the book back and thought, and thought. Flipped open the pages and pointed. 'There's your title, you little scamps.' Her fingers had alighted on a passage about the tree with its many layers and its deeply hidden heart – *The Ripping Tree* – and she nodded, so be it, it was done.

ACKNOWLEDGEMENTS

Bringing a book to life involves a vast collaborative effort. This one took over a decade as life crashed spectacularly into the process. An unplanned new baby alongside three older kids intervened continually, with all the noisy clutter of their music, skateboards, footy boots and prams in the hall. Over a very disjointed decade the various editors who've worked alongside me have felt like a gift of clarity, wisdom and narrative instinct. Frankly, they've saved me.

This book – all my books – would have been much the poorer without the suggestions of various editors and publishers along the way, sometimes over a dining table, sometimes in private clubs and cafes, once on a beach because we both decided that, well, it was absolutely the best possible place to be (Anna V, I'm looking at you). This book would never have seen the light of day without careful editorial shaping over the years and several magnificent women have firmed its story. They made some big suggestions, which I've been happy to take on board because I've felt in very safe hands. It's all about trust.

So huge thanks to my publishers Anna Valdinger and Catherine Milne, and editor Maddy James, for guiding this story into the light. Also to proofreader Scott Forbes for the meticulousness and fine sifting skills when it came to all those colonial words and expressions; ditto Annabel Adair. Rounding out a superb team, the lovely Alice Wood and Kimberley Allsopp in publicity and marketing.

Emeritus Professsor John Maynard, of the Purai Global Indigenous History Centre at the University of Newcastle, read my manuscript with great compassion, rigour and sensitivity. I was so grateful for the thoughtfulness, loved the to and fro and learnt so much in the process. Respect, sir.

There's a heart-in-mouth moment for any writer when they're presented with a cover idea for the first time. Darren Holt has created two of my previous book covers, which I adored, and once again he didn't disappoint. There was a gasp of joy when I saw his latest creation – a tree trunk, lit from within, and only later did I discover it had been created from strips of paper dipped in ink during lockdown. Darren is a marvel.

To the Great Godwin, my agent over several decades and many rollercoaster writing adventures – well, it's been quite the ride and I thank him for taking a punt on me way back in the day. I respect his judgement and bolshiness and am so grateful to have him as a trusted (eminently teasable) advisor.

To my four scallywags, Lachie, Ollie, Thea and Jago, for keeping me laughing through the long years of writing this. I don't think they quite realise that they've been put on this planet for their parents' amusement. And we have little Thea to thank for the title of this tome. She was transplanted from Blighty to the strange, spiky land known as Australia at a tender young age, and instantly noticed the wonder of the Melaleuca Quinquenervia, or paperbark tree. 'Mummy, look at the ripping tree!' she exclaimed. Her magpie writer-mother instantly seized upon the description as rather a magnificent title for a novel. Made the mistake of asking Thea if it could be 'borrowed' for possible use one day. 'If you pay me,' responded that canny child, rather too quickly, and the little bugger never forgot. The day Darren's beautiful cover appeared on my laptop screen she reminded me again. So, pay-up time.

To her father, the chap in my life, for giving me the space to be who I really want to be. And to write. Over several decades he's sent me off for weeks at a time, to carve out some solitude whenever he senses motherhood closing over me too much. 'Just get lost. Go. Write.' Because he knows that after a week or two of words and not much else I'll return calmer, quieter and stronger – and a better mother all round. To this working mother his generosity, self-sufficiency and perceptiveness are a marvel. Literally, I couldn't do it without him.

And, finally, to the man this book is dedicated to. My father, Bob, who died just as the horror year of 2020 ended. He was a coalmining man who came first in his primary school class yet went down the pit at sixteen – because it was expected of him. He worked as a miner for almost sixty years and was eventually killed by the black dust lodged in his lungs. In my early twenties I told him I wanted to write novels; 'Waste of time, that,' he declared. After reading the first page of my debut novel, *Shiver*, he shut the book because it had a word in it he didn't approve of. He never attempted to read any of my books again. Yet Bob's selfless, non-judgemental love of his untameable daughter was the greatest gift of my life. He was a good man, and I'm so grateful to have had such a role model of generous and tender masculinity in my life. He was always there for me and for that I want to say thank you. I loved him so much. And suspect *The Ripping Tree* would have been the first book of mine he would have actually read. It's his kind of tome. Daddy, my darling daddy, this one's for you.